A CAPACITY FOR FALLING IN LOVE

CARRIE CLARKE

eBook Format: 978-0-6456982-4-4

Print Format: 978-0-6456982-5-1

Cover Design: Akapit Ryan Alexander Gilchrist

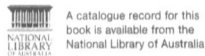
A catalogue record for this book is available from the National Library of Australia

This book is written using Australian English. You might find unfamiliar spelling or phrases. If anything in particular perplexes or interests you, please contact me at hello@carrieclarkeauthor.com.au. I'd love to hear from you.

CONTENTS

To my three beautiful children,
who encouraged me to follow my dreams.
I hope you are always inspired to follow your own.

CHAPTER ONE

Rosanna

A hand reaches into the car and takes mine in a firm grip, helping me slide towards the door. The fingers are long and elegant with short, neat nails. The skin is pale, covered in golden freckles. There are callouses on the palm. It's not my boyfriend's soft and slightly puffy hand, and a frisson of something I've never felt before runs up my arm and pools in my lower belly.

As my head emerges from the limo, I see the body the hand is attached to. Benedict Carter.

Marco, my boyfriend, who you could argue should've been the one to help me out of the car, stands a few feet away, adjusting his jacket, eyes scanning the long line of hopefuls waiting to get into this uber-trendy new club. Oblivious to my need for assistance. Or maybe disinterested is a better word.

Ben's other hand slides under my elbow, steadying me on the sky-high heels even I know are ridiculous. It doesn't help that the skirt of my dress fits like a second skin, giving my knees all of two or three inches of movement. Yes, impractical. But so, so gorgeous.

Lulu follows me out of the car, much more agile in a micro mini that shows off her perfect legs, with her husband, Nick, hot on her heels.

"I can't stop looking at you, Ro. That dress is gorgeous," she gushes, ever supportive, knowing I both designed and made it.

"Next time, maybe you should double-check the measurements," Marco mutters, his gaze leaving the line of waiting women to give me a cursory once-over.

Lulu's eyes narrow and she opens her mouth to respond, but to my shock, Ben beats her to it.

"It looks perfect to me. You're a lucky guy, Marco."

Heat licks up my neck and onto my cheeks, and I can't take my eyes off the clutch purse in my hands. I don't know whether it's embarrassment at Ben hearing the belittling way Marco spoke to me, which is becoming more and more frequent, or the thought Ben must now be looking at me, realising I could, in fact, do with losing a few kilos. Or ten. Because Ben is male perfection. Tall and lean and pretty much the handsomest man I've ever seen.

"That's one word for it," Lulu says under her breath. Just loud enough for Marco to hear. There's no love lost there from either side.

By now, the rest of the limo's occupants are on the pavement: Ben's brother Will, his sister Greer and her partner Josh, and Nick's sister, Claire.

I have no idea how it came about, but somehow we scored VIP invites to the opening of a club that's been the talk of Sydney for months.

In my periphery, I can see flashes going off, and I look around to see if there are any genuine celebs arriving. No. Just us. But you could easily mistake Lulu, Claire and Greer for models or actresses. And anyone getting a good look at Ben could be forgiven for assuming he's a model.

We make our way up the wide staircase and through the doors without the bouncers even batting an eyelid or asking for our invitations.

"How did a ratbag like you score invites to a gig like this?" Will jabs Ben in the ribs and flicks his chin out, indicating the spectacular surrounds of the club.

Something I can't place passes over Ben's face before he grins, although it doesn't quite reach his eyes. "I have contacts."

"Well, whoever this contact is, I hope he's legit. This place is amazing. I'd hate to get thrown out before we've had a chance to enjoy it."

Ben scowls, and I can see the muscles in his jaw working. "He's legit."

I don't understand the tension, but it's almost visible in the air between Ben and his brother.

"Well, I'd like to say thank you right now, Ben." I jump into the conversation, keen to dispel the odd energy between them. "In case I have too much champagne and forget later. This is amazing. I appreciate the invite." Ben smiles, and this time it does reach his eyes.

"No skin off his nose. They'll make money off us. No doubt the prices are stupid expensive," Marco snarls without pausing his scan of the enormous room.

"Everything is on the house tonight," Ben corrects him as he shepherds us around the perimeter of the enormous space, towards the second level, where lush booths with low tables line the balcony overlooking a dance floor that sparkles like a night sky in the outback.

The club extends for another two floors, each level stepping back over the one below so the ceiling in the centre of the space is three stories high. Five massive chandeliers with hundreds of lights hang at varying heights, reflecting off the mottled bronze mirrors on the walls. It's unbelievably chic and moody and glamorous. Nothing is overdone or tawdry. If a high-end private club and a nightclub had a baby, this is what it would look like.

We're barely settled in a booth in prime position when servers appear with two bottles of champagne in glistening silver buckets. Marco checks the label, and I cringe inside.

"Don't worry. It's the good stuff." Ben pours a perfect half-full glass and hands it to me. This guy knows his way around a bottle of champagne.

"Jeez, bro, who are you sleeping with to get this kind of treatment? Seriously." Will grabs the other bottle, shaking his head and chuckling as he pours a glass for Lulu and Claire.

The tension I noticed when we first arrived is back.

"Lay off him, Will." Greer takes a gulp of champagne and stands, holding her hand out to Josh. "Let's dance," she adds with a shimmy. It's not long before the others follow and it's just me, alone with Ben and Marco, who has downed the first glass and is well into his second.

"Would you like to dance?" Ben puts his glass on the table and stands, holding out his hand. "You wouldn't mind, would you?" he asks Marco, who doesn't even look our way.

"Nah. Have at it."

I follow his gaze, and it's fixed on a tall, waif-like blonde draped over the railing a few feet away.

Ben helps me stand and guides me down the stairs to the dance floor, his hand never leaving the small of my back, but never straying far enough south to be offensive. And there's that tingle again.

I love to dance. Marco doesn't. So I don't often get the opportunity. It's no surprise that Ben is a great dancer. His moves are smooth and confident without being showy, and we have a lot of fun.

By the time we head back up to the table we're exhausted, and Marco has disappeared. But he's back in no time, seemingly in a much better mood. In a move that's completely out of character, he pulls me onto his lap.

"Did you have fun on the dancefloor, babe?" he asks, slipping his fingers under the wide straps of my dress for everyone to see. He never calls me babe. Or touches me this way. I don't miss the fact that the tingle I felt from Ben's touch is missing. Nor do I miss the smug grin Marco shoots at Ben. If I didn't know better, I'd think he was jealous.

Ben looks away as Marco pours an almost full glass of champagne for me, urging me to drink up.

I can see Lulu's mouth hanging open in confusion on the other side of the table. All I want to do is get off Marco's lap and sit in my seat, but I don't want to cause a scene. When Marco is in this kind of mood, he doesn't care who he offends or how badly he behaves. So I sit quietly on his lap while he strokes my bare arm, drinking champagne and wishing I was pretty much anywhere else.

More champagne arrives, and Marco guzzles it like it's lemonade. Tension is rolling off Ben until he stands abruptly.

"I'm going downstairs and catch up with a couple of people," he says and makes his way down the stairs to the main floor where he's quickly swallowed up by the heaving crowd.

Abruptly, Marco dumps me in an awkward sprawl on my chair, spilling my drink across the thick carpet.

"Marco!" leaps from my lips as I struggle to sit upright, which causes everyone to look our way. Great. I'm now the centre of attention, with champagne running down my bare leg.

"You're heavy. My leg's gone to sleep." He rubs his thigh without taking a break from slurping from his refilled glass.

"Are you okay?" Claire, who is sitting across from me, asks.

"Yeah, I'm fine. I might go to the bathroom, though." I surreptitiously swipe at the drops of liquid on my leg and skirt as I stand.

I'm sure there are bathrooms nearby—this club is not short on amenities—but I take the flight of stairs up to the next level where it's a little quieter. A headache is brewing, and I need a minute or two of peace.

The bathroom is as beautiful and luxurious as the rest of the club, all dark marble and low lighting, except for the spotlights over the mirrors. I flip the lid on the toilet down and sit, closing my eyes, relieved to have a moment of privacy. I hate it when Marco is in this kind of mood. And to behave like that in front of Nick and Will and Claire? Lulu is used to it, but I can only imagine what they're thinking.

As beautiful as this club is, and as much as I enjoyed the dancing, and most of the company, I can't bring myself to get up and go back downstairs. Marco's behaviour is embarrassing, and it's making me uncomfortable. I wish I could've come without him. God knows he goes out without me often enough. But when he got wind of the invitation, there was no stopping him.

I'm busy gathering my courage to return to the table when a wave of sound surges in with the opening of the door, swirling around me before receding as the heavy door thumps shut. I press my fingers to my throbbing temples. Quiet again. Except for the sharp clack of high heels on the marble floor and the banging of stall doors on either side of me. I'm about to open the cubicle door when a high-pitched nasal voice raises over the partitions causing me to drop back on the closed toilet lid and wait. I don't think they realise there's someone else in the bathroom.

"So, you remember how I told you about a guy I fucked last week? The one who tied me up?"

"Yeah, and then ghosted you?"

"That's the one. Well, he's here."

"What?" The conversation stops. Toilets flush. Doors bang. Heels clack. Taps turn on. I so don't want to hear this. But coming out of the stall now would be embarrassing. So I wait. Hoping they'll leave quickly.

"He's here. At a big table in the VIP section. Near the railing. Good looking, dark hair. Wearing a Tommy Hilfiger T-shirt and a leather jacket." My ears prick up. Fuck. I know who they're talking about. My heart starts to pound, and I feel sweat gathering under my arms. I peer through the gap in the door and see two skinny girls in short dresses with bright blonde hair, fixing their lipstick in the antique mirrors.

"Oh yeah, I know who you mean. He's hot. Are you sure it's him?"

Please say no.

Except, in my heart of hearts, I know what's coming next.

"Hey! I know I get around, but we only fucked, like, a week ago." They both snicker.

"Did he say anything?"

"No. Just gave me the side eye. He was with a girl."

"No shit! Which one?"

"The fat one squashed into that red satin dress."

Squashed?

I want to storm out of the cubicle and confront them. But I don't think I could face the humiliation of looking them in the eye.

"With the long dark hair?"

"Yeah, that's the one."

I look down at my red satin dress. Fat? I know I'm curvy. Sure, I could do with losing a few kilos, as Marco is fond of reminding me. But fat? It occurs to me this is a strange thing to focus on, given what they're talking about. I hold my breath, waiting for them to continue.

"Fucker. After you let him, like, tie you up and everything."

Tie her up? The man who won't touch me because he 'respects' me too much is tying women up?

"Yeah. I don't mind it a bit rough, you know, but I don't usually go for bondage on a first date. He was just so hot. Big dick energy, you know? I thought maybe we had a connection. Then, I never heard from him again. Fucker. And now he's here with some other chick." I'm shaking so badly I couldn't stand up if my life depended on it.

"Fuck him, then. He doesn't deserve your sweet self. And if that's his taste in women, you're better off without him, babe."

"Yeah, fuck him."

The voices recede as the opening and closing of the bathroom door lets in another wave of sound. I'm alone again. Still sitting on the toilet lid. Looking down at the red satin dress I loved when I put it on. Now I want to rip it off. That's my boyfriend they're talking about—the cheating bondage fan who treats women like trash. And I'm the fat girl in the red dress.

I stagger to my feet and manage to flip up the toilet lid seconds before I lose the expensive champagne we've been drinking.

CHAPTER TWO

BENEDICT

The club is packed. Pulsing. We should make pretty good bank tonight, even accounting for the freebies we're handing out to VIPs. I put a lot of money into this venture. But I'm confident it will pay off.

I lean on the railing of the upper balcony, looking down over the VIP area and the main floor. A girl I hooked up with a few weeks ago—the night before I first met Rosanna, in fact—is standing at the bar, scanning the crowd. We had fun. She was hot and eager. As always, I had made it clear this was a good time, not a long time. I suspect she's looking for me because I told her I'd be here. I could head down there, and I'm pretty sure she'd be keen to hook up again. The problem is, an almost-anonymous hook-up is not what I'm looking for anymore. Unfortunately, what I want is something I can't have.

From where I'm standing, I have a bird's eye view of the table where Will, Greer, and my friends are sitting. Along with Marco, the arsehole. He's no friend of mine. I scan the table again. No sign of Rosanna, but Marco is eyeing off some blonde at the end of the bar. What a shock.

It's still early, and I should be pumped, but I've had enough for tonight. I can't seem to shake off Will's comments about how a loser like me scored an invite to such a swanky club. There was a time, not so long ago, when I would've been amused. These days it stings. I'm aware of the role I've played in my family's impression of me, but it would be nice if one of them thought to actually look at me. See me.

I'm also not enjoying seeing Marco man-handle Rosanna. For the life of me, I can't work their dynamic out.

I'm about to head down the corridor to the office when the door to the ladies' room flies open and Rosanna staggers out, stopping in the middle of the hallway. She looks disoriented. I know she didn't have that much to drink because I was watching her.

Yes. Okay. Creepy, I know. But what can I say? I haven't been able to take my eyes off her since I first saw her at our mutual friends Nick and Lulu's Australian re-wedding. I've never felt anything quite like it. A surge of raw, physical energy and a kind of knowing rolled through me. All of a sudden, those feelings of romantic love I thought I had no capacity for are coursing through my veins, infusing every cell. Supporting every breath.

But right now, she's clearly not okay. If someone has roofied her drink in this club, there will be hell to pay.

She doesn't seem to notice me until I take her arm. Her whole body is trembling.

"Rosanna, are you okay?"

She turns to me with a glazed expression and shakes her head, mute.

"Wait here. I'll go and get Lulu." I start to lead her towards a small sofa on the landing, but her feet dig in, and she shakes her head again.

"No. No Lulu. I don't want ..." But she doesn't finish the sentence.

I can't leave her here so I reverse course and head back towards the office at the end of the corridor.

"Okay. No Lulu. Why don't you come with me?"

She moves slowly, swaying a little, but remains on her feet. I unlock the door. Whoever was in here last has left the desk light on, so I leave the overheads off and lead her towards the chair in the corner sandwiched between towers of boxes containing wine and spirits, guiding her into it. I drop into the desk chair and roll towards her, bracketing her knees with mine, taking in her pallor and wide eyes. If I had to guess, I'd say she's in shock.

I pick up the phone, dial the kitchen and order a pot of tea. All the while, Rosanna sits still and silent, her hands clasped so tight the knuckles are white. I don't want to wait for the tea, so I pull a random bottle out of one of the boxes. It's Drambuie, of all things. Doesn't matter what it is, though. She needs a shot of alcohol. I slosh a couple of fingers into a glass that looks mostly clean.

"Here. Drink this." I go to hand her the glass, but her hands are shaking so badly I have to hold it directly to her lips and she gulps it down, coughing violently as the alcohol burns her throat.

"Thanks." It's all she can manage around the spluttering.

We sit in silence. My mind is racing over the possibilities for the state she's in, but there's no point speculating. She'll tell me when she's ready. By the time the tea arrives, Rosanna seems to have relaxed a little. At least the shaking has stopped, and she wraps her hands around the cup, gulping it down despite its heat.

"Better?"

She nods and keeps drinking.

"Do you want to tell me what happened?"

"I don't know. Not yet." She keeps drinking, and I watch her until she finishes the tea and looks around at the cramped room. "Where are we? Are we allowed to be in here?"

"Yeah, it's fine. I know the owner." That's an understatement. And on a need-to-know basis, she doesn't. "Are you sure you don't want me to get Lulu?"

"No. She hardly ever gets out without the baby. And if you tell Lulu, Marco will hear ..." And the glazed expression is back. My blood starts to simmer.

"Did he do something? Hurt you?" If he hurt her, I'll kill the fucker. Even if it isn't my place.

"Yes. No. Kind of." Well, that's clear as a bell. In my experience, the best way to get someone to talk is to leave space for them to do it, so I say nothing. I lean forward with my elbows on my knees and wait. Eventually, she starts up again. "I went to the bathroom. I have a headache. I sometimes get migraines. And there were some girls in there. Blonde girls. Pretty. So thin. Like models." She stammers to a halt. In my mind, I've already put two and two together and come up with a cheating prick.

Marco is an arsehole, and I'm pretty sure I've seen him on the club circuit more than once. With skinny blondes, and I use the plural deliberately. I wait some more.

"He slept with one of them. I heard them talking. About how he tied her up. And then ghosted her." Big tears are starting to leak from her eyes, and her hands are shaking again so I pour her some more tea and slosh a big hit of Drambuie into it before handing it back over.

"How do you know they were talking about him?" It's possible she was mistaken. Unlikely, but possible.

"Because he's the only arsehole who still wears Tommy Hilfiger T-shirts." Looks like the booze hit the spot. "That lying, lowlife creep. And you know what else? They called me fat." The tears are really flowing now.

"What? They said that to you?"

"No. I was in the cubicle. But the one he ... you know ... told her friend he was here with a fat girl in a red satin dress." She sweeps her hand down her body and across her waist to illustrate her point.

I don't know what to address first. The fact that her boyfriend is cheating, or she was called fat. Since I can't do anything about the cheating boyfriend, I go with the fat comment.

"That sounds like jealousy to me. You are nothing short of spectacular. There isn't a man in this club who hasn't given you the once-over. Well, except for Nick. Oh. And Josh. But you know, they can't see anyone but Lulu and Greer. So ..." I shrug.

I know I've given her the once-over. More than once. More than twice. But she doesn't need to hear that.

Her melted chocolate gaze locks with mine, and I can read the disbelief as clearly as if she had spoken. Looks like Marco has done a real number on her self-esteem. This guy keeps getting better and better.

"I don't think that's true, but thanks."

"It is true. Between you and me, you've got the best boobs I've seen in, well, ever." This has the intended effect. She laughs. I think she's calm enough now for me to sort out what to do with her.

"I'm guessing you don't want to go back to the table. Do you want me to take you home?"

"Oh, no. That's okay, Benedict. I don't want to ruin your night. I can get a cab."

"No, you won't. Lulu would skin me alive if I didn't make sure you got home safely. And I've had enough of tonight anyway. But what are you going to do about Marco? Do you want to have it out with him now?"

"Oh, God, no. I couldn't bear it." She picks up the evening purse she had dropped on the floor and pulls out a phone. "I'll text him and say I've got a migraine and I'm going home."

"Seriously? He'd let his girlfriend go home alone with a migraine?" What a prize he is. A prize dick. I can't fathom what a gorgeous, funny, intelligent woman like Rosanna is doing with a shit like Marco.

"We'll soon find out. I'll message Lulu too." Her fingers fly over the screen, and within seconds, a message bounces back from Lulu, offering to take her home. They message back and forth for a few minutes before she looks up at me. "Yep. Looks like he would let me go home alone." She turns the phone, and I see the most recent message. From Marco. A thumbs-up emoji followed by 'cool'. That's it. As I said, arsehole. In fact, there aren't enough expletives in the English language to describe him.

While Rosanna was texting, I ordered a car and messaged the club manager and told him I was leaving. We take the back way out into the alley, where the car is already waiting, surprising Rosanna.

"You didn't need to order a car for me."

I shrug. It's the least I can do.

By the time we pull up outside her building, Rosanna is cycling through teary and moving on into angry again. She seems a bit too fragile to leave, so I tell the car to go and follow her upstairs.

"I'm okay, really," she says as she lets us into her apartment. "Don't feel you have to stay."

"I don't. I do want to make sure you're okay, though. You said you had a migraine. Where do you keep your headache tablets?" I ask, opening the kitchen cupboards until I find a glass, which I fill at the sink. Rosanna stands in the middle of the living room, looking like she doesn't quite know what to do.

"In the bathroom cabinet." She waves a hand in the direction of the hall beside the kitchen.

As I look for the tablets, I spot a huge bathtub surrounded by bottles of oil and bubble bath. Obviously well-loved and well used. I turn the water on, pour in some oil that smells like lavender—isn't that good for headaches?— and take the tablets back to Rosanna.

"Take these. I'm running a bath for you. Then we'll get you settled in bed."

Lucky for me, Rosanna is able to undress herself and get in the tub. That's a sight I would never be able to unsee, and it would not be good for our friendship if I had a vision of her, naked, burned onto my retinas. Maybe one day we might be more than friends, but right now is not the time to be thinking those kinds of thoughts.

Worried the combination of alcohol and headache tablets might make her drift off and drown, I slide down the wall outside the bathroom door and try to keep her talking. I don't need a Whitney-style tragedy on my hands.

"So, you must have missed Lulu while she was away in Scotland."

I figure it's best to stay away from the subject of Marco if I want to get her calmed down enough to sleep. Her best friend

Lulu recently married and had a baby with my friend Nick, which is how we met.

"So much. But I went to Scotland when Isla was born, so I did get some time with her then, which was lovely." She sighs, but it sounds more like a happy sigh than a sad one. "Nick is a great guy. But you'd know that, I guess."

"Yeah, he's solid. He's always been a pretty closed book. Lulu has really opened him up. It's good to see him so relaxed and happy. They seem really good for each other."

Another deep sigh. "Yes. They are. He loves her so much. It's beautiful to watch." She doesn't say anything for a while, but I can hear the gentle swooshing of bathwater so I know she's okay.

The rhythmic sound of the lapping water continues. After a while I hear the tap running, as though she's topping up the heat. More swooshing and sighs. I try not to imagine the sight of Rosanna in the bath, but it's a losing battle. And then there's a sudden rushing water sound, like maybe she's struggling. I'm up and into the bathroom before I even have time to think it through. Only to find her standing in the bath, reaching for a towel. And holy hell.

Whatever I had envisioned about Rosanna's body, I was wrong. Apparently, my imagination is lacking. Her bitter chocolate hair is piled in a messy bun on her head. Her body is all soft, lush curves, with a tiny waist nestled between perfect breasts and rounded hips. Her smooth olive skin is flawless, and the dark curls between her legs glisten with water droplets. I can't help but lick my lips. Other than that tiny movement, we're both frozen.

Clearing my throat, I break the tension. "What those girls said about you being fat? Couldn't have been more wrong. You're fucking perfect. From a man's perspective." I can hear lust in my voice and can only hope she's disoriented enough by the pills not to notice. The last thing I want is to make her uncomfortable. Or to feel like I'm hitting on her.

I pull the towel off the rail and put it in her outstretched hand, which seems to bring her back to reality, and she quickly covers herself up with the fluffy white fabric.

"Sorry to burst in. I thought ... anyway. I'll let you get dried off."

Back in the lounge room, I will my hard-on to subside before she comes out of the bathroom and notices the massive bulge in my pants. Fortunately, she heads to the bedroom and it's a few minutes before she comes back out wearing cute cotton pyjamas. Which shouldn't be sexy. They're like librarian clothes for bed. But knowing what's under them? Sexy as fuck.

"I don't think you should be alone tonight. You still don't look right. And you've had a bit to drink as well as the headache medication. I'll sleep here on the sofa, if that's alright?" I've already spread out the knitted throw I found on the arm of the sofa and arranged a couple of the many colourful cushions. Lucky for me, the couch is big and looks comfortable.

"You don't have to do that. I'm okay." She's roller-coasting again, tears flooding her eyes but not yet falling.

"I want to. You hop into bed. I'll be right here. Call out if you need anything." A huge part of me wants to tuck her safely into her bed, but that's way too dangerous, and she doesn't need me drooling over her at a time like this. I lie down and put the rug over myself as she heads into her bedroom, leaving the door ajar.

I lie awake, listening to her toss and turn for a while before the crying starts. It's a quiet kind of sniffling at first, but when it turns to strangled sobs, I can't listen anymore.

"Hey, hey, it's going to be okay." She's facing the middle of the bed, her back to the door, so I circle round and sit on the other side, stretching my legs out and propping my back against the padded velvet headboard.

Without a word, Rosanna slithers closer, and the sobs get louder for a while, before petering out to hiccups. I've slid down the bed a little and her head is cradled against my shoulder, the fabric of my shirt soaked with tears and probably snot, her hand resting on my chest, clutching a bunch of soggy tissues. But I wouldn't move for the world. I don't know how long it takes, but eventually, I realise she's drifted off to sleep and I lie there enjoying the warmth of her body snuggled against mine.

Somehow, I seem to have fallen into the knight in shining armour role for the loveliest princess in the land. And it feels good. Now all I have to do is not screw this up.

CHAPTER THREE

ROSANNA

W eird. I wake to the smell of coffee and bacon. For a moment, I can't quite get my bearings. And then I remember. Last night. The club. The ladies' room. No wonder my head feels like it's full of wet cement. But none of that explains the smells until a head full of messy red-blond hair appears around the door. Benedict Carter. Holy hell. Now the rest of it comes flooding back, and my cheeks start to burn.

"Oh, good. You're awake. I got you some breakfast." The rest of him appears, arms laden with a tray full of plates, cups and glasses. "I didn't know what you might like, so I ordered a bit of everything."

As he sits beside me on the bed, I recognise the berry pancakes from the café across the road. My favourite. There's also bacon, scrambled eggs, what looks like freshly squeezed orange juice, and two enormous takeaway coffees in keep-it cups with their logo on. As if all that isn't enough, sitting on a neatly folded piece of paper towel are two headache tablets.

"How are you feeling?" His gaze is earnest as it scans my face.

I must look a mess. I can feel how swollen my eyes are when I blink, and my lips are dry and cracked. No doubt my hair is a poorly constructed bird's nest, and my breath probably smells like roadkill. But there's no sign of distaste in his expression. Nothing but concern.

"Okay. I think." It's all I can manage to scrape out of my raw throat. He puts the tray on the floor and plumps up the pillows.

I'm grateful he doesn't open the heavy curtains. I can see by the light sneaking in through the gaps that it's bright outside, and I don't think I could deal with the light just yet. And right now, the harder it is for him to see me clearly, the better.

"Up you scooch. That's it." He arranges me comfortably against the mountain of pillows, tucks the doona around me, and slides the tray onto my lap before handing me a juice and the tablets. As I gulp them down, he settles on the bed beside me, stretching out his long legs, and helps himself to one of the coffees. Grabbing a fork, he starts to dig into the eggs. "These are really good." He couldn't be more relaxed.

Even if I wasn't suffering from a crying session hangover, his kindness would be overwhelming. I barely know Ben. He's a friend of Lulu's husband—we've met maybe three times. Including last night. And now he's seen me at my absolute worst. Not to mention naked.

"I'm really sorry about last night. I ruined it for you."

"Ahh, don't give it another thought. I'd had enough anyway. And I couldn't leave you to get home on your own. You'd had a terrible shock."

"I appreciate that more than I can tell you. And you certainly didn't have to stay and listen to me bawl my eyes out for hours. And get breakfast. You hardly know me. It's above and beyond."

The tips of his ears turn pink, which seems at odds with the cool and carefree guy I pictured him to be, based on everything I've heard about him. And yet, totally in keeping with the way he's treated me in the past twelve or so hours. It's strange, but everything about Ben tells me I can trust him, despite our limited acquaintance.

"It was my pleasure. Now, eat up before all this gets cold."

We eat in silence for a while, sharing from the plates as though we've done this a thousand times before. Despite my sorry state, I'm not at all uncomfortable or embarrassed, which is nice. If Marco had seen me like this, I would've been mortified. He would've insisted I shower and dress before we ate. Ben seems oblivious.

And while I undoubtedly look like something the cat dragged in, he looks delicious. His hair is a rumpled mess. The slight scruff he wears is a little longer than normal, edging towards the beginnings of a beard and his clothes are rumpled. Even the purple circles under his eyes seem to enhance their deep, deep blue, and brighten the red-gold hair. However you look at it, Ben Carter is a dish.

I think back to the first time we met at Lulu's wedding. He was dressed in a very sharp suit, and I couldn't help but ogle him. Which is odd. I rarely notice most men. But for some reason, Benedict stood out and had me feeling things I shouldn't. He's the complete opposite of Marco. In every way, it would seem.

The thought of Marco has some not-so-nice emotions bubbling up inside me. None of which are grief or hurt, strangely. Anger. Embarrassment. Shame. More anger. But not sadness or hurt. Benedict must see something of my inner turmoil on my face because he stands and reaches for the tray.

"Why don't you go and hop in the shower? You'll feel much better after a good long wash. I'll clean this lot up." Heads into the hallway to the kitchen.

I do feel much better after a shower. Ready to face what needs to be done. Although I'm still not sure what that is. I'm kicking Marco to the curb, that's for sure. How I go about it, and how I break it to my parents, is another matter altogether.

Marco not only works for my father, but since Dad got sick, he's more or less taken over the business on the understanding he and I would be getting married at some point. Which has been Dad's plan for me since childhood. Marry his best friend's son. A good Italian boy. When Dad finds out, he won't be happy. And when Dad isn't happy, nobody is. Which is why I've put up with Marco for so long. Because I'm the good Italian girl, and with Dad's health the way it's been, particularly since he had a terrible turn earlier this year, I've lived in fear of the potential consequences of upsetting him.

I find Benedict in my spare room, which I use as a workroom. It's stuffed to bursting with fabrics and finishes, two sewing machines, a big worktable and three dummies. The dummies are wearing half-finished costumes for a drag queen I work for on the side. He turns to me with a smile.

"Sorry. I hope you don't mind. I couldn't resist. Lulu told me you're a costume designer. I didn't realise you work from home."

"Oh, I don't. I work for a small ballet company as an assistant designer. I do work on the side for friends, even though technically I'm not supposed to."

"These are stunning." He gestures to the three dummies. "For a drag queen, I'm guessing?"

"How did you know?"

"They're just so ... extra, I suppose." His smile tells me he likes them despite how 'extra' they are.

"Have you heard from Marco this morning?" he asks.

"I doubt it. He plays golf on a Saturday."

His eyebrows rise as we head to the kitchen where he has thoughtfully put my phone on charge sometime since we got here last night. As I expect, there's no message from Marco. But two from Lulu asking me to call and let her know I'm OK.

I think about calling her. I love Lulu. She's like a sister to me. Which is why I can't call her. She'll be furious when she finds out what Marco has done. And I'm not ready to deal with her militant support right now. Curiously, the undemanding company of Benedict is exactly what I need.

"Do you have plans today?" I ask, while at the same time wondering what on earth I'm thinking. Why on earth would Ben want to spend more time taking care of my sorry arse?

"Nothing in particular. Would you like to hang out?" His single dimple makes an appearance. It's like he read my mind.

"I was thinking of heading up to Paddington Markets. Maybe I could buy you lunch as a thank you. If you're interested." It's the kind of day Marco would consider torture, but for some reason I get the impression Benedict might be up for it. Maybe it's the relaxed way he moves, but it seems like not much would faze him, and he could find pleasure in the simple things.

"That sounds great. I love the markets. Although you don't have to buy me lunch."

While he has a quick shower, I text Lulu.

Me: Hey, I'm OK. Just need to rest. Will call you tomorrow?

Lulu: Are you sure? Isla and I could come over and take care of you

Me: I'm sure. I'll be fine. Talk tomorrow

Lulu: OK, but call me if you need anything xxx

I may not have great taste in men, but I can sure pick a best friend. I don't know what I'd do without her. And I hope I never have to find out.

It's a beautiful summer's day in Sydney. Benedict and I stroll to the markets, stopping at all the odd little shops on the way. He's great company, keeping up a light banter and stopping me from dwelling on my shitful situation. When we reach the markets, he heads straight for a stall and picks up a vintage Nirvana T-shirt.

Wrinkling his nose, he sniffs the armpit of the shirt he had on last night. "This shirt stinks." And seemingly without a second thought, he whips it off in the middle of the market, passing it to me as he takes his new shirt from the stallholder. My mouth goes dry as I watch him slide it over his head and, crime of the century, cover up his incredible chest and a ladder of abs. He's tall. Maybe six two or three, and muscular, without being bulky. Unlike a lot of men now, he's left his golden chest hair, which covers his pecs and dwindles to a narrow trail disappearing into his jeans. Giving myself an internal shake, I hand him back yesterday's shirt and he stuffs it in the cotton bag the stallholder gives him.

"That's better." He settles the shirt across his shoulders.

I can't agree. He didn't stink—he smelt incredible. And it's definitely not better that he put a shirt on. There should be a law or something.

The markets are packed, as usual, and we wander aimlessly from stall to stall. Ben insists I buy a silk scarf in deep reds and burgundies with splashes of turquoise, and then treats me to some gorgeous rose geranium bath salts, because he noticed the geranium bodywash I use in the shower. I pick him up a cap to protect his face from the Sydney sun, and we load up on loaves of sourdough. When my stomach begins to rumble, despite the huge breakfast, I check the time and discover it's already mid-afternoon.

"How about some lunch? There's a great empanada truck beside the park near my place, and we could sit on the grass?" It's odd that I feel no self-consciousness around Ben. Just comfort and ease, despite my current circumstances.

"Hell, yes. I love empanadas. Impromptu picnic, here we come."

We find a shady spot at the park and despite my intention to buy lunch, Benedict insists I sit while he heads over to the truck and buys what looks like enough food for six.

"I couldn't decide." His ears turn pink again.

Once we've tucked into the food, Benedict clears his throat. "So, I realise it's none of my business, but have you thought about what you're going to do about Marco? Do you want to talk about it?"

"I don't know." I sigh. "I'm going to break up with him, obviously. But it's complicated. He works for my dad—our parents are friends—and Dad is unwell at the moment. The doctors have said no stress. I need to work out how to tell him without upsetting him."

"That is complicated." Is all he says, giving me space to work this out in my head.

"I know I cried a lot last night, but to be clear, it was more anger and embarrassment than anything else. I can't believe I didn't see what he was like."

"Hey, nothing for you to be embarrassed about. He seems like a smooth operator, and not in a good way."

"Well, I feel like there is. Can I be honest with you?" Ben nods for me to continue. "He's been my only boyfriend. We've been dating since I was eighteen. And ..." My cheeks start to burn, and I'm not sure if I can continue. I look down at my unfinished empanada.

"And?" Benedict urges.

"And we've never had sex," I blurt. "I wanted to, but he said he wanted to wait till we were married. That's why I'm embarrassed. I bought his stupid, cheesy lies. I'm such an idiot." I look up to find Ben's mouth hanging open. It takes him a minute to respond, and I'm not sure what to expect when he does.

"Hold on. Wait a minute. I didn't know you were engaged." He looks pointedly at my bare left hand.

"We aren't."

"So, wait, what? I'm having trouble getting my head around this. He wanted to wait till you got married, but he didn't propose, and you've been together, what, eight years?"

By now the heat from my blush runs all the way from my chest to my hairline.

"Yes," I choke out, gulping my drink before continuing. "When you put it like that, me staying with Marco sounds ridiculous. It *is* ridiculous."

"Fuck. That's ... that's fucked up. What an arsehole. I mean, I knew he was a bit of a cockhead, but that's ... Wow."

"So now I discover he's been with someone else, probably lots of someones, all the while telling me he wanted to wait." My anger is rising again, along with a heaping dose of embarrassment.

"Can we ... Do you mind if we back up a bit?" The wheels are turning in Ben's mind, struggling to catch hold of something that can't be made sense of.

I nod and shrug my shoulders, showing him he has free rein to ask what he wants.

"How did you two get together in the first place?" Ben asks, tentatively feeling his way through a minefield.

I pick at my empanada and think about how to answer.

"Growing up, I idolised Marco. He's four years older than me. He seemed so grown up and handsome. When he asked me out, I think I was a bit starstruck. I had no idea he'd ever noticed me. I was flattered, grateful for the attention. Plus, Dad has had his heart set on me marrying Marco since I was a little girl."

Saying it out loud, I realise how old-fashioned and sad it sounds. But Ben shows no sign of judgement.

"I get it so far. But why wait around for so long with no proposal and ... no sex?"

I wish I had a simple answer for him. But it's complicated.

"Good question. Honestly, I've been unhappy for a while. I was going to break it off a few years ago, but before I got the chance, Marco's father got cancer and died. I couldn't do it then. By the time things started to settle down, my father was sick. I guess I missed my window of opportunity. Which is no excuse. I should've left him years ago. Regardless of the complications it would cause for the family or Dad's business." I stop short of telling him about my fear nobody would ever want me if Marco wasn't interested. It's too humiliating.

"Has he always treated you like he did last night?" It doesn't surprise me Ben noticed the way Marco was with me. He seems to pick up on things most people miss.

"No. At first, he was kind. Attentive. Although, looking back, he was always a little distant, never affectionate. He always said he didn't want to disrespect me or my dad. As time went on, I don't know ..."

"I get it. You were the frog in cold water. You didn't notice when it started to get hot in that pot."

For the first time, I realise that's exactly what's happened. It's taken last night's revelation to show me how far things had deteriorated. "A stupid frog. I can't believe I didn't work this out sooner."

"Hey, that's how these guys work. It's so stealthy, you don't see it coming. I don't know what else to say. Except that this is not on you. At all. Because any guy who would date you and not make it his mission to get you into bed—fast—is an idiot."

Despite my anger at Marco, I laugh. "Well, thanks. I appreciate the compliment."

"Just calling it as I see it. And I get that it's complicated with your parents and all, but that prick needs to be made to suffer." Ben's defence of me strengthens my spine a little.

"Agreed."

We eat in silence for a few minutes. I can see from Ben's shifting expressions he's working through what I've told him. And then his face lights up. He dusts his hands off, takes a swig of his Coke and turns to me with a dazzling smile.

"He needs to suffer. You need vengeance. And I've got an idea."

Judging by the look of glee on his handsome face, it's a good one.

CHAPTER FOUR

BENEDICT

All day I've been pondering The Cockhead, as Marco shall be known from now on. Unless I can think of a better name for him. He's even worse than I imagined. I'm incensed on Rosanna's behalf, although she seems angry and embarrassed rather than hurt. Regardless, something has to be done to redress the balance. And I have an idea.

"Vengeance? Isn't that a little dramatic?" Rosanna laughs, although there's no joy in the sound.

"No. Not at all. Guys like him need to understand you can't treat women like this. You need to take back your power. So, do you want to hear my idea?"

"Sure, hit me with it." She uncrosses her legs and stretches them out, leaning back on her elbows on the grass. Which does great things for her breasts, and bad things for my trousers. I pull my knees up and rest my forearms on them to hide my response and focus on what's left of my lunch instead of her magnificent figure.

"You said it yourself; he won't have confined his cheating to a one-off." She flinches, and I feel terrible that I've inflicted more pain, but I continue. "So, where does he meet these women? In clubs, maybe, yes. But also on hook-up sites. So, we catch him with his own net. We set up a fake profile that looks like everything he might want in a hook-up—using the woman from the club as a template—and we lure him in. Arrange to meet. You're there, and he's caught red-handed."

Rosanna lets out a nervous laugh. "That's not a bad idea. But how do we know which site he might use? And how do we set up a fake profile? We can't just use anyone's picture; that wouldn't be right."

"We put the profile up on a number of sites and see if we get a bite. As for the picture, I might have that covered. I have a friend who I think would be more than happy to let us use her picture if we asked."

"But what about her profile? What if he sees it's the same girl?"

"He won't. For one, she's super careful about her online footprint so she doesn't do dating sites, and for two, she's a lesbian. So even if she were to go on dating sites, it probably wouldn't be the same ones."

Rosanna's eyes start to gleam. "You really think this will work?"

"Can't hurt to try. And yes, I think it'll work."

"So we arrange to meet somewhere, and when he gets there, I confront him?"

"Yep. He won't be able to weasel out of it because you've caught him in the act, and your parents will understand why you broke up with him because you have proof he's a cheater. So no blowback on you."

"I like it. When do you think we should do it?" It hasn't escaped my notice that she's talking as though we're in this together, which I don't mind at all.

"No time like the present. It might take a while for him to connect, and the sooner you catch him, the better. The trick will be not to tip him off before he's hooked. Do you think you can do that?"

"Ha. Sure I can. He won't have a clue."

Standing, I reach down and take her hand to help her up. I'm happy she's agreed to my plot. Partly because seeing a lowlife like Marco get his comeuppance will be fun. And partly because it allows me to spend time with Rosanna. Getting to know her better is a definite win.

On the way back to her apartment, I call the friend I have in mind, Sabrina, and leave a voice message, filling her in on the situation without using any names. Sabrina is a really cool chick I met years ago while I was travelling. She's not only beautiful but is a scary smart hacker turned app developer, and we've done a bit of business together over the years. She calls me back in minutes.

"Benny Boy. How the hell are you?"

"I'm great, Sab. You? Got anything new to run by me?"

"Maybe. Soon. I'll let you know. In the meantime, yeah, of course you can go ahead and use my picture. I'll send a few through. You can use them however you want. Let me know where they're going and once you're done, I'll wipe everything clean."

"You're a gem. It shouldn't take too long."

"I hope it all works out for your friend. Don't be a stranger."

A few seconds after we hang up half a dozen pics come through on my phone, most of which show a little more of Sabrina than I needed to see, which surprises me. For some reason, I hadn't expected she'd have such sexy pictures of herself lying around. She's always been a bit of a tomboy. Regardless, they're perfect for our purposes.

"We're good to go." I show Rosanna the pictures and her eyes nearly pop out of her head.

"Is she a model?"

"Nah. She's an app developer. Great girl. And once we're done, we let her know, and she'll clean up after us."

"How do you know her?"

"We do a bit of business together, from time to time."

"Oh. I thought ... Lulu said ... Never mind." Rosanna looks confused and embarrassed. I can imagine what she's been told about me. Normally, I wouldn't care, but I don't like the idea that Rosanna might have the wrong impression of me.

"Don't believe everything you hear about me, Rosanna."

· ♥ · ♥ · ♥ · ♥ · ♥ ·

It takes a couple of hours, but in the end, we put a profile up on six different sites. Between what Rosanna knows about Cockhead, what we piece together from the conversation of the girls in the club, and my knowledge of what men are looking for on hook-up sites—any single man who tells you he's never used one is lying—we come up with a pretty good profile if I do say so myself.

"What time does Cockhead finish golf?" I ask as Rosanna pours us a glass of wine. It's getting on towards dinner time, and we both need something to relax after the roller coaster of the last twenty-four hours or so.

"Oh, he'd be finished playing. They'll be in the clubhouse now. But I'm sure we won't get a hit today. He has his monthly poker game with the boys tonight." She's putting the bottle of wine back in the fridge when we hear a chime from her computer and we both jump. Our gazes lock.

"You've got to be kidding me." She doesn't move towards the computer but stands frozen in the middle of the kitchen. It's been less than twenty minutes since we went live on those sites. As I said, cockhead.

"Do you want ..." I gesture towards the laptop, not sure if she would want me to see it.

"No. I can't. Can you look?"

"Okay. It's not him. Jesus. This site is really disgusting. Some guy has sent a dick pic already." I nearly gag at the hideousness of the picture. What women have to put up with.

"Yuck. Can we swipe ... is it left?" Rosanna scrunches up her nose.

"He's already history." I take my wine and guide her to the sofa. "Maybe we should watch a movie while we wait?" I suggest.

We get another couple of random hits, and the tension in the room is off the charts before we hit pay dirt. Less than an hour after we loaded our fake profile.

I click on the icon, and there it is, on the nastiest site we chose, a message from a user whose profile picture is clearly Marco, shirtless. I throw up a little bit in my mouth at his profile name. Oh, and the pic. Which makes him look much taller and more built than he actually is.

"Is it him?" I can't tell if she looks hopeful or horrified. We deliberately didn't approach him directly. We put up the profiles in the hope he'd find them and do the rest himself. This needs to be entirely on him, with no wiggle room at all.

"I'm afraid so." I turn the laptop so she can read the message. I can almost see the steam coming out of her ears. Even I'm surprised by the speed of his response.

"He's got to be kidding. ItalianStallion69? That's his profile name. And this message?" She puts on a voice scarily like Marco's. "Hey gorgeous, you are hot AF. You down to meet?"

If this goes on too long, I think I'll have to get used to the taste of bile. But something tells me it will all be over very soon.

"Bastard. Okay, what do we do now?"

"We engage." I hand the laptop to Rosanna. I think it's important for her to be in control of the process from now on. She positions her hands on the keyboard. "What do I say?"

"Something that will encourage him to dig himself a big hole."

Rosanna flexes her fingers and starts typing.

Us: I don't know. I might need to see the goods before I get hot enough for that. (winky face emoji)

Rosanna looks at me before hitting send, her bottom lip caught tight between her teeth. We don't have long to wait.

Him: You won't be disappointed

This is followed by a dick pic. I've seen plenty of these in my day—a story for another time—but this one is a standout. It almost looks like a professional shot. Scratch that. It's absolutely a professional shot. Definitely not a quick selfie taken in the men's locker room at the golf club. His cock is oiled and hard, standing up out of pubic hair trimmed to within an inch of its life. His hand circles the base as though he's about to give himself a handie. But it's the lighting that sends it over the top.

Very moody, with the shadow of his average-sized dick lying across his thigh.

I laugh. "Wow. That's full on. Looks like a professional cock shot. He must have had it ready and waiting. No way to know for sure it's his cock though."

"Oh, it's his alright. Stupid prick left his signet ring on." Rosanna roars with laughter and I can't help but join her when I notice the ring on his pinkie finger. A huge, ostentatious gold thing.

"Do you want to go straight for the kill or toy with him for a bit?" I ask, hoping she'll choose the latter. I'm starting to enjoy this.

Taking a gulp of her wine, she moves to the dining table where she can type comfortably, and I head to the kitchen for the bottle of wine. "Oooh, let's toy with him."

"Yeah, baby. Let's get him so hot and bothered that by the time he meets you, he can't think straight."

Rosanna grins and starts typing. Before she hits enter, she reads out to me what she wrote.

"You wicked, wicked girl." I didn't expect that from Rosanna, but I'm totally on board with it. Despite the fact that he's an arsehole, and I'm not gay, or even bi, being part of this strange foreplay is weirdly arousing.

Us: What? No cum shot? (sad face emoji)
Him: Your wish ...

I nearly choke on my wine as she turns the screen to show me another pic. The photo he sends is obviously from the same photo shoot. And I do mean shoot. This one has captured a stream of cum shooting from his cock, some already having landed on his belly. Rosanna's cheeks are red, but her eyes are narrowed in thought as she starts typing, giving me a running commentary as I hover in the kitchen.

Us: (sad face emoji) I was hoping for a little live action
Him: You'll get plenty of live action when we meet baby

Us: Those pics are hot as fuck. I'm getting so wet. I need to finish

Him: How about I see a little of that wet pussy?

"Oh my God. We can't send him a picture. What are we going to say now?" Rosanna squeaks, wringing her hands together.

"Easy, we distract him. He won't be able to resist talking about himself."

She takes the ball—excuse the pun—and runs with it.

Us: What are you going to do to me?

Him: Oh baby, you're going to suck my cock. Right down your throat. Then I'm gonna fuck your tight cunt from behind while I spank your perfect arse

Rosanna stumbles over the c-word, which doesn't surprise me. She's not a prude, but it's not a word I can imagine her using.

Him: Hot enough for you, baby?

Us: So hot. But you should know, I like it a little rough. Think you can handle me, Stallion?

Him: I was built for a bit of rough, baby. Name the time and I'll be there to take you so hard you won't be able to walk

Rosanna and I look at one another and crack up laughing again.

"So, when do you want to meet the Stallion?" Rosanna needs to decide how much of this she can take. We must take too long to answer because he messages again.

Him: I'm up for a fuck tonight

"But tonight's his poker night." Rosanna looks confused.

"When he said he was playing poker, I don't think he meant cards, honey." I squeeze her hand. For a second, she doesn't catch my meaning, and then she's rolling her eyes.

"Of course, he didn't. I'm such an idiot. He's off fucking his brains out, and I think he's playing cards with his mates."

"Hey, look at it this way. At least you don't have to get an STI test, so it could've been worse. Also, objectively, his cock isn't that impressive."

Rosanna grins at me, slides the laptop towards her again and ups the ante.

"Let's see how committed he is to this. He usually comes to my parents' for dinner on a Sunday night."

Us: I can't tonight. I'm working at the club. How about tomorrow night?

We had called our avatar Kylie, and she works as a dancer in a strip club.

Him: What club and I'll come and watch

Us: I don't mix business and pleasure. Tomorrow night or nothing

Him: Tomorrow night it is. I'll have blue balls by then thinking about you stripping for other men. When and where?

"Oh. Shit. Where shall I tell him?" Rosanna panics. We hadn't expected this to move so fast. I don't want Rosanna meeting him in a bar where they'll be hard to keep track of, so we choose a restaurant nowhere near her place or his. That way, he won't worry he'll be spotted. Buying a woman a meal isn't in Marco's game plan.

Marco: Why not meet at a bar?

Us: You can buy me dinner first. I'm worth it

Marco sends a string of emojis that make it clear he's keen. We can't resist one last message.

Us: See you then Stallion. Have to go and finish myself off before work if you know what I mean ...

Marco logs off with another pic; this one isn't part of the photo shoot series. It's of his hard-on straining at the seams in bad-taste briefs.

"Ugh. He just took that. I recognise the tiles from the bathrooms at the golf club, the filthy pig." Rosanna is scowling so hard her forehead is in danger of splitting and her cheeks are flaming.

"To paraphrase my granny, arsehole is as arsehole does."

That cracks her up, and we both have a good laugh over what a complete waste of oxygen this guy is.

"Can you believe how quick that was?" Rosanna's understandable roller coaster of emotions is on the downswing again, and she looks a little shell-shocked.

"Sadly, I can. Guy's a total dickhead. And in no universe does he deserve you."

Before I can even take another mouthful of wine, Rosanna's phone is chirping with a text message:

Marco: Really sorry, but I won't be able to make dinner with your parents tomorrow night. Dennis from golf has broken up with his wife and I said I'd take him out for a meal. Catch up during the week, yeah?

Then there's the afterthought.

Marco: BTW, how's the headache?

"Wow. Took him less than two minutes to think up an excuse. Guess he's had lots of practice."

"Now, how are you going to meet him when you're supposed to be with your parents?"

"Easy. I'll go over there early, then tell them I have to leave because I promised to watch Isla for Lulu. They love Lulu, so they'll be happy for me to head off and babysit. They'll be heartbroken when I tell them we've broken up. They adore Marco."

She looks sad all of a sudden and despite what she said, I wonder if maybe some part of her still loves Marco and is too hurt or angry or humiliated to admit it. After all those years together, I couldn't blame her for being conflicted.

"Well, they won't once they hear about all this. The censored version, I'm guessing. And you're better off without him, you know."

"I know. And thank you. For saying that, and for today. And last night. Would it be weird to say I had a really good time?" Rosanna ducks her head and looks up at me from under those incredibly long lashes. If I didn't know it was embarrassment, I might think she was flirting with me. I wish.

"Hey, I had a great time too. Picked up a cool new shirt, chowed down on some tasty food, and catfished a total arsehole.

Not to mention I got to spend time getting to know you. Epic day." She doesn't look a hundred percent convinced.

Little does she know, despite the pain she's in, this has been the best day I've had in years.

CHAPTER FIVE

ROSANNA

After Ben leaves, I take a long, hot shower and climb into bed. I'm so grateful he found me in the hallway at the club. I can't believe his generosity in spending the whole day with me, although he did seem to get a lot of enjoyment out of catfishing Marco.

There are a couple of texts on my phone from Lulu checking in on me. I hate lying to her. She's more than my best friend and is always there for me when I need her. I have to tell her what's going on, but I'm so tired I can't do it right now, so I text to suggest brunch tomorrow.

Snuggling down into the pillows, I finally have time to think about how I feel. For someone coming so fresh off the breakup of an eight-year relationship, I'm in pretty good shape. I'm ashamed to say my pride is hurt rather than my feelings, which says a lot about our relationship. As does the fact that I had more fun with Benedict Carter today than I've had in a long time. And no, it has nothing to do with the fact that he's drop-dead gorgeous.

I also can't deny there's a vague sense of guilt that I'm trapping Marco. Does his bad behaviour justify mine? At the same time, I feel like he gave up all rights to be treated with respect when he behaved so appallingly. Not only to me, but to my father, who trusts him to take care of his daughter and his company. What will happen there, I have no idea. Dad's not well enough to run the company, but can Marco keep working there after what he's done?

With each twist of my thoughts, I turn over, punching my pillow, pushing the covers off, and pulling them back. My body is as unsettled as my mind. Maybe if I don't tell my parents why we broke up, he could stay on? The problem is, then I'd still have to see him regularly. And my parents will dig and dig until they find out why we broke up. Having my humiliation laid bare for them to see would hurt. I don't need their inevitable feelings of betrayal being added to mine. It's a tangled mess.

First things first. Break up with Marco. Then work out what to do about the rest of it.

Lulu is already at our old favourite brunch spot when I arrive the next morning, pram pulled up close to the table. She's so wrapped up in the contents of the pram that she hasn't spotted me. Like all new mums, I guess, she looks tired, but happier than I've ever seen her. As I watch, she pulls out her phone and snaps a picture, before settling back in her seat which is when she finally sees me.

"Hey you. How are you feeling?"

Her eyes search my face as I lean in for a kiss. It takes me a second to remember she's under the impression I had a migraine.

"I'm good. Starving. Let's order," I lie as I peer into the pram to check on the soundly sleeping Isla.

We make small talk—mostly about Isla—until our food and drinks are in front of us.

"So, I wasn't entirely honest with you on Friday night," I start. Lulu's fork pauses halfway to her mouth and I get what can only be described as a disapproving mum look. That didn't take long. Isla is barely five months old, and she's got that shit down already.

"What do you mean, you weren't honest?"

"I did have a headache, just not a migraine. But that's not why I went home early." I take a big gulp of the table water. This is going to be tough.

"What happened? Did Marco do something? After you left the table, he disappeared downstairs and only came back to the table to refill his glass, the cheap git." Lulu's eyes roll.

"It was Marco. But nothing he did at the club. While I was in the bathroom I heard two women talking. About him." I take a deep breath.

"Go on." Lulu leans forward, eyebrows raised. If I didn't know better, I'd think Lulu is expecting what comes next, but to be fair, she always expects the worst from Marco. Turns out she was right.

"About him and how one of them hooked up with him last week."

"What?" Lulu drops her knife and fork onto her plate with a loud clatter, causing Isla to jump in her pram and let out a squawk. Lulu pats her back to sleep and leans across the table towards me with a face like thunder. "Details, please."

She sits silently as I fill her in on what I heard in the toilets and what's gone on since. As soon as I mention our catfishing expedition—minus some of the dirtier aspects—she completely gives up on eating and puts both hands over her mouth, elbows on the table, probably to stop herself from interrupting. I can't tell if she's horrified or thrilled, but knowing how Lulu feels about Marco, it's probably the latter.

When I finally come to the end of the story, her eyes are wide with disbelief.

"What the actual fuck?" she whisper-shouts.

"I know. It's beyond mad."

"I don't even know where to start." She huffs and looks like she's about to speak but stops herself a couple of times before slumping back in her chair.

"And Benedict Carter helped you out with all this?"

"Yep. He was fantastic. Just the right balance of kind and thoughtful without being too sympathetic."

"Huh. Who knew? But why didn't you call me?" Lulu looks a little hurt.

"I didn't want to ruin your night. It's not often you get to go out without Isla. And I didn't want to make a big scene. I wasn't ready to deal with Marco. I needed to get away, and Ben was there, so ..."

"And those women called you fat? You know that's not true, Ro. You're gorgeous." Her mind is jumping all over the place, trying to piece the whole thing together.

"That's what Ben said."

Lulu sits up straight in her chair. "Ben said what? Did he hit on you?" Her tone is so 'accusing mum', I have to laugh.

"What? No. Of course not. It wasn't like that at all." I use the excuse of stirring my coffee to not look her in the eye.

"Good. Because you don't want to get mixed up with him. He's a nice guy and all, but he's a pants man. He's got no direction. All he does is party. You don't need that in your life right now."

"He doesn't see me like that. We're friends." Which is true. So why the twinge of something that could be disappointment? And I find I don't like her assessment of Ben. He doesn't come across as a directionless pants man to me.

We both tuck back into our food. Now that the drama of the story is over and the weight of my subterfuge is lifted, I really am starving.

"Well, I'm glad you had someone to look out for you." Lulu drags a piece of sourdough toast through what's left of her hollandaise sauce. "So. Tonight. You're going to be there when Marco thinks he's meeting this supposed stripper. Do you have a plan?"

"Ben has insisted on driving me, so I won't have to drive home if I'm upset. He's picking me up at seven. Showtime is seven thirty."

"What are you going to say?"

I lean back in my chair and run my hands through my hair in frustration and confusion. "Other than I never want to see his lying, cheating face again? I don't know. It depends on what he says, I guess." I've been having the conversation in my head since Ben left last night. Sometimes, I go with a less is more approach, and give him little more than a contemptuous look before walking away. Other times, I give him the serve of a lifetime. I have no idea which will give me more satisfaction, so I'm going to wing it and do what feels right at the time.

"If you think you're doing this alone with Ben, you can think again, sister. I'm coming with you. And afterwards we can de-brief with lots of gin. For you anyway. I'll stick to ginger beer." Lulu developed a craving for ginger beer during her pregnancy. It helped with the nausea, and she's been addicted ever since.

"Really? I know it's tough to get away when you're breast-feeding. I'll be fine, honestly."

"Oh, no you don't. I'm coming. I have plenty of milk ex-pressed, so Nick can give Isla a bottle if she needs it. You'll be doing him a huge favour. He loves to have her all to himself."

As if the sound of her father's name has alerted her, a brief wail comes from the pram, and Lulu checks her phone. "Right on time. You could set your clock by this girl."

As she gets the baby settled in for a breastfeed, I take a mo-ment to text Ben and let him know Lulu wants a ride-along with tonight's operation. Which I love her for. Although I'd be lying if I didn't admit a teeny tiny part of me was looking forward to being alone with Ben. Which sets off a cascade of guilt. But I can't analyse that right now. I have bigger problems to solve. Namely, Marco.

Once she's finished feeding, I get some cuddle time with the baby while Lulu inhales a Danish and another cup of chai. I couldn't love this baby more if she were mine. I'm not ready to be a mum. I have too much I want to do in my career. But I always thought one day I would give my parents grandbabies. That dream's a little further off than I had hoped now that I'm back to square one in the relationship department, I guess.

"So, what are you wearing tonight? Ooh. I know. Let's get you something new. It has to be super sexy to rub his nose in what he's thrown away. That little shop up on Oxford Street has some great stuff." Lulu starts to pack up the baby paraphernalia and gestures for the bill.

An afternoon shopping with my girls sounds like exactly what I need. We head off along Oxford Street, stopping in any boutique that takes our fancy.

You might think shopping with a baby would be a nightmare, and maybe with some babies it would, but Isla the Wonderchild is an angel. Not only does she lie happily in her pram watching the proceedings, she's so damn cute she charms every shop assistant—and many of the customers—we come across. By midafternoon, we've found a sensational black silk dress and some killer new heels. Mission accomplished. I'm a firm believer in the confidence of a spectacular outfit, and this one will carry me through for sure.

Nick comes to pick Lulu up, and we decide we'll all head to my parents' place. They've been after me to bring Lulu and the baby over since she arrived back in Sydney. They haven't met Nick, so we're killing two birds with one stone. Bonus—having the baby with us gives me the perfect excuse to leave early. No need for fibs.

Lulu fills Nick in on the Marco situation and plans for tonight on the way. It warms my heart how angry he gets on my behalf.

"If there's anything I can do for you, Ro, let me know. I've had some pretty questionable clients over the years. Maybe one of them could arrange for Marco to have an accident." I know he's kidding, but it sure is tempting.

We pull up outside Mum and Dad's and no sooner has Nick lifted the baby carrier out of the car than my mother is running down the front path, arms wide, heading straight for Lulu.

"Lulu, *bella*, it's so good to see you. It has been too long. So much excitement for you. *Un matrimonio. Una bambina*. We are so happy for you." Mum wraps Lulu in a crushing headlock, kissing whatever part of her face she can find. I roll my eyes at Nick, who is standing stunned by the display. "The *bambina*, let me see the *bambina*."

"Mum, calm down. The baby's here."

Lulu staggers to Nick's side and takes his free arm. "Flavia, this is my husband, Nick Pierce. And this is Isla." Taking the carrier from Nick, she lifts it so my mother can see the baby. How she slept through all this noise is beyond me.

"Oh, *è bellissima, molto bellissima.*" By now, Mum is crying, Lulu is laughing and Nick and I are waiting patiently for it all to stop. But of course, then Mum realises she hasn't paid Nick the attention he so clearly deserves.

"Ah, *Nico, Nico, Nico. Benvenuto alla casa nostra.*" And my tiny little mother is wrapping her arms around him. I snort out a laugh at his look of bemusement.

"She said, welcome to our home. She lapses into Italian when she gets emotional. Or excited. Just nod and smile and you'll be right."

"Thank you so much for having me. I'm sorry we arrived unannounced. I hope that's alright?" Nick was raised in a pretty buttoned-up waspish home. Since he met Lulu, he's relaxed a lot, but those private school society manners still kick in from time to time.

Mum makes a tsking noise in her throat, waving away his concerns. "*Non è un problema.* Come in, come in and meet Andrea." Mum whips the baby carrier away from Lulu and starts up the path.

"You'll get used to the language changes," Lulu says, kissing Nick on the cheek. He takes her hand and follows behind my mother, who is shouting—despite the sleeping baby—for my father. Seeing the way Nick is with Lulu gives me hope. One day, maybe I'll find a man who cares for me that way.

As always of late, Dad is in his favourite recliner. Years of smoking and working on building sites have taken their toll on his lungs, and he's in the early stages of emphysema. He still goes to work a few days a week, otherwise, he can usually be found in this recliner watching European soccer. It's hard to watch a man who ruled our house with an iron will be reduced to a frail shadow. Although his fiery temper and determination still make the occasional appearance.

Before anyone has a chance to stop her, Mum is unbuckling Isla from her carrier as though she's been doing it her whole life and handing the now stirring baby to my father.

"*Questa è la figlia di Lulu, Isla. Non è bellissima?*"

Dad starts to tear up. He loves Lulu and he loves babies. "*Sì, sì. Che belli capelli rossi.*" Dad strokes his shaking fingers over the red curls on Isla's head. Seeing Isla sets them off on a rant about why I haven't given them a grandchild yet, adding another dimension to my anxiety about telling them about Marco, and causing a lump to form in my throat.

For the next hour, I sit back and watch my parents fuss over Lulu, Nick and Isla, plying them with food, cuddles and more attention than they might be comfortable with. Isla is, as always, an angel and spends her time smiling and making cute baby noises at my parents, before falling asleep in my father's lap. I hadn't thought of it, but bringing Lulu, Nick and Isla was the best thing I could've done today. It stops me from dwelling on what might happen this evening and distracts my parents enough that Marco's name is barely mentioned. Other than to say how beautiful the babies I'll have with him will be. Ugh.

Soon enough, we're struggling out the door with full bellies, boxes of leftovers, bottles of home-made Limoncello and promises to visit again soon.

Back at my apartment, Lulu gives Isla one more feed and sends her on her way with Nick so we can get down to hair and makeup.

I take a long shower, using the moments of privacy to think about the situation I find myself in and mentally prepare for battle.

By the time I'm putting the finishing touches on my makeup, the anxiety is starting to kick in big time. I'm relieved when I hear the buzzer from downstairs. Ben is here. I know he won't let this go sideways. Which is strange since I hardly know him. Yet another thing I can think about later.

CHAPTER SIX

BENEDICT

On my way home from Rosanna's last night, I messaged Sabrina and filled her in on what had happened with Marco. With any luck, by Sunday evening, I'll be able to give her the go-ahead to wipe all traces of what we've done from the internet. They say once it's on the internet, it can never be truly removed, but that isn't strictly true. And if anyone can get rid of all traces, it's Sabrina. Before she turned her talents to good instead of evil, she was a first-class hacker.

I considered swinging by one of my clubs to check on things but decided I needed an early night, so I got the car to drop me at my place. I didn't get much sleep last night, what with Rosanna's curves nestled in beside me. I told her she was perfect when I interrupted her bath last night and I meant it, and just like that, my cock was perking up at the memory.

Getting in the shower, I lathered my hands with soap before taking hold of my hard-on. Part of my brain told me I shouldn't be giving in to these thoughts about Rosanna for a whole host of reasons. Not least of which is she needs a friend right now, not some creeper hitting on her. But I also knew I'd never get to sleep unless I took care of this situation, so I closed my eyes and pictured her as she looked standing in the bath, wet and naked. It didn't take me any time at all to come like a charging bull, heart racing, legs shaking. I consoled myself that what Rosanna doesn't know won't hurt her, and I sure as shit won't be telling her about what I did.

As I tried to settle into sleep, it occurred to me this Marco creep might not take too well to what we have planned, and we need to be prepared. I shot off a voice message to one of my security guys and arranged for him to be nearby in case things go pear-shaped. I also put a note in my diary to do a bit of background work on Marco. Just in case. Never go into a situation without ammunition is my philosophy.

First thing Sunday morning, I call Rosanna to check she's okay and still good for this evening. I'm happy to hear she's spending the day with Lulu. I don't know Lulu well, but I've known Nick all my life. Although we couldn't be more different, I do know he's as solid as they come. So if Lulu is good enough for him, she's good enough for me.

Then I settle into doing some due diligence on Marco. The more I uncover, the less I like him and the shadier he looks. It's clear his business ethics are flexible, at best. This situation requires more investigation. I decide to keep what I've found to myself for the time being. Rosanna doesn't need to be any more upset than she already is.

Once I've set up a file on Marco, I get down to some real work. The comment Rosanna almost made yesterday and her surprise at me 'doing business' hurt more than it should because I know the impression my family and friends have of me is entirely my own doing. A persona I constructed years ago to protect myself. And maybe to protect them as well. I couldn't bear to let them down again. If their expectations are kept low, well, they won't be disappointed.

Pushing those thoughts aside, I put in my earbuds and crack on with reviewing some proposals that have been sent to me. I have a fantastic assistant who works part time out of my home office during the week, and she's left me with an organised list of things to review. I record a few notes for her to follow up before turning to the quarterly report. Things are looking good. What does it matter if my parents think I'm a flake who can't settle down? I know the truth.

By midafternoon, I'm restless. After twenty minutes of pacing, I throw on my running gear and hit the streets for an hour. I arrive back home sweaty and exhausted. While I'm waiting for the lift, I chat with the doorman. Not many Sydney apartments have a doorman, but I love having a gatekeeper on top of the electronic security. This particular guy is my favourite. He's old school, and I'd trust him with my life.

"Hey, Ray, how're you doing?"

"Not too shabby, Mr Carter. How about you?"

"I'd be doing better if you'd call me Ben." I've asked him a thousand times, but he won't budge.

"That's the beginning of a slippery slope, Mr Carter. I start calling you Ben, and before you know it, I'll be having coffee with Mrs Phillips in 12C and calling her Daphne, and then where would we be?" He grins because we both know Mrs Phillips in 12C would never stand for being called Daphne, let alone have coffee with the doorman.

"Good point. By the way, could you add someone to my security list please?" I have no idea why I ask this, but for some reason, it seems right. Maybe it's my unease about Marco, but I'd rest easier if I knew Rosanna could come here if she needed somewhere to go in case of an emergency.

"Of course. What's the name?"

"Rosanna Moretti. Give her full access, Ray. Even if I'm not home. You can let her in any time."

Ray gives me a sly grin. "No problem, Mr Carter. I'll put it in the system and make sure the other guys know. I'm guessing she's pretty special?"

I can't think of anyone else I've given this sort of access to other than my assistant. Not even my mother or father. Certainly never a woman. What does that say about how I'm feeling?

"She is, but it's not like that. She's a friend going through some stuff and might need a place to stay. That's all."

He attempts, and fails, to wipe the grin off his face. "Certainly, sir."

The elevator dings before I have a chance to reply. I get in and swipe my card for access to my floor, where I have one of the two penthouse apartments.

Before I hit the shower, I message Mum to tell her I won't be at our regular Sunday night dinner tonight. I find this family ritual both comforting and excruciating. At least this week I have a good excuse not to go.

I should be thankful. I know my family love me, which is more than a lot of people can say. They just don't understand me. Not surprising since I hold them all at arm's length. Which hasn't bothered me much until recently. I don't know why, because business couldn't be better, but I'm feeling unsettled by the status quo in my life. Maybe it's time to come clean and stop lurking on the periphery of my family, pretending to be something I'm not. It's starting to get lonely outside the tent.

I look around my apartment. I'm proud of what I've achieved. So why do I continue to let them think I've blown all the money Granny left me and am freeloading a room from a friend with a multi-million-dollar apartment? My smoke and mirrors act has served its purpose and managed expectations for quite a while now, but it's time to step up, I think.

I arrive at Rosanna's apartment ten minutes early. I tried to wait downstairs, but I'm too hyped. Also, I want to make sure she's okay before we get going. Lulu answers the door.

"Hey Ben. Come on in." She steps back so I can enter. "Ro's ready. She's doing one last nervous wee." She laughs. I don't mention I've needed to do a couple of those myself.

"That might be more information than I needed, but thanks. How has she been today?"

"Surprisingly good, for someone who just found out their boyfriend of eight years is a lying, cheating manwhore." I can tell by her expression she'd like to get her hands around Marco's neck. Get in line, lady. "And by the way, I want to say thanks. She told me what you did for her and how much support you've given her. I'm glad she didn't have to deal with this alone."

I might be imagining it, but her tone almost seems to be saying *I've got this from here*. Well, if that's the case, I've got news for her. Before I have a chance to respond, the bedroom door opens, and the woman we've been discussing is standing there. In a figure-hugging black dress that screams *touch me* and sky-high heels that add *fuck me*. She looks sensational. My brain short circuits for a moment, and the best I can do is let out a long, gusty sigh.

"Fuck," I huff. Rosanna fiddles with a large gold hoop earring, looking a little nervous and uncertain but a whole lot of sexy.

"Ro, you look incredible," Lulu says, so much more articulate than me.

"It's not too much?" Rosanna smooths her hands down her skirt and looks at us both, one perfectly shaped eyebrow raised. Her long hair is up in a messy bun and her lush lips are painted fire-engine red. She looks like a movie star.

"Not too much. Perfect. If he doesn't fall to the floor and kiss your feet and beg for forgiveness, he's more of an idiot than I thought. Which would be quite a feat." Lulu goes in for a hug.

"What she said," I add, finally reconnecting my brain and mouth, although not very effectively. "But if he does, you kick him in the face with those fuck-me shoes and walk away. Nothing he could say or do makes him good enough for you."

Rosanna smiles wide, and her shoulders straighten. Right there is the woman who sat with me yesterday and lured Marco to his demise. Nobody seems to know what to do next, so I clap my hands.

"Okay, ladies, let's get this show on the road." I hold open the door for Rosanna to exit, and Lulu runs back to the kitchen for a couple of bottles of water as though our stakeout will take hours instead of minutes.

We have to circle the block a few times to find the right parking spot for Lulu and me to have a good view of the restaurant entrance without being seen since Marco knows both of us.

"My palms are sweating." Rosanna grabs a tissue from her bag and wipes her hands before getting out.

"You've got this," I say. "Channel your inner fiery Italian, and you'll be fine. And remember—we're right here. We can be in there in five seconds if things get ugly."

We've all agreed Rosanna will keep her phone on her lap. We'll text when we see him coming; then, she'll call us so we can hear what's being said. This was my idea and Rosanna thinks it's a bit of overkill. But she doesn't know what I know about Marco. I don't honestly think he'd hurt her, especially in public, but you never know. Lulu voices my thoughts as Rosanna enters the restaurant and she hops in the front with me.

"You don't seriously think he'd get physical, do you?" Sadly, she looks like she believes he might.

"No. Not in a public place. But it could get ugly. If he starts anything, I'd rather be prepared. See the guy at the bus stop? In the black hoodie?"

Lulu peers through the windscreen. "Yes ..."

"He's a seccie. One word from me and he'll have Marco out of there in less than a minute."

"Wow." Lulu's mouth drops open. "You're really taking this seriously, aren't you?"

"You didn't see the conversation I saw yesterday. And I've never had a good feeling about that guy. So yes, I'm taking it seriously."

"Does Rosanna know about the security guy?"

"Of course not. No need to scare her any more than she already is. But I've got her back. I can't control what The Cockhead says, but I can sure as fuck control what he does." I don't like her going in there alone, but I've done what I can to minimise the risks. At least from a physical standpoint. The emotional risks are something I'll deal with later.

I reach over to the back seat and hand Lulu one of the two black baseball caps I brought. "Here, put this on. In case he looks over here. That hair would give you away in a second." Lulu has wild blonde curls. Once seen, they're not soon forgotten. She stuffs them as best she can into the cap and pulls it low on her forehead.

"You've thought of everything. Were you a spy in a previous life?"

"No, but I was a boy scout for a while, so..." I shrug.

That makes her laugh, despite the tension rising in both of us.

"She doesn't deserve this," Lulu whispers.

"No. She doesn't. But she does deserve someone who loves her. Respects her. And if going through this will get her to that, then I guess it will be worth it. Better now than when they're married with kids."

I can feel Lulu's gaze searching my face, but I keep my eyes forward in the direction we expect Marco to come from.

Adrenaline has had me as jumpy as a scalded cat all day, but now that it's time, I'm laser-focused. In a matter of minutes, Rosanna will be free of this creep.

The street isn't busy, so we spot him easily as he swaggers towards the restaurant. Lulu bashes out a text to Rosanna while I call Tama at the bus stop and let him know it's on.

"Looks like it's show time."

CHAPTER SEVEN

ROSANNA

I nearly jump out of my skin as my phone silently vibrates. One glance at the screen tells me it's time. I bring up Lulu's number, hit dial and speaker, and place it face down on my lap. By the time I look up, the front door is swinging open. I chose this table because it's right in the middle of the restaurant, with my seat facing the door. Marco couldn't miss me sitting here.

The look of panic on his face when he sees me is comical. I struggle to suppress a shiver of revulsion at the sight of him. He scans the restaurant once and then again, no doubt noticing there's not a sexy blonde sitting alone at a table. He's fifteen minutes late, I'm guessing so he could pull a no-show if it turned out that in person 'Kylie' is not as advertised on the website.

I smile and wave, so he's in no doubt I've seen him, although I suspect my smile is more like a grimace.

He stalks over to the table and scowls at me. "Rosanna, what are you doing here?" Apparently, it still hasn't dawned on him what is happening. He's dumber than I thought.

"I could ask you the same question."

"I'm here to meet up with Dennis from golf. I told you. He got the sack and needs some cheering up." The whole time he's talking, he's scanning the restaurant. A bead of sweat runs down the side of his cheek.

"Hmm. I thought you said his wife had left him. Still, I'm sure a night out with the Italian Stallion will make him feel *much* better." Finally, Marco's head snaps around, and he looks me in the eye. I can almost see the penny rolling towards the slot and dropping in.

"What the fuck do you mean?" he hisses, sliding onto the chair opposite me, his body language suddenly intimidating, making it clear how little I really knew the man.

"Just that a night with the Italian Stallion seems to be in great demand. Although I did think it was Kylie you were meeting, not Dennis. I have to be honest; I had no idea you swung both ways." I smile with as much venom as I can muster, which, judging from the panic on his face, must be a lot. "But I guess there are a lot of things I had no idea about."

"What are you talking about? I'm meeting a mate. You're supposed to be at your parents'. Why are you here?" I can't believe he's still trying to bluff his way through this.

"I came to let you know you won't be meeting Kylie tonight. She had a better offer. Which wouldn't be difficult, really."

He's still not ready to give in. "Who's Kylie?" His fingers drum the table in a fast, uneven beat. He won't be giving Henry Cavill any sleepless nights over his next acting gig, that's for sure.

"Kylie is a friend of mine. Nice girl. But not interested in you. She's got far too much sense. Oh, and she prefers the company of women."

His face is now a mottled red and sweat is pouring down both temples. I'm a bit worried about his eyeballs. They look like they're going to burst out of his head.

"I don't know what the fuck you're talking about." He leans closer, and I notice froth gathering at the corners of his mouth. Ewww. "I don't know any Kylie. You're batshit crazy." Aaand, there we have it. How did I not see how he'd been gaslighting me all these years? Suddenly, I'm weary of the whole thing.

"You do know. She's the pretty blonde stripper you sent those very arty dick pics to yesterday. But not the blonde from the club on Friday night, who you fucked last week and then ghosted. So, I thought perhaps I should tell you, in person, because I'm principled like that. This,"—I wave my hand between us— "is over." I go to stand, but his hand whips out and grabs my wrist, pinning it to the table, forcing me to stay in my seat. An electric current of fear runs down my spine, and I remind myself we're in a public place. Ben and Lulu are listening. I'm safe. Even if it doesn't feel like it.

"You don't get to decide this is over," he hisses.

"I believe I just did." It takes every ounce of self-control I have, but I don't give him the satisfaction of trying to stand again or struggling to get my wrist free. Based on what I've recently discovered, I have a feeling he'd enjoy that. Our voices are low, but it must be obvious to everyone we're arguing because I can feel the silent stares from other tables. My heart is pounding, but I try and keep my expression and my voice calm. Cold. Unlike Marco's boiling anger.

"I don't think so. You're going to sit down and shut up. What you want is irrelevant. I'm in charge here. It's best you get used to the idea now. Before we get married."

"You're deluded. Why would I marry you? Christ knows what diseases you've picked up. Not to mention you've spent the last however many years lying to me and fucking other women." I lean as far back in my seat as his grip on my wrist will allow.

"You're the woman I'm going to marry, not the woman I want to fuck." Marco spits, eyes wild.

"Excuse me? Here I was thinking I should be both." I clench my fists to stop my hands from shaking. I'm hoping the server will come over, but unsurprisingly, they seem to be avoiding us.

"You're being ridiculous. We'll have sex once we're married." Contempt is dripping from every word.

"Have sex? Not fuck? Not make love? I may not have much experience—well, apart from those occasional deeply uninspired trips to third base with you—but I do know there's a difference. And I'm not prepared to settle for second-best duty-sex. Not now, not ever. Neither will I tolerate a liar and a cheat." I take a deep breath. "Now let go of my arm before I scream for help." I look up to see a giant of a man in a black hoodie and jeans standing beside Marco's chair.

"You heard the lady. Let go of her arm and get out, before you can't walk out on your own legs." Even his voice is menacing, yet when he glances at me, I see kindness. Which is in stark contrast to the look he gives Marco.

I have no idea who this guy is or where he came from, but thank Christ he's here. Marco stands up and straightens his shirt.

"Fine. Have your temper tantrum. When you calm down and can think rationally, call me," Marco sneers, his face having gone from mottled red to a strange shade of green. "Because we both know you will. I'm your only option. Who else would want you? And breaking up with me will upset Daddy, and we wouldn't want that, now would we?"

"Oh, I'm thinking rationally for the first time in years. It'll be a cold day in hell before I ever call you!" A little of my cool has left, and I've shown him the anger underneath. I want to stand and go toe to toe with him, but I'm not sure my legs will hold me.

"Don't be too sure of that, *Princess*," he shoots at me as he walks away. Princess. From most people, that would be considered a term of endearment. From Marco, it's a dig at how my parents treat me. But if he thinks such a cheap shot from him could hurt me, he's sadly mistaken.

The giant in the hoodie follows Marco out the door, and I lose sight of them both as they turn down the street.

I take a gulp of the water the server put in my glass. My hands are shaking so hard that I spill it down the front of my dress. It matches the cold sweat trickling down my back. A few people are still staring, but most have returned to their dinners, although the restaurant is unnaturally quiet. I sense a presence at my elbow and turn to find a server putting a glass of red wine on the table.

"On the house." She smiles. "You were awesome, by the way."

I've got a whole-body shake going on now, so I thank her and gulp down the wine, then head for the door on unsteady legs. I look up and down the street but can't see any sign of Marco or the giant, only Ben and Lulu waiting by the bus stop right outside the door.

"Oh my God. Are you okay?" Lulu grabs me in a hug as my knees give way.

"Yes. I think so. A little rattled, but I'll be okay." More than a little. My smile is wobbly, and I'm not sure if my legs will hold me up, much less take me across the road to the car. I'm grateful Lulu keeps an arm around me.

Ben takes the phone still clutched in my frozen hand and ends the call still connected to Lulu's phone. "You were incredible. You held your nerve and didn't take any shit. And you maintained your dignity. You should be really proud of yourself."

"Thank you." Keeping a smile on my face is like trying to nail jelly to a tree.

"You know what I think? I think we've all earned a drink." Ben bundles me into the car and pulls into the traffic. It's a relief to sit down again.

"A drink sounds good. I was fine at first, but towards the end, I started to feel a bit threatened. Then, this giant of a guy appeared. Out of nowhere. And told Marco to leave or he wouldn't be able to walk."

There's silence from Ben and Lulu, although I see them exchange a look in the rear-view mirror.

"Wait a minute. Do you know something about that?"

"It was only a precaution," Ben says, concentrating on the road.

I look back at Lulu, and she shrugs, tipping her head towards Ben. "Don't look at me. That was all Ben's doing. And I'm so glad he did it. I was beginning to think things would get physical towards the end."

"You arranged him?" I can't believe Ben organised protection for me.

Ben looks a bit sheepish. "I wanted to make sure you were safe. Like I said, I got a bad vibe from the guy from the start. Just as well because it was all seconds away from going nuclear."

"I think everyone in the restaurant was a bit worried about that, to be honest. You should've seen his face. It went from white to red to green. And he was sweating bullets. What I can't believe is how long it took him to give up arguing. He never even admitted what he'd done." My hands are gripping the seatbelt, and I force them to relax. "Still, it's all over now, so I don't ever have to think about him again. Well, once I've told Mum and Dad. Shit. That won't be easy. But at least he gave me plenty of ammunition." I know I'm babbling, but the adrenaline is starting to subside, and I'm scared I'll break down if I don't keep my mind occupied. I have no idea what I would do without the solid presence of Ben and Lulu.

Ben parks in front of a fancy-looking pub and we head inside. The guy on the door greets him politely by name, and within seconds, we're seated at a freshly set table in a quiet corner of the bistro.

Before we have a chance to order, a bottle of expensive Australian sparkling wine arrives in an ice bucket with three glasses. Curious. Almost like they were expecting us. All the staff seem to know Ben by name, so I guess this must be one of his locals.

"To Rosanna and to taking back your power." Ben holds up his glass in a toast, and Lulu follows suit. I'm still thoroughly shell-shocked but tap my glass against theirs and knock back the better part of the glass. The bubbles, sitting on top of the red wine, start to take effect and my shaking finally settles.

As I put the now empty glass down, I see a familiar large figure standing in the doorway on the other side of the bar.

"Hey, there's the guy who came to my rescue." He catches my eye and makes his way over to our table.

"How are you? Did he hurt your arm?" He gives me a kind smile that looks oddly sweet on his tattooed face.

"I'm fine. Really. Thank you so much for coming to the rescue. My arm is okay. No real harm done." We all look down at my arm where bruises are already starting to show. Ben and Lulu exchange glances like daggers before he gets up and excuses himself, walking away with the giant.

"What was that about?" I turn to Lulu, who's attempting to look innocent and failing.

"No idea. Guess they have something to discuss. Ben's very protective of you for someone he's only met two or three times," she comments, raising her eyebrows.

"Well, he's a really kind person." I can't explain to her what's going on between Ben and me because I don't even understand it myself. I've barely escaped what can only be described as a toxic, if not abusive, relationship, so any feelings I may or may not be having towards Ben are entirely inappropriate and unwelcome. At least they should be.

But that doesn't mean I don't have eyes in my head. However you look at it, Ben is a good-looking guy. No, scratch that. Good looking doesn't even begin to cover it. He's gorgeous. But he's more than that. He's charming and kind and funny and generous. What he isn't, I'm sure, is interested in me as anything more than a friend. Which is fine with me. Right now, I could use all the friends I can get. Especially when they have such great taste in wine. Still, I can't deny there's a connection.

"Be careful, Ro. Yes, he's good looking. And he's been incredibly kind and supportive. But like I said before, he's a party boy. Nick says he's never had a girlfriend, just a long line of one-night stands and fuckbuddies. Not to mention he doesn't even have a job, so God knows how he supports himself. The last thing you need right now is a man-child."

For some reason, even though I know what Lulu has said is true, and she has my best interests at heart, it rubs me the wrong way. Maybe Ben is a man-child. Nick's known him all his life, so he would know, I guess. But I've seen a different side of Ben, and it doesn't quite gel with what Lulu is saying.

As much as Ben is protective of me, I feel the same way about him. It doesn't mean I'm going to jump into a relationship with him—even if he was interested, which he probably isn't—but I don't like people shit-talking my friends. Even if it is Lulu.

CHAPTER EIGHT

BENEDICT

I follow Tama away from the table. Neither Rosanna nor Lulu need to hear this conversation, but I keep them in my line of sight in case Rosanna folds. After what she's been through, who could blame her?

"What happened in there?" As soon as Marco told Rosanna to sit down and shut up, I sent Tama into the restaurant.

"Nothing too bad, boss. He grabbed her arm. Fucker. But she was holding her own, that's for sure." He grunts in disgust. Men who hurt women or children are pretty much his least favourite things.

"And when you followed him down the street?"

"Got in a souped-up soft-top BMW as fast as his little legs could carry him and drove off without looking back. Chicken-shit. You want me to put a watch on him?" Cowards would be his second-least favourite.

"Not sure. Let's wait and see what he does over the next few days. Maybe keep your ear to the ground. I know he's a regular at a couple of the clubs, so let's keep an eye on him. I'll let you know if I need you to step in again. Thanks for your help tonight, man."

"Always happy to help a lady in distress, boss. I'll keep you posted."

Tama heads back out to chat with the seccies on the doors. He's head of my security team and runs the guys who work at all my clubs and pubs. I'd trust him with my life. And Rosanna's, if it comes to that, which I hope it won't. I make a mental note to put a little something extra in his pay this week.

Before I return to the table, I call Sabrina to thank her again, let her know the mission was a success and she can take down the profiles we created. I could get my PA to do it, but if Sab does it, I know all traces will be wiped, which is the way I'd like it.

Rosanna looks a lot calmer and more in control of her emotions when I sit back down. Lulu's glass is still half full, as is mine because I'm driving, but I notice most of the bottle is empty, so Rosanna's knocked back a few glasses. God knows, she's earned it.

We order a quick meal, and although Rosanna protests she doesn't think she can eat, her meal disappears in record time.

When Lulu starts checking her phone, I know it's time to pack this up.

"You ladies ready to head out?"

"If Rosanna is okay?" Lulu gives her a searching look.

"Yeah, yeah, I'm good to go. I've had just the right amount of wine to help me sleep." She's a little pale, but it looks like she's starting to come down off the adrenaline high, letting out a couple of big yawns.

We drop Lulu back at her loft apartment, which is above a warehouse. I can see the lights on upstairs where I know Nick is waiting with their baby. We don't drive away until we see her wave through the window so we know she's safely inside.

Rosanna is quiet on the short drive to her place. I follow her inside and up to her apartment door. I wouldn't put it past Cockhead to ambush her. You can't get into the building without being buzzed in, but all you have to do is wait for someone else to open the door and you can slip in. Which is why I love having a doorman. Nobody gets past the guys in my building.

"Would you like to come in for a cup of tea?" Rosanna asks as she turns the key and eases her apartment door open.

I'm reluctant to leave her alone so soon after her confrontation with Marco, so I'm pleased she asked. I don't want to come off as controlling. She's just come out of a relationship like that. But based on the way she was after the club the other night, I also know she could crash and burn any minute.

Not to mention, spending more time with Rosanna is always welcome. I only hope I can continue to keep my hands, and my feelings, to myself. I'm walking a fine and unfamiliar line.

"Thanks. I'd love a cup."

Rosanna makes us a couple of mugs while I wander her apartment, looking at the art on the walls and the masses of photos on the tables and bookshelves, which are also stuffed with a worn and battered collection of books.

One picture, in particular, grabs my attention. It's a slightly younger, grinning Rosanna and Lulu in graduation gowns, flanked by an elderly couple. They don't look quite old enough to be her grandparents but are older than I'd expect her parents to be. As she brings the tea into the lounge room, she notices the picture I'm holding.

"Are these ..." I start.

"My parents," she interrupts, handing me a steaming mug. "I was a menopause baby. They'd tried for years and given up hope. And then, surprise!"

I put the picture back on the shelf and move towards the sofa. I'm starting to get a clearer picture of her family life. This gives context to her anxiety about upsetting her parents. Treasured, longed-for only child. And a good Italian girl. It's a potent mix. I want to know everything there is to know about Rosanna, but I also want to keep our conversation light. Give her some space to calm down from the evening's drama.

"You have no idea how lucky you are. Growing up with my brothers and sister in my face constantly, there were times I would've given my right arm to be an only child."

That gets a laugh out of her, and we settle into our seats, trading stories about whether being one of four or an only child is better.

As we finish our tea and the conversation winds down, I realise that, even though I started out genuinely wishing I had been an only child, being one of four isn't so bad. And not because of the funny or horrible stories it provides. Despite the distance I keep my family at and the irritation and tension that choice creates, I know each of my siblings would be there for me in a heartbeat if I needed them. I'd wondered why Rosanna put up with Marco for so long. Maybe the loneliness of being an only child had something to do with it.

Our tea is finished, and it's getting late. I have no excuse to stay, so Rosanna sees me to the door.

"Thanks again for everything, Ben. I know it was full-on, but you made it bearable." She leans in and gives me a long hug. Christ, she smells good. It takes all my willpower to let go and step back.

"No need to thank me. I had fun. In a weird way."

"Yeah. Me too." She laughs. "Oh, and please thank Sabrina and ... the giant guy; what was his name?"

"Tama."

"Tama. Please say thanks to Sabrina and Tama for me. Maybe I can buy them a drink sometime?"

"That would totally embarrass Tama, but I'm sure Sabrina would love to. I'll organise it next time she's in town. Are you sure you'll be okay on your own tonight? It was pretty traumatic for you." I search her face for lingering signs of the roller coaster, but she's calm and relaxed.

"Yeah, I'm fine. I promise."

"Okay, well, I'll give you a call tomorrow to check in. You call me any time if you need to talk." With one last hug, I head back to the lift, taking the spicy scent of her perfume with me on my clothes. Looks like another hand job in the shower for me tonight.

· ♥ · ♥ · ♥ · ♥ · ♥ ·

Over the next few days, Rosanna and I fall into a bit of a rou-tine. I call her every morning to see how she's doing and make sure she hasn't had any unpleasant contact from Marco. Which means any contact at all, really, because nothing from him could ever be classed as pleasant. So far, nothing. His silence concerns me. If he was worried he might lose Rosanna, he would be in damage control. But he's giving her space, which suggests he's either delusional and potentially dangerous, or he has an ace up his sleeve.

She hasn't told her parents yet either. Which is low-key con-cerning. She may have finished her relationship with him, but this is far from over until her parents know what's going on.

We chat again in the evenings when she finishes work about all sorts of things, avoiding mention of Marco as much as possi-ble. We make each other laugh, which is something she probably needs right now.

I also keep up a back-channel communication with Lulu, who has lunch with her a couple of times and talks to her daily. Between the two of us, we keep a good eye on her.

On Thursday, Rosanna surprises me—pleasantly—by sug-gesting we catch up for dinner. I'm trying to walk a careful line here. She needs a friend, not someone hitting on her. I'm also aware she's probably heard stories about me from Lulu and Nick. Which might be true, as far as they go. But the thing about the truth is it doesn't always give you the whole picture.

On the other hand, I don't want to be friend-zoned for all time. Rosanna is the first woman I've ever considered having an actual relationship with. I knew the minute I laid eyes on her she was the one for me, and getting to know her over the last few days has only confirmed it.

I'm also aware that, as an almost thirty-year-old man who has never had a real girlfriend, I might not be considered a safe bet. The last thing I want to do is hurt her. She's had enough hurt in the past week to last a very long time. For the first time in my life, I'm swimming in the deep end of the emotional pool, and I have no real game plan. Other than to be there for her. Whatever she needs.

We meet up at a bar on Oxford Street. Rosanna's come straight from work and looks sensational in a sleeveless cream knitted dress that clings to those curves like Gladwrap and brown suede ankle boots with sky-high heels. Her hair is in a ponytail, hanging halfway down her back.

"Hi, Ben." She leans in and kisses my cheek. Not a nearly-there air kiss, but a real, lips-making-contact kiss. They're soft and full and leave a tingling imprint on my face. I'm so focussed on the lingering sensation and the smell of her perfume that I have no idea what she's talking about. I smile and nod like a ventriloquist dummy. Luckily, Ro seems happy to carry the conversation.

After a couple of drinks, we move on to one of my favourite restaurants, which is a few doors up the street. It's owned by a friend of mine so we get a great table and the food and service are fantastic. In the end, we're the last table left, and Rosanna insists we leave when she realises all the other tables have not only been cleared but are reset for tomorrow's service.

It's been a great night. With definite date vibes, giving me a tantalising glimpse of what a future with Rosanna could be like if we can get clear of the Marco shitshow. Once she's had a chance to catch her breath, I'll show her what it feels like to be adored.

I order a car and drop Rosanna at home, again escorting her to the door of her apartment. We haven't talked about Marco tonight, which was deliberate on my part. I wanted her to have fun, and I wanted all her attention on me. Because even though it's probably way too early, I hope she's feeling for me at least a fraction of what I'm feeling for her.

That said, I do want to check in about the situation. It bothers me she hasn't told her parents about the breakup yet. I'm about to bring it up when Rosanna takes care of it for me.

"By the way, I've still heard nothing from Marco. So that's a good sign. The trouble is, once I tell Mum and Dad, I don't know what will happen. How can he continue working for my dad after all this?"

"Bottom line is, he can't." From my sleuthing around Marco's dealings I know he's been practically running Moretti Construction since Rosanna's dad got sick. I also know not everything is above board. And I'm convinced Mr Moretti doesn't know that. "But you really need to tell them, Rosanna. It won't get any easier." I try to infuse my voice with some urgency without alarming her.

"The thing is, since Marco was going to marry me—or so we all thought—the plan was for Dad to leave the company to the both of us one day. This is not just about breaking his heart. It leaves nobody to run the company for him. And nobody to leave it to." Which explains not only why Marco maintained his relationship with Rosanna but why he was so angry with her when she ended it. The threat he made as he left the restaurant is never far from my mind.

"I don't have an answer for you there. But what I do know is you need to be careful. Marco showed his true colours on Sunday night. Things are likely to get nasty. I wouldn't put much past him." I try to sugar-coat what I'm thinking, but it's a fine line. She needs to be aware that this could get uglier than it already is. Uglier than she could imagine.

Rosanna laughs nervously, twisting her hands on the handle of her handbag. "You sound like you think he might ... I don't know. Do something to retaliate?"

"I think it's a distinct possibility, honey. So, you need to act fast and watch your back."

Rosanna looks shocked by what I've said. I don't want to leave her on such an unsettling note.

"How about we catch up on the weekend and do something fun? Maybe do yum cha and a movie. How does that sound?"

"Yes." She beams at me. "I love yum cha and haven't been for ages. Saturday?"

"Great. Why don't I pick you up around ten thirty?" I suggest.

Spending this much time with Rosanna isn't easy. My self-control is getting a real workout right now. Because every cell of my body wants to hurl itself at her and show her what it is I want. Which can't happen. Yet. But not spending time with her? Well, that seems worse.

"Sounds perfect." She does an excited little wiggle that goes straight to my jeans. Jesus Christ, I'm in trouble.

I kiss her on the cheek and head for the lifts.

"Ben?" she calls as the lift door opens. "I don't know what I would've done without you this week." Her smile is blinding, and I'm pretty sure mine matches. Hopefully, as long as I don't screw this up, she won't have to do without me for a long, long time.

CHAPTER NINE

ROSANNA

I have dinner at Lulu and Nick's on Friday night. I need her advice. It's been nearly a week since I kicked Marco to the curb and I still haven't worked out how to tell my parents. Which might seem silly, but I've never found it easy to disappoint my dad.

It's also an opportunity to do a bit of digging about Ben since Nick's known him for so long. Something's not quite adding up, which should be unsettling, but somehow, I know I can trust him. My experience of Ben is very different from the picture Lu has painted. If he doesn't have a job, where does he get the money for the cars that have picked us up? Not to mention the new Audi he drove on Sunday night. My curiosity has been well and truly piqued. And if I'm honest, my hormones have too. Which is a totally new experience for me.

Nick takes Isla the Wonderchild for a walk to give Lulu and me time to talk. She wastes none of it.

"So, why haven't you told your parents about the breakup?" she asks, settling on her plush red sofa with a glass of ginger beer. She notices me eyeing it. "Don't look at me like that. I'm not pregnant again. Yet. But I'm addicted. And don't try and change the subject."

"I don't know how to break it to them. If it was only me and Marco, I'd tell them what a bastard he is and be done with it. But I know as soon as Dad finds out, he'll fire his arse."

"As he should." Lulu nods at my assessment.

"Yes, but that means Dad will have to go back to work full time. He's not up to it, Lu. He's doing better now, but you know we nearly lost him earlier this year." The memory of that time sends a shudder through me. "The doctors wanted him to give up work entirely. But he won't. So, if Marco goes, what happens?"

"He could sell the business. I'm sure he'd find a buyer." Lulu puts her glass down and takes my hands, which I realise I've been wringing together.

"He could, but I don't think he would. He's too stubborn. He sees the business as his legacy, and he's determined to leave it to me. Since, you know, I wouldn't be able to support myself, being a woman and all." Dad is old-school Italian. Which, to some extent, is how I ended up with Marco in the first place.

"Yeah, I see your dilemma. How many days a week is he working?"

"Two. In a good week. I'd never forgive myself if he went back full time and something happened to him." It's been tough watching a vital man become so frail, a decline that seems to be speeding up.

"I get it." Lu squeezes my hand to bring home her point. "But you know, he loves you more than anything. If he found out you kept what Marco did from him, he'd be furious. Which wouldn't be good for his health either. I think you just have to rip the Band-aid off. Although, I think I'd keep the details to a minimum."

That makes me laugh.

"You're right. I'm going over there for dinner on Sunday. I'll tell them then, minus the details."

I'm no closer to working out how to break it to them, but I do feel more resolved. Maybe when I see Ben tomorrow, he'll have some suggestions.

I wait until Isla is in bed, we've finished dinner and we're relaxing on the sofa with a last glass of wine to start interrogating Nick.

"So, Nick. Tell me about Ben." Subtlety is not my strong suit.

"Ben? Why do you ask?" Nick skewers me with a lawyer look, and I get a glimpse of the hard-arse Lulu first met.

"Oh, no reason. Only he's been so kind this last week, helping me out with the Marco thing and everything. I don't know much about him, other than he's Will's youngest brother." Will was in the same year as Nick at school and worked with him in the law firm their grandfathers established years ago.

"You know, it's odd. I've known him all my life, but I can't honestly say I know much about what he does." Nick's gaze is unfocused as though his mind is sifting through the years he's known Ben. "Other than he doesn't take much seriously. He doesn't seem to have a job and spends his time jetting off around the world at a moment's notice. Partying till all hours with all sorts of people. He seems to be well connected from what I can gather, but I have no idea how."

"How can he afford that if he doesn't have a job?" I have to stop myself from leaning forward into Nick's answer. I don't want to alert him as to how interested I am.

"His grandfather was canny with money. When his grand-mother died, she left a substantial chunk of it to each of the grandchildren. I guess he lives off that, although Harry seems to think he must have blown through it years ago." I remember Ben's father from Lulu and Nick's wedding. He struck me as a pretty switched-on guy.

"It all seems very odd ..."

"Ben had a bit of trouble at school. I don't think he even fin-ished in the end. Just upped and took off after his grandmother died. He stayed away for a few years, and now he comes and goes at random. Harry tried to get him to take up a trade of some sort, but he refused." I haven't known Ben long, but no way do I see him as a tradie.

"Stella told me he had a rough time when he was young. They lost a baby between Ben and Greer, and Stella didn't take it well. So, Ben didn't get much attention. Things like that can scar a person," Lulu adds.

"Please tell me you're not interested in Ben, Rosanna. He's a great guy and would do anything for anyone. Except settle down. After what you've been through, you don't need more heartache." Nick gives me the sort of look I might get from a big brother, if I had one.

"I agree," Lulu chips in. As if she hadn't already expressed the same opinion. More than once. "Getting toyed with by a charming playboy is the last thing you need. Do you want Nick to have a word with him?"

The thought of being toyed with by Ben sends a fizzing sensation through my veins. I cross my legs, squeezing my thighs together. Oh, my.

"No. God, no. It's not like that. Honestly. Something about him isn't adding up for me, that's all." The thought of Nick warning Ben off is horrifying. Not only because I'm sure he doesn't see me that way but because hurting Ben by implying he's not good enough for me is all kinds of wrong.

I make my excuses and head home not long after. People with new babies start to yawn around nine o'clock. And I need to be alone with my thoughts. Process what I've heard from Nick against what I know of Ben myself. I'm sliding my key into the lock when I hear the lift doors open. Glancing over my shoulder, I freeze. It's Marco.

I don't know where I find the presence of mind to pull my key out of the lock and instinctively grip it between my fingers like I learnt in a self-defence class. There's no way I'm opening the door. The last place I want to confront Marco is behind the closed door of my apartment.

"What are you doing here?"

"I came to see if my *girlfriend* had come to her senses yet." He's not entirely steady on his feet and is slurring his words. His normally perfect hair is a little untidy. Great. A drunk Marco. I have experience of how belligerent he can be when he's had a few drinks. My stomach bottoms out.

"I'm not your girlfriend. We're over." Brave words, but my knees are shaking and I have to brace myself against the doorframe to stay upright. The bruise on my arm from Sunday seems to throb, reminding me he's capable of more than I had imagined.

"We're over when I say we're over, *Princess*. A fact I think you know, since you haven't told your parents yet." His voice is quiet but menacing and he's coming closer, caging me in against the door. Too late, I realise I should've moved towards the stairs. There's no escape now.

I lift my chin and eyeball him. "I haven't told them yet because I'm trying to work out how to break it to them. They love you, and it will crush them to find out what a lowlife you are." It takes all my effort to keep my voice strong and even. Inside, I've turned to jelly. Half set, wobbly jelly.

"I'd be very careful what I say if I were you." He's pressing against me now, making me shudder with revulsion. "Right now, I'm giving you some time to work out what a silly little girl you're being. But my patience won't last forever. Tell your parents we've broken up and you'll be very, very sorry." He punctuates each word with a sharp finger jab to my chest. My teeth start to chatter. I'm in real danger of wetting my pants. There's no Ben or Tama to bail me out this time.

I start to contemplate my chances of success if I try and knee Marco in the balls. My heels are too high to run in. Can I slide my shoes off without him noticing?

Just as panic starts to set in, the lift doors open and the two guys who live across the hall spill out with their girlfriends. I don't know them well, but we smile and say hi whenever we come across one another. Marco must look as threatening as I imagine because they both step towards us, even as their girlfriends back up down the hall. I hear a whimper and realise it came from me.

"Everything alright here, Rosanna?" one of them asks.

"Yes. All good, thanks. Marco was just leaving. Weren't you, Marco?" There's a tremor in my voice now that rescue seems to be at hand.

Realising he's outnumbered, Marco swings away. "You've been warned, Rosanna. You won't like what happens if you cross me," he hisses as he gets into the lift.

"What a dickhead. Who was that?" one of the guys asks.

"My ex-boyfriend. Very ex. Thanks so much. I don't know what I would've done if you hadn't come along." My cheeks are flaming with embarrassment, my eyes burning with tears I refuse to let fall until I'm alone. It takes a couple of tries to get my key in the lock; I'm still shaking so hard.

"No worries. He gives you any more trouble, let us know. And we'll keep an eye out for him. He looks like bad news."

"You got that right. Thanks again." I hightail it into my apartment and barely make it to the sofa before my knees give out.

I upend my bag on the coffee table, desperate to find my phone. My finger hovers over Lulu's number, but it's late. They have a baby. Without giving it any more thought, I call Ben. He answers on the second ring, but I can hardly hear him over the thumping dance music.

"Wait a sec. I'll go somewhere quiet." The noise starts to recede. "Better?" he asks.

By now, I'm feeling guilty for interrupting his night out. Oh shit. Maybe he's on a date. I'm interrupting a date. I should've called Lulu and Nick. They wouldn't mind. I don't know why I called Ben. It's Friday night. Of course, he'd be out partying.

"I'm sorry. I've interrupted your night. It's okay. I'll see you tomorrow." I can hear my voice shaking. I'm about to disconnect, but he stops me.

"Hey now. None of that. What's wrong? You sound upset? Are you okay?"

"Yeah. I'm okay. I'm ... Marco came over." I don't know what else to say, but there's no need.

"Where are you?"

"At home."

"Is he still there?"

"No, my neighbours appeared, and he took off."

"Right. Lock the door. Don't answer it for anyone but me or Tama. Pack an overnight bag. Can you do that? I'll be there in twenty minutes."

"No. No. It's okay. I'm sorry I bothered you. I'm being silly. I don't want to put you out. I'll be fine." Even as I say the words, I know Ben won't take no for an answer. And I'm selfishly grateful.

"You're not putting me out. I'm glad you called. You shouldn't be there alone. I'm on my way."

Now I'm crying. With gratitude. "Okay. Thank you. I'm sorry." He can hear the sobs breaking up my words.

"No need to be sorry. Do you want me to stay on the line until I get there?"

This man. Honestly.

"No. I'm alright. I'll pack a bag. I'll see you soon."

It's such a relief to think I won't have to spend tonight here where Marco could come back any minute. Talking to Ben has calmed me down.

I don't even think to ask where he's taking me. I get myself together, pull out a bag and start packing.

It's barely fifteen minutes before Ben's buzzing to be let into the building. I'm still rattled and check the peephole in my apartment door to make sure it's him before opening it.

"Hey, sweetheart. It's going to be okay. I won't let anything happen to you," Ben says, folding me up in a big, firm bear hug the moment I open the door. The solidity of his arms and chest make me feel safer. Yet strangely, they also make me cry again. He lets me get it out of my system for a couple of minutes before sitting us both on the couch.

"Is the front door the only access to the apartment?" he asks, which seems a strange thought.

"Yes. Unless you climb over from one of the other balconies, but we're very high up here."

He checks the lock on the balcony door. "Do you have your bag?" Following my gaze, he spots the overnighter beside the door and picks it up. "Right. Let's get going then. Did you remember your phone charger?"

"Yes, Mum." I can't help but laugh. Which surprises both of us.

I fell apart tonight, but only because Marco caught me unawares. It won't happen again. I straighten my spine and follow Ben to the car.

It's not until we're on our way that I ask where he's taking me.

"We're going to my place. I have better security. A doorman. And Marco doesn't know where I live, so he won't know where to find you."

That makes a lot of sense. He'd find me in a hot second at Lulu's or Mum and Dad's.

Before I know it, Ben is swiping a card and we're pulling into an underground carpark where he nips into a spot right next to the lift. He waves a card against the reader on the wall and the doors open on a stylish mirrored lift. In seconds, we are smoothly and soundlessly coming to a halt.

There are only two doors on the landing by the lift, along with a marble table holding an enormous arrangement of glorious lilies scenting the air. Ben punches in a code and the door clicks open.

"Here we are. Home sweet home." He's trying to be jovial, but his face has been tense since he picked me up.

Despite the state I'm in, I register that we're in probably the most beautiful apartment I've ever seen, with floor-to-ceiling windows looking out towards the Opera House and Sydney Harbour Bridge. The view alone would make this place worth millions, never mind the size and style of the place.

Ben heads straight down a wide hallway carpeted in plush carpet so thick his footsteps don't make a sound. He opens a door and stands back.

"Will you be comfortable in here?" he asks, almost sheepishly.

Like the living room, the bedroom is lots of white on white with a spectacular deep teal velvet headboard mounded with plush pillows, a couple of matching velvet chairs and a beautiful sideboard. Open doors on either side of the bed lead to an ensuite bathroom and an empty walk-in robe. It's so beautifully decorated that I would've assumed it was the master suite, if not for the complete lack of clothes or personal items.

"Oh, wow, it's beautiful. But I ..." He holds up a hand to stop me.

"No buts. The room is yours for as long and as often as you need it." He drops my overnighter on an ottoman in the walk-in robe and heads for the door.

"I'll go and put the kettle on while you get settled. Or would you rather have a glass of wine?"

"Tea would be great. Thanks, Ben."

I sit down on the bed and try to catch my breath. Less than an hour ago, I was backed up against a wall by my deranged ex. Now I'm the guest in a five-star—correction, six-star—apartment. After checking out the beautiful bathroom, complete with a bathtub plenty big enough for two, I change into more comfortable clothes and head back out to the open plan living room where Ben hands me a steaming mug of tea.

"Do you want to talk about it? Tell me what happened?"

CHAPTER TEN

BENEDICT

I'm kicking myself. It crossed my mind to have Tama and some of the boys watching Rosanna's apartment, but I discounted it on the basis that Marco is a bully and, therefore, a coward. I honestly didn't think he would approach her like that. I underestimated his stupidity. Or desperation. A mistake I won't make again.

On my way to pick up Rosanna, I called Tama.

"We need to put a tail on the Cockhead." I don't need to use his name. Tama knows exactly who I mean. "I also want someone watching Rosanna. Don't approach or freak her out; just be around when she goes to work and comes home. I'll try and get her to agree to a car if I can."

"Sure thing, boss. Don't worry. He won't get near her again. You want me to go over there now?"

"No, not right now. I'm picking Rosanna up and taking her to my place. Have someone standing by when she goes to work on Monday, if you would."

"Easy."

I also put a social media alert on Marco. Whenever he's active or mentioned, I'll get a notification.

Rosanna was clearly rattled when I picked her up, but by the time we're drinking tea in my living room, she's changed into yoga pants and a T-shirt and is back to her feisty self. She fills me in on what happened at her apartment.

"What the hell makes him think it's okay to threaten me?" she fumes.

"Honey, he's an arsehole. We've already established that."

"You know what really gives me the shits? I wasted so many years of my life on such a creep. I could've been out there having fun, meeting guys, maybe falling in love for real. All I ever wanted out of a relationship was someone to love. Who loved me. Instead, I stuck it out with him. Deluding myself. To keep my father happy. How did I not see what he was?"

I hate that she feels any level of responsibility for this cluster-fuck.

"Hey, don't beat yourself up. He's a sociopath. You'd have to be a psychologist to pick up on what he was up to." I don't mention that I had a hunch about him from the minute we met. And it had nothing to do with the fact that he was her boyfriend—although that didn't endear him—or that I was sure I'd seen him around the club scene, and not with Rosanna. There was something about him that didn't sit right. Which brings me to the next issue. It's time to fess up.

"Listen, there's something I need to tell you. I would've told you earlier, but at first I wasn't sure, and then there was so much going on and I thought you had enough to deal with, so ..." I put my cup on the coffee table and turn to face her.

"What is it, Ben? What more could there be?" She looks as though she's at the end of her rope, and I hate to add to her burden, but if she found this out down the track, I'd never forgive myself. Best get it all out there so she knows precisely how heinous this guy is now rather than later.

"When I first met Marco, I thought maybe I'd seen him somewhere before, but I couldn't work out where. The night at the club, when you overheard those girls, I worked it out." She's not going to like what I have to say.

"And?" She clutches her mug tighter as if bracing herself.

"I've seen him around the clubs. Quite a lot. For a while now."

"How long?" She stiffens her spine, ready for the blow.

"Couple of years, at least. Maybe three. Always with a different girl. Although they all look the same. Young, skinny, blonde. Short skirts, boobs out. Like the girls last Friday night, essentially."

She takes a moment to absorb this.

"Well. He's got a type, that's for sure. And it's obviously not me." She lets out a bitter laugh. "He really did mean all those digs he made about my weight."

It's all I can do not to roar with anger. This guy gets worse with every tick of the clock.

"It says a lot more about him than it does about you, honey. Like I said, he's a sociopath, and girls who are not real bright and not real picky give him what he needs. A big boost to his ego. I'm sorry I didn't tell you earlier, but I honestly only worked it out that night, and by then, you'd already heard the headlines from the girls in the bathroom. I just didn't want to keep anything from you."

She puts her tea down and pulls her knees up to her chest.

I weigh up whether to tell her I think he might be doing dodgy deals through her father's company. Maybe it will help her come clean to her parents. But I might do some editing of what I suspect. She has enough to deal with.

"Do you think there's any chance this will all just go away? Maybe he'll find another job and leave us alone?" Her voice is uncharacteristically small. I wish I could say something to allay her fears, but if I did, I'd be lying. While I might withhold the whole truth, I can't outright lie, so I pat her knee, hoping to soften the blow at least a little.

"I think it's unlikely. I also think it's unlikely he confines his arseholery to his private—or not so private—life. So it might be wise to be prepared for the worst." Rosanna buries her face in her hands, letting out a small whimper. It's time to give her a bit of a break. "You know what? It's late and you've had a shitty evening. How about we put a pin in the problem and come back to it tomorrow when we're fresh?" I pick up our mugs and hand hers over, taking a gulp from my own.

"That sounds like an idea. Although I think I'm too wound up to sleep, to be honest."

I know I'll have trouble getting to sleep with her in the next room. In bed. In those sexy-librarian pyjamas.

"Alright. How about a movie, then? Something light and fluffy to take your mind off it? Or are you in the mood for car chases and explosions?"

In the end, we settle on a *Brooklyn Nine Nine* marathon. There's not much a good laugh can't fix. Rosanna drifts off towards the end of the fourth episode, her head on my shoulder. I sit through another three episodes, not wanting to disturb her by moving, before I drift off myself. Plus, it gives me the opportunity to stroke her gorgeous, silky hair and breathe in that earthy, spicy scent of hers.

The sun is barely up when I wake to an unfamiliar ringtone coming from the coffee table in front of me. Rosanna and I are curled up around one another on the sofa. Our legs are tangled, her head is on my chest, and I have a monster case of morning wood.

Trying not to disturb her—she's sleeping like the dead—I reach out for the phone and see it's her mum calling. Even I know answering that call is not a good idea.

"Ro, honey, wake up. Your mum is calling." I push the hair back off her face and gently shake her shoulder. The call goes to voicemail, but she's starting to stir.

"What? Oh my God. I fell asleep on you. I'm so sorry. You should've woken me."

"No problem. But your mum called. I'm guessing it's important since it's not even seven am."

Rosanna sits bolt upright, narrowly missing my hard-on as she pushes herself up. Taking the phone, she fumbles with it, but before she has a chance to dial, it's ringing again.

"Mum? *Cosa c'è? Stai bene?*" Hearing her lapse into Italian does nothing for the situation in my pants, despite what I can see from her worried frown; it's not good news.

The rapid-fire Italian from the other end of the line continues for a minute or two, punctuated by gasps from Rosanna, who is standing up and heading towards her bedroom. I follow, worried this might be about Marco.

"Where are you?" Ro asks in English, followed by another burst of Italian. "*Si. Si. Vengo subito.*" By now, tears are running down Rosanna's face. Disconnecting, she throws her overnight bag on the bed and rifles through it, pulling off her T-shirt and sliding her yoga pants down her legs without hesitation.

"It's my dad. They've taken him to hospital." She's swiping on deodorant and running to the bathroom with a toothbrush, still in nothing more than her knickers and bra, oblivious to the effect she's having on me.

"Shit. Which hospital?" I'm already out the door towards my bedroom and ensuite.

"St Vincent's," she calls as I take a quick pee and clean my teeth. I've pulled on a fresh shirt and jeans in seconds, and grabbing socks and a pair of boots I meet her at the door. Her eyes are so full of tears, she can't get her own shoes on, so I sit her down and do it for her.

"Right. Let's go." I grab my car keys and open the door.

"You're coming with me? You don't have to do that. I can get a cab." She's jabbing the button for the lift, seemingly seconds away from a full-blown panic attack.

"I go where you go, honey. If you think I'm leaving you to face Marco alone again, you've got rocks in your head. You never know where he might turn up."

"Thank you," she sniffles as we get in the lift.

We pull out of the garage and swing towards the hospital before I have a chance to ask her what's wrong with her dad.

"He has emphysema. Apparently, yesterday, he decided he wanted to do some gardening. Mum woke up at four am, and he was struggling for breath, so she called an ambulance. Looks like he overdid it." A piece of the puzzle slots into place. No wonder she's worried about telling her parents about Marco if her dad is sick.

We arrive at the hospital less than half an hour after the call from Rosanna's mother. Neither of us give a thought to how it looks, me being there with Rosanna at the arse crack of dawn.

Rosanna's father is asleep in the bed, his grey face all but covered by the oxygen mask.

"Mama," Rosanna wails. "*Comè sta?*"

A flood of emotional Italian follows from the tiny woman who had been clutching her husband's hand but is now gripping Rosanna like a boa constrictor.

I take a step back and wait by the door, not wanting to intrude on a family moment, even though every part of me wants to wrap Rosanna up and protect her from whatever is going on.

A nurse comes in and tells us the doctor will be around shortly, which seems to calm Mrs Moretti down enough for her to notice me. Her eyebrows hit her hairline, and she turns a stern look on Rosanna.

"This is my friend Benedict. He's a friend of Lulu and Nick." Her scowl clears. Seems like Lulu and Nick are the magic words.

"Ah. Lulu and *Nico*. *Si. Benedetto*. It is nice to meet you. I am Flavia. This is my husband, Andrea." She takes both my hands in hers and gives me the once-over.

"*È molto bello, ma dov'è Marco?*"

It's quite disconcerting not to understand what's being said half the time, especially when I have the distinct impression she's talking about me. And The Cockhead.

"At golf, Mama. Marco is at golf." Rosanna rolls her eyes at me. She's calmer now that she's seen her father. While he's clearly not in great shape, he doesn't look like he's in imminent danger.

Flavia makes a sound of what I take to be disgust. I know Rosanna thinks her parents adore Marco, but based on Flavia's response, I wouldn't be surprised if her mother has some doubts about him. Before I have time to travel down that line of thinking, the doctor arrives and confirms that, yes, Andrea overdid it yesterday and needs to rest and avoid all stress. The kicker for everyone is that work is no longer an option. Even part time.

Rosanna's eyes meet mine over her mother's head. I can almost hear what she's thinking. And it's exactly what I'm thinking. Damn.

The good news is, with any luck he should be home in a day or two. Rosanna visibly relaxes, and once she's explained in Italian what the doctor said, her mother relaxes too.

"She speaks English perfectly well. But when she gets emotional, she reverts to Italian," Rosanna whispers as Flavia fusses with the blankets on Andrea's bed.

"Do you think it likely Marco will turn up? Will they have called him?" I whisper, as quietly as possible so her mother won't hear.

"I don't think so. They'll have left it to me to call him. Someone from work might let him know, but probably not till Monday. Marco pretty much runs things these days, so they'll all probably defer to him anyway." At least I can relax about the likelihood of Marco turning up.

What Rosanna has said pretty much matches what I've been able to piece together about Marco, Andrea and the company.

"What the hell do I do now? I can't believe this timing. There's nobody else to take over." Rosanna's voice is loaded with frustration and more than a little fear.

"We'll work it out. The important thing right now is to get your dad back on his feet." I don't entirely believe what I say, but Rosanna needs reassurance, and I need time to work out a plan because Marco has a hold on this family that won't be easy to break.

It's a really bad idea to have Marco running things, but now is not the time to drop that bombshell. I can only hope the right opportunity presents itself before Marco makes good on his vague but troubling threats. Because Rosanna might not be aware of the damage he could do, but I am.

CHAPTER ELEVEN

ROSANNA

Is the universe trying to tell me something? That's three times now Benedict has been on hand to save my bacon in a crisis. And I have to say, I am so glad he was. Mum and I are in a bit of a state, but Ben takes care of all the practical stuff. He runs down to a local café and gets us some breakfast and a decent coffee. And he comes back with flowers for my mother. Suckup.

While Dad is still sleeping, he suggests we go to Mum's and pick up some things Dad might need, like pyjamas and a toothbrush.

"*Si. Si. Un bravo ragazzo*," Mum gushes and pushes us out the door together.

"I think your mum likes me." Ben gives me a cocky grin as we travel down in the lift.

"Of course she likes you. You brought her flowers. And coffee." I nudge his shoulder with my own, and he leans into it, his warm, muscular arm pressing against mine. Gulp.

"I think it had more to do with the magic words."

I raise my eyebrows in question.

"Lulu and Nick."

"Ahh. Yes. Well, she does love Lulu. And she fell in love with Isla at first sight."

"Why wouldn't she? That is one adorable kid." Those are some powerful pheromones he's giving off. If he bottled them, he could make a fortune.

I realise he's keeping up a light banter to stop me from worrying, and I could kiss him for it. Which would be bad. But also, I suspect, really, really good.

It doesn't take us long to pack a bag for Dad. With any luck, he'll only be there a couple of days, so he won't need much. It's a good kind of weird having Ben in my childhood home. His presence fills the space left by Dad's absence. I shouldn't be thinking like that, especially with my dad so sick, but I can't seem to help it.

We're back at the hospital by lunchtime and find Mum trying to coax Dad into eating some ugly green jelly. He's scowling until he spots me coming through the door.

"Rosanna. *Bella mia.*" He turns to Mum. *"Basta, Flavia, per favore."*

"He wants Mum to stop fussing," I translate for Ben. "We brought you some *sfogliatelle*, Papa." I put a Tupperware box full of his favourite treats on the table next to the lurid jelly. Dad has a wicked sweet tooth. It's a constant source of wonder he doesn't have diabetes. Reaching for the box, he grabs one of Mum's delicious pastries.

"Dad, this is my friend Benedict." Dad is busy stuffing his face with the pastry. I yank the box out of his hands to offer one to Ben, whose eyes roll back in his head as he takes a bite.

"Mmm. These are delicious, Mrs Moretti." He gives her his most charming smile and my mother blushes. Actually blushes. Good God.

"Flavia says you are a good friend of Lulu and Nico." Dad's not quite as easily won over. Not that there's any reason for him to be won over. It's not like Ben and I are anything other than friends.

"Yes, I grew up with Nick. Our parents and grandparents were good friends." Ben sneaks another sfogliatelle with a mischievous smile.

Dad grunts through a mouthful of pastry. Mum continues to fuss and Ben looks amused by the whole scene. Any minute now, Dad will ask where Marco is, but I'm saved from having to lie through my teeth by the nurse, who tells us all we have to leave Dad to rest.

Ben drives Mum—and her flowers—home and waits patiently while I get her settled. I offered to stay, but she insists she'll be fine on her own and is looking forward to a nice long nap since she didn't get much sleep last night.

It's not till we're getting in the car that I think about Marco. "What if Marco turns up and Mum's there on her own?" I start to unbuckle the seatbelt to go back in, but Ben puts a hand on my arm.

"He won't get anywhere near her." He inclines his head, and across the street, I see a sleek black car with tinted windows.

"What do you mean? Who's that?" And then it dawns on me. "Wait, is that the security guy?"

Ben nods as he pulls away from the curb. "Or one of his team. You know I don't trust Marco. I just want to make sure your mum is safe at home on her own."

This blows my mind. I watch the car disappear in the wing mirror. It's blindingly obvious there's more to Ben than he lets on, even to his family. Which makes no sense. I'm confused but not concerned. I mull over everything I think I know as we head back to his apartment. By the time we're in his swanky living room, I'm no closer to solving the puzzle. It's not any of my business, really. But I'm burning with curiosity.

"Who are you, Ben?" I ask, eyeing him across the wide marble island bench. Again, subtlety is not my usual MO.

He looks me in the eye. "I'm your friend." I know he's telling the truth, but a long way from all of it.

"I know you are. And despite the fact there are red—or at least orange—flags popping up all over, I trust you completely. But Lulu and Nick say you don't have a job. Yet you have these security guys apparently on standby. Then there's the way restaurants and clubs know you by name. And you're friends with an app developer you 'do business' with. Not to mention the flash car and this expensive apartment."

He shrugs and continues to make us each a cup of tea, but I can see the tips of his ears have gone pink again. "You sound like you think I'm some kind of drug lord."

"No. I don't think that. I don't know what I think, but not that." I try and drill him with a mum look like Lulu's, designed to get the truth out of him, but I fail miserably. He smiles and hands me a steaming mug, in which the tea is the exact colour I like.

I'm struggling with this whole situation. On the one hand, Ben is entitled to his privacy. He doesn't owe me anything. On the other, it's barely a week since I discovered I've spent almost my entire adult life being lied to and deceived and I won't tolerate it again. My instincts tell me Ben can be trusted. But if the past week has taught me anything, it's that I my instincts are faulty at best.

We order lunch to be delivered, and while we're waiting, Ben excuses himself and heads onto the balcony to respond to some messages. Which, of course, gives me the perfect opportunity for some low-level snooping.

The whole apartment is done in white on white, with touches of blue ranging from soft Wedgewood to sapphire to teal to French blue. The kitchen is sleek and modern with white cabinets and spectacular marble benchtops, a huge walk-in pantry and built-in appliances.

The living room manages to combine comfort and homeliness with style. Spectacular original artworks fill the walls, along with an enormous wall unit jam-packed with vinyl records, and a Bose stereo and speakers that must've cost as much as my car. Strangely, there's not a book in sight.

I saunter as casually as I can down the hall. As well as my room—which I haven't even used yet apart from to clean my teeth this morning—there are two other bedrooms. One is almost identical to mine, although here, the blue is a beautiful dusty tone. The other is clearly the master and is enormous. Even from the doorway, I can see the personal items on the bedside table. Coupled with the clothes I spot through the open door of the closet, it's clear this is the room Ben uses. The thing is, if this apartment belongs to a friend, which is what Lulu told me, why is he using the master suite?

At the end of the hall is an office, which looks like a real working space, with two very different desks. Both have what look like state-of-the-art laptops, but one is piled with files and folders while the other is bare except for the laptop, and what looks like an old-fashioned Dictaphone.

As I head back to the living area, a buzzer sounds in the foyer. Ben is still on the balcony, so I answer.

"Oh, hi Ms Moretti. Just letting you know your food is here. Do you want to come down and pick it up, or shall I send the guy up?"

Ms Moretti? How does this guy know my name? Curious, I tell him I'll come and pick it up.

When I get to the foyer, the delivery guy is gone, and our food is sitting behind a sleek marble and wood reception desk. This is the first time I've been in the foyer, and it's stunning. All sleek marble, warm woods, and spotless glass. An antique table with an enormous display of flowers like the one on Ben's floor stands in the middle of the vast space.

"Hey, Ms Moretti. Here's your food." The guy behind the desk hops up and hands over the bag. "I'm Ray, by the way. Nice to meet you. Oh, and here is your card. You'll need it to access your floor." With a friendly grin, he hands over a white envelope containing a plain black plastic card.

"My card? Okay. Wow. Thank you, Ray. How did you know my name?"

"Mr Carter put your name on his security list last weekend. I figured I'd get a card made up, just in case. If you misplace it, please let me know straight away so I can get it cancelled and issue a new one. You can't be too careful these days."

"No. You can't." It's as though I've fallen into an alternate reality. Who the hell is this guy?

"Oh, and if you ever need a car or a taxi, buzz down to the desk and we can arrange it for you. Have a good afternoon."

Before I have a chance to say more, Ray answers the buzzing phone on his desk.

The little black card works perfectly in the lift, but when I get to the apartment door, I realise I don't know the code to get in, so I knock on the heavy wood, hoping Ben has come back in from the balcony.

The door swings open and I don't miss the look of relief on his face.

"Ray called and said the food was here, so I went down to collect it. He also gave me this." I hold up the card, raising my eyebrows in question.

"Oh, good. Glad he got that organised. We can change the code for the door to something we'll both remember, if you like."

"You want to change the security code. For me." It's meant to be a question but it sounds more like a statement laced with disbelief.

Ben takes the food and heads towards the sofa as if none of this is at all strange. "Sure. It will be much easier that way."

I can't argue with that. It will be easier. If he's expecting me to stay for days. Or weeks. Which is crazy. Isn't it?

After depositing the bag on the coffee table, he goes to the kitchen and grabs a roll of paper towel from the pantry and a couple of beers from the fridge. I give the pristine white sofa a look of sympathy before deciding if he doesn't mind the risk to his upholstery, neither should I.

We tuck into the Vietnamese noodles and beer, but I don't even make it halfway through mine before I'm groaning and pushing it away.

"You aren't going to finish those?" Ben asks, dragging the container towards himself. "Mind if I do?"

I shake my head. "How do you eat so much and not get fat?"

By my reckoning, he put away three sfogiatelle at the hospital; my mother shovelled a sizeable chunk of lasagne into him when we dropped her at home, and now the noodles. And his abs are washboard flat.

"No idea." His grin is shameless as he tucks into what's left of my meal.

While he's eating, I continue to ponder the puzzle that is Ben Carter. He supposedly doesn't have a job, but I'd bet money this is his apartment. He's a party boy but thinks nothing of leaving a night out early to come to my rescue. He's never had a girlfriend but has taken care of me in ways my own boyfriend wouldn't have dreamt of. And I'm not buying any of it.

My head is spinning, and I know I need answers. Now.

I tuck a foot under my bum and turn to face him on the sofa. "So, Ben. You're going to tell me who you really are. Because I'm not buying the charade which seems to have everyone else fooled, and I won't tolerate another liar in my life."

CHAPTER TWELVE

BENEDICT

Well, fuck. That's not what I was expecting her to say. It's lucky I have a mouthful of noodles, which gives me a minute to think before I answer. Unfortunately, Rosanna has thrown me enough that I've got nothing. I'm not used to people looking below the surface. I'm not used to being seen. Her earlier question should've been a warning, but it seemed like she'd dropped it. I should've known better.

"I don't know what you mean." I take a gulp of my beer and busy myself with another mouthful of noodles.

"Seriously? You're pleading the fifth?" Her tone is somewhere between incredulous and amused, with a dusting of annoyance. "You said we're friends." Ouch. Low blow.

"We are." This couch used to be comfortable. Right now, I can't stop squirming.

"Then tell me, honestly, who the hell are you?"

There are no noodles left for me to use as a buffer. But I find I can't answer her. Do I deflect or do I tell her the truth? Deflection has always been my go-to, not that I've needed to use it often, but how much longer do I want to be so isolated? Maybe telling this perceptive woman might not be so bad. God knows I want her to know me. All of me. But changing the habits of a lifetime doesn't come easy.

"Okay. How about this? How about I tell you what I think is going on with you, and you can either confirm or deny?" She's not going to let this drop, and I'm inching closer to the cliff.

"Sure." I brace for impact because Christ knows what she's going to come out with.

"I think this apartment"—she waves her hand around to indicate the space—"doesn't belong to a friend. I think it belongs to you. I also think the club we were at the other night belongs to you, at least in part. And maybe the pub. And that girl, Sabrina the app developer, you said you do business with her, so maybe you fund or buy her apps. Which I guess makes you some kind of venture capitalist. What I don't get is why you let your friends and family think you're living off your connections."

Well, fuck again. She couldn't be closer to the truth if she'd read the script. How did a woman I met a matter of weeks ago see through all my smoke and mirrors when even my brothers can't? My ears start burning.

"Those are some pretty big assumptions." I try to stop gnawing on my bottom lip.

"I don't hear you denying any of them."

Long, silent moments go by. Rosanna holds my gaze despite my desperate desire to look away. Her words about not tolerating another liar ring in my ears, louder even than the fear of pity and judgement. Decision made, I let the breath I didn't realise I was holding out in a gusty sigh.

"Yeah. No. There'd be a good reason for that."

"So, I'm right? About all of it?" Her gaze is like a laser beam, searing right through my skull and dissecting my grey matter.

"You are. I don't know how you figured it out, but you're right."

"How can that be? How does nobody else see what you're up to?" She's incredulous, which is not surprising, really, given the size of my deception. "And why keep it a secret?"

"People see what they expect to see. Even family. Maybe especially family. I spent so many years at school being the family fuckup; none of them have ever expected anything else."

Her mouth drops open, and for a second, she's speechless.

"Okay. I'm going to need you to explain that for me. About the family fuckup. Because from where I'm sitting, you look … I don't know … remarkable?"

That gets a laugh out of me. "I think we might need another beer for this conversation." I head to the kitchen and grab a couple more beers. "Are you sure you want to talk about this now? You've had a shocking couple of days. Maybe you should—"

Rosanna cuts me off with a hand up, palm out.

"Oh no, you don't. You're not getting out of it that easily. To be honest, it would be a welcome relief to think about something other than Marco and my dad and all the shitfuckery going on in my own life for a while. So, spill." She holds out her hand for the beer.

"Right. Well, you asked for it." I settle in next to her, prop my feet on the coffee table and decide to start with the basics. If she can't handle that, the rest is a moot point. My stomach clenches, and my throat threatens to close over. I clear my throat. "First things first. I'm dyslexic. And I have dysgraphia, which is kind of related." For a long time, I didn't like to admit this. I felt judged and pitied. And people don't really understand what it means. More often than not, they assume it means I'm stupid. But while I've come to terms with my condition, I rarely tell anyone because it doesn't often come up.

I look over at Rosanna, terrified I'll see the pity I usually get when this comes out, but her face reflects nothing but concentration, so I take a swig of beer and continue.

"The thing is, they didn't pick it up until I was in high school. The teachers thought I had ADHD, so they put me on Ritalin. Which, of course, didn't work since that wasn't the problem. Anyway, by the time someone picked it up, I was already labelled the naughty kid, and the damage was done. Mum and Dad tried to get me to stay at school, but I was having none of it."

"How did nobody pick it up earlier?"

"It's mild-ish, so hard to spot. And you'd be surprised how easy it is to compensate and deflect. I got pretty good at that. And things at home were pretty brutal when I was little. Mum had a baby when I was two, and she was stillborn, so Mum and Dad were distracted. Mum, in particular, was inconsolable. It wasn't till later she was diagnosed with postnatal depression. Then, when Greer came along, there was a new baby to care for. Mum was pretty anxious about keeping her safe. I guess you could say I slipped between the cracks."

"How old were you when Greer was born?"

"Four. For a while there, Mum didn't have much time for me or my brothers, but Will and Ethan were a bit older, so I guess it didn't impact them quite as much."

"I'm so sorry. That must have been terrible. For all of you."

"It was. But most especially for Mum. She's a great mum. She loves us all so much. Would do anything for her kids. But she was really struggling then. I know she feels guilty about not picking up on my dyslexia earlier, but the school told her I was acting out because of the loss of the baby, and the supposed ADHD, and she had no reason not to trust them. And Dad was working long hours growing the firm. So he was never around."

"But what about later? As you got older?"

"By the time things started to settle down, I was already behind. And then Greer started getting bullied, so she was the focus again." As I say this, I realise how it must sound. "But please don't think I blame Greer at all. She's my baby sister, and I love her. I don't begrudge her even a minute of their time."

"So, you kept struggling through." Rosanna puts her hand on my leg. I know she's intending it to comfort me. And it does. But it also has an entirely different effect. I try and ignore my physical response and focus on our conversation.

"Anyway, when I was in year eleven, my grandmother died and left money for each of her grandchildren. School was still a struggle for me, so I left. Took the money—Dad was livid that I had access to it straight away—and headed to Europe."

"Wow. That was brave. All by yourself?"

"Yep. By this time, Dad had given up on me ever 'achieving anything' and was trying to convince me to get a trade. Plumbing or something. But that was never going to happen. So I thought getting away was the best solution." I look at her for signs of pity, but see nothing of the sort. Only curiosity and compassion.

"I stayed away for years. Over there, no one thought I was a screw up or stupid. I was the fun guy everyone liked to be around. The family thought I was burning through my inheritance, which was quite a bit of money, and for the first year or so, I was. But then I ran into these guys in a hostel in Prague. They were on a gap year before heading to MIT. They had this great idea for an app. I had money and nothing to lose, so I gave them the money to develop it. Six months later, we sold it to a big software house. I met Sabrina through them. She had an idea too, so I invested. And it made millions. Before I knew it, I was meeting people from all over who had ideas. If I thought they were good, I invested. If not, I didn't."

"That's incredible. Did you ever invest in anything that didn't work out?" Rosanna's eyes are wide with amazement.

"Once. It wasn't a complete fail, but it didn't quite break even. Otherwise, pretty much everything has at least made me some money. Sometimes, a lot of it."

"So, why not tell your family?"

"Ah. That's the thing. Like I said, I was the family screw up. Which is tough in a family full of lawyers, architects and academics. It's hard to shake that voice out of your head. And every time I invested, I thought, 'This is it. This is the time I'm going to fail'. I didn't want to prove my family right. Which is ridiculous, I know, because letting them think I'm nothing but a party boy *is* proving them right. But I couldn't bear to get their hopes up that I would make something of myself and then let them down. Eventually, it got to be a habit."

"And none of them ever asked what you were doing? None of them ever wondered how you were living?" Her knitted brows are a clear indication of how strange Rosanna finds this whole scenario. Laying it all out like this, I can see why.

"Nope. I guess they convinced themselves I was still living off Granny's money. Letting them think this place belongs to a 'friend' helped. They think I live here rent-free and am scraping by on the last dregs of my inheritance. And that makes it easier to not invite them here."

"They've never been to your apartment? None of them?" Rosanna's tone is incredulous. Which I guess is not surprising. It's not your usual family situation.

I shake my head.

"So, here you are, probably the most successful of their children, and your parents think you're partying your life away."

"To be fair, I kind of do. When you own clubs and restaurants, you tend to do a lot of partying. Which is how I got into that business in the first place."

"Does your dad still tell you to get a trade?" Her brow is furrowed in concentration.

I laugh out loud. "Yeah, he does. On the regular. It's kind of funny." I don't tell her how much it hurts. The last thing I want is for her to pity me.

"And kind of sad," she adds. Truer words. "That explains it." And her brow clears.

"Explains what?"

"The books. I noticed you have no books. And the Dictaphone. On the desk in the study. That's how you get round the dyslexia. You use a Dictaphone."

"Huh. You did a bit of snooping while I was on the phone earlier? Yes, I use a Dictaphone. My assistant transfers most of the written proposals and other documents onto tape for me to review, or we use Dictate in Word, and we go from there."

"You know, I get how you slipped through the cracks when you were little, but what I don't get is how nobody can see how smart and switched on you are. I've never met anyone who can read people the way you do."

"That doesn't make me smart. I had to learn at an early age to spot the people who would bully me for being stupid and the ones who would be cool."

"You were bullied?"

"Yeah, of course. Anyone who's different gets bullied. Worse than bullying was the pity." I've had plenty of that in my lifetime, but I don't think I could deal with it from Rosanna.

She takes a few moments to respond. Moments during which I can't take my eyes off her face. I can almost see every thought as it lands. Everything I learn about this woman increases my attraction. Not only is she gorgeous, but she's kind and perceptive. How could a mortal man resist such a combination?

"Why on earth would someone feel the need to pity you? I can't even tell you how much I admire you. Overcoming dyslexia and turning a tough start into an incredible story of resilience and success? I'm in awe of what you've achieved and the man you are."

There go the burning ears again. I don't doubt her words. She's an honest person, and the sincerity shining in her eyes makes me feel all kinds of wonderful.

It's so good to have got this off my chest. If I can tell Rosanna, maybe one day I can tell the family. When I'm ready. Which raises a good point.

"I'd really appreciate it if you kept this to yourself, Rosanna. I don't like asking you to lie to Lulu. I know how close you are, but she'll tell Nick, and he'll ..." I trail off, knowing she can see how it will unfold.

"Hey. Not my story to tell, my friend. Your secret is safe with me. I'm just honoured you shared it with me."

I let out a breath of relief. I had no doubt I could trust Rosanna, but there's always a fear lurking in the back of my mind that it will all come out. It's important to me that I control the narrative. I'll tell them. When and how I'm ready.

"Shared it? You practically tortured it out of me." We both laugh.

"What I will say is what you've been saying to me about Marco. You need to tell your family. Soon. You deserve better than the way you're being treated. And when you're ready, if you need me, I'll be there for you."

"Thanks. I will. One day."

"Soon. And some time you'll have to tell me what dysgraphia is. But not now. Right now, I want you to tell me how I can get Marco out of my life and tell my parents without Dad ending up back in hospital."

"Tama probably knows someone who could disappear him ..."

We crack up laughing, brought closer by my opening up and her beautiful response. If I thought I was in deep before, I had no idea. I am so gone on this girl I don't know which way is up.

CHAPTER THIRTEEN

ROSANNA

After Ben's revelations, I decide I need a nanna nap, and Ben has some work to do, so we go our separate ways for a couple of hours. He's organised for Tama or one of his guys to take me back to the hospital for a visit this evening to give me time alone with Mum and Dad while still providing protection from the threat he perceives Marco to be. Although I've known Marco all my life, and would never have thought him capable of anything violent, I'm no longer sure. And I trust Ben's instincts. More than my own at this point.

Of course, when I get to the hospital, Mum grills me on who Ben is, why he was here this morning and where Marco has been. I fob her off with a story about how I stayed at Lulu's last night and Nick and Ben went for a run together this morning. Her expression says she doesn't believe me, but I manage to divert her with pictures of Isla I took last night.

Tama doesn't come into the room, just waits out of sight in the hallway, but there's no sign of Marco. It's not until I get back in the car and check my phone that I find a text from Ben.

Ben: The guys spotted Marco at your place. He tried to get in but eventually took off. Be careful.

Me: On my way back now. No sign of him here.

Ben: I have to go out for a while. Make yourself at home. My credit card is on the kitchen bench if you want to order yourself something to eat. Should be home by midnight.

It's nice to have some alone time. I've got a lot to process. Not just about Marco and my life but about Ben and his. The emotional intensity of the past week has brought us together quickly, and I'm surprised to realise he's become my go-to when I have a problem, ahead of even Lulu. Partly because she has a baby and a husband now, and I don't want to interfere. But it's also because of who Ben is. I guess it should feel odd, since I barely know him, but it doesn't. Something about him settles me.

Ben's concern about what Marco might do is a little unnerving. Which makes me think maybe he knows something I don't. But whatever Marco may throw at me, I know two things. Ben has my back, and I trust him completely.

I heat up some of the gnocchi Mum sent home with me for dinner, wolf it down, and head straight to bed. Despite my afternoon nap, I'm exhausted. And bed is a good place to process. As it turns out, it's also a good place to think about how hot Ben is. Because of this morning's events and how the day has unfolded, I haven't even thought about how we were tangled together when we woke up. But lying here in the quiet and dark, my mind wanders back there, with a little help from my lady parts.

Holy hell, he's gorgeous. I can still smell his citrusy scent and feel the rock-hard pecs and abs where I laid my head. I also didn't miss the impressive morning wood he was sporting.

Could I pick a worse time to develop a crush on someone? Although, to be honest, I've been crushing on him a little since I met him. Hey. I have eyes in my head. But since we've become friends, my crush has morphed into something more. Attraction doesn't seem like a big enough word. Lust? Nope. It's more than that too. Fascination? Getting warmer. Which is what I do whenever I think about him.

This is bad. For so many reasons.

I think he finds me attractive. He did say so when he saw me naked—ooh, where's a fan when you need it—in the bath. Which could've been him being kind. The problem is, I have so little experience I can't tell for sure. And there's another problem. My experience. According to Lulu, Ben gets a lot of attention from women. How could I ever compete? My own boyfriend didn't want to have sex with me. Why would a guy like Ben?

Not to mention, he probably doesn't even want a relationship, and I know enough about myself to know I'm not a casual kind of girl.

Right now, what I need is less drama, not more. Of course, if I wanted to take care of the pesky issue of my lack of experience—which I now realise I do—I could hardly find someone better than Ben. He knows what he's doing, he's kind, he knows my history. And he's hella hot.

But no. I don't need to complicate things, and I don't need to lose him as a friend. So I'll continue to keep my inconvenient crush—or whatever it is—to myself. Sigh.

I spend most of Sunday at the hospital listening to Mum fuss and Dad grizzle. It would be torture if it weren't for Lulu, who arrives to break the tension and provide someone else for Mum to torment. Anyone would think Mum was the only woman to have raised a child and she gives Lu every piece of old-fashioned, out-dated advice she can muster. Then starts in on her about baby number two.

Dad will be sent home tomorrow, pending a visit from the doctor in the morning. Which is the good news. The doctors have doubled down on their view he needs to give up work—and stress—entirely. So, the fact Marco and I won't ever be getting married couldn't have come at a worse time because Marco is, unfortunately, the only option for running the business.

I can't distract them from the situation much longer, but the other benefit of Lulu being there is she can redirect like a boss, and whenever the conversation strays towards Marco, she creates a diversion.

Lulu and I leave together, and as we head down in the lift, Tama stands silent in the corner. I fill her in on what's happened since I left her place on Friday night, which seems like a lifetime ago.

"You're staying with Ben?" Her jaw drops.

"Calm your farm. He's offered me somewhere to stay where Marco won't find me. And we're friends."

"Well, yeah, that is nice of him. But staying with him? Is the person who owns the place okay with it? Has he had any parties? What if he brings one of his randoms home and you have to listen to them having wild monkey sex?"

I can't help but laugh. Her idea of who Ben is and mine are quite different. I know he probably has wild monkey sex—gasp—but for some reason, I don't think he would do it in his apartment with me there. Which I don't think I can explain to her since I don't understand why myself.

The lift doors open and we wander through the hospital foyer and out to the carpark, Tama trailing at what I imagine is considered a safe but respectful distance. The idea of having a security detail blows my mind when I think about it. And makes me wonder exactly what Ben thinks Marco might do.

"What Ben does is his own business. Yes, the owner is fine with it." She doesn't need to know who the owner is. "And no, he hasn't had any parties. I'm grateful for him stepping in after Marco cornered me on Friday night. I don't think I'd feel safe at home by myself."

"You could come to our place."

"Which Marco knows is a possibility. I wouldn't do that to you and Nick. Also, then I'd have to listen to you two having wild monkey sex."

"Fair point. Do you really think he's dangerous?"

"A week ago, I wouldn't have said so, but you didn't see him on Friday night. It's like a switch has flipped and he's gone full-on batshit crazy. Now I don't know what he might do. And Ben seems concerned."

"Oh, I know. You could stay at Nick's old apartment. Marco doesn't know where it is."

"Isn't it up for sale?" I can't tell her I don't want to move out of Ben's, even if there is a viable alternative.

"Yes, but until it's sold, you could stay there."

"Thanks, Lu, but honestly, I think it's safer being at Ben's with him coming and going. The doorman is great too. He knows not to let anyone in." If I moved, I wouldn't see Ben every day, which is a thought I need to examine. Or not. Perhaps it's more of a thought I need to squash.

Lulu hops in her car and heads home, and I climb into the car Tama brought me in. No sooner have I buckled in than my phone vibrates with a text. My first thought is Ben. But it's not Ben. It's Marco.

Marco: Where the hell have you been? I went to your place yesterday and you weren't there. You aren't answering my calls

That's true. I've had several missed calls from Marco. I have no desire to call him back. I haven't even listened to the voicemails. My instinct is to ignore his text too, but then I remember Dad and what the doctors have said. I at least need to keep Marco calm enough to carry on with his job—and not cause trouble for Dad—for the time being. But I do ignore his question about where I've been.

Me: Dad has been in hospital. He's coming home tomorrow, we hope. I assume you'll be ok to keep things going at work?

In all honesty, he'll probably be thrilled to be the one in charge without having to explain his decisions to Dad.

Marco: So, you haven't told them yet how stupid you're being?

Wow. Just when I think this guy can't get any worse. No concern for Dad, who gave him a job and trained him in the property business right out of school. Who has treated him like a son for years. Arsehole.

Me: No. They don't need any drama right now. Dad needs to avoid all stress

It crosses my mind to ask him not to tell them about the breakup either, until I realise it wouldn't be in his best interest to do so anyway—what with taking over the business as a beloved son-in-law being off the table.

Marco: Fine. But I meant what I said. You've got till Andrea is better to come to your senses or you'll be very sorry

A shiver runs down my spine despite the vagueness of the threat. I have no idea what he means or what he might be thinking of doing, and I'm not sure I want to. Ben implied there might be more to Marco's behaviour than the cheating. If I find out he's been cooking the books or doing dodgy deals, I won't be responsible for what I do. Dad has always run a tight ship, but with how absent he's been lately, Marco could've done anything he liked without being found out.

Ben is getting ready to go to his parents' for dinner when I arrive back at the apartment.

"Why don't you come with me? You already know Will, and Greer and Josh. Mum and Dad would love to get to know you."

"Are you sure? I don't want to impose ..." But neither do I want to spend the evening alone after the text conversation with Marco. Also, I'd be lying if I said I'm not dying to get to know his family. I met them briefly at Nick and Lulu's wedding, but I'm curious about the family dynamic. It astounds me they can't see through Ben's flimsy smoke and mirrors routine.

"You absolutely won't be imposing. They'd love to see you again, and you'd be doing me a favour. I could do with a good buffer." He gives me his most charming smile.

"Okay. Give me ten minutes to change, though. I smell like a hospital."

"Take your time. No rush." He settles on the sofa to wait while I spend a good five minutes agonising over what to wear to dinner with the family of a not-boyfriend. It's a good thing I'm an over-packer because the overnight stay I packed for has morphed into three so far. If things keep going the way they are, I might need a few more items. Work clothes for one. And if I keep feeling the way I'm feeling, maybe my vibrator.

I'm sure Ben won't mind stopping at my place on the way home. Surely Marco won't be hanging around late on a Sunday night?

CHAPTER FOURTEEN

BENEDICT

I t doesn't escape my notice that Will's eyes practically jump out of their sockets when I walk in with Rosanna, but he's smart enough not to say anything. Mum and Dad are predictably thrilled to see her, and in the same way I didn't miss Will's expression, I don't miss Mum and Dad exchanging meaningful looks. This is the first time I've ever brought a woman home, friend or otherwise. It feels better than I imagined having someone in my corner, on my team, for once. It's kind of ridiculous, but I feel indestructible.

On the way here, Ro filled me in on her exchange with Marco. The climax of this whole sordid story is edging closer, but with Ro's dad still unwell, I don't want to be the one to escalate things. Who knows, maybe once Rosanna tells her parents what's happened, Marco will slink away like the coward he is. Or not.

"Rosanna, how lovely to see you again." My mother draws Ro into the kitchen where Greer is whipping cream. "I had no idea you and Benedict were ... friends."

Subtle. I roll my eyes, and Ro suppresses a grin.

"Is there anything I can do to help, Mrs Carter?"

Having met Rosanna's parents, I spot what she's doing straight away. She has plenty of experience in deflecting. She'll get along fine.

"Oh, thank you, dear. You could trim the beans." Mum pushes a board and knife towards her. "I understand you've been friends with Lulu since college. She's such a lovely girl. It's nice to see Nick happy. He had a bit of a tough time growing up ..." Mum continues to prattle on while Ro makes noises of agreement.

I pour us both a drink and get out of there. It amuses me to hear her talk like that about Nick, whose father was an arsehole, no mistake, but who finished top of his class at law school and went to Oxford on a scholarship. It's all about perspective, I guess.

Having taken care of the beans and the cream, Rosanna and Greer are shooed out of the kitchen while Mum finishes dinner and we have a few minutes to catch up. Greer and Rosanna get on like a house on fire, which is great, and I find myself imagining how good it would be if Ro was here every week. As more than my friend. I give myself a mental slap. It's way too soon to be thinking like that.

"Wee, Bee, Gee, you're up." Mum calls from the kitchen.

"What did your mum just say?" Rosanna asks, laughing.

"Oh. Those are our nicknames," Greer tells her as she, my brother and I all head to the kitchen. It's our job to bring the food to the table.

"Nicknames, huh? That's cute." Rosanna smiles and nudges me in the ribs as we sit.

"Yeah, when Will—William—was little, he couldn't say his own name. All he could manage was Wee-yam. Which, of course, got shortened to Wee. Then when Ethan came along, he became Eee, Ben is Bee, and I'm Gee." Greer is already heaping food on her plate.

Will groans in embarrassment. "I wasn't even two. Am I ever going to live this down?"

"No!" we all chorus.

"That's adorable. Bee." Rosanna gives me a cheeky grin. She looks more relaxed than she has in days. I'm glad I brought her. I might have a fractured relationship with my family, but they're good and loving people. "So, where's Ethan?"

"Ah. The ever-elusive Ethan. He's away even more than you these days, Bee," Will says, loading himself up with a second helping before most of us have finished our first. Eating big is a Carter family trait even though we're all lean. One day we're going to wake up and find we've exploded overnight and look like Dad. But I'll worry about that when I don't have a table full of Mum's cooking in front of me.

"Ethan has just finished his PhD in archaeology. He's always heading off on a dig or a conference somewhere or other. But he should be home again at the end of summer," Greer explains.

"I certainly hope so. Otherwise, he'll miss his own wedding," Dad harrumphs. Dad doesn't like it when any of his kids are not within lecturing distance. In the most loving way, of course.

Gee, always the one to smooth over awkward moments, pipes up.

"Did I tell you Lulu and I have been talking about collaborating? Not sure about details on how yet, but it's exciting." And the conversation turns to Gee's career as an architect and how she and Lulu might work together.

By the time we're finishing dinner, I almost think I might have got away without the usual interrogation when Dad starts in on his favourite subject.

"So, Ben, have you given any more thought to looking into an apprenticeship?" More than ten years we've been on this merry-go-round.

"Dad, I'm nearly thirty. I'm too old to be an apprentice."

"Yes, and you're too old not to have a job. You should've got onto this years ago instead of wasting your time wandering the world." He's about to break into a full-blown lecture. Normally, I can tune it out for the most part, but I don't relish the idea of Rosanna hearing a humiliating dressing-down. I loved seeing the admiration and respect in her eyes when I told her my story yesterday, and I'd like to keep seeing it.

"Harry ..." Mum's hands start to flap on the table, a sure sign she's anxious. These discussions—which normally turn into arguments—upset her. And no wonder. They upset me too. I didn't think Dad would go there with Rosanna here. Which goes to show how much it bothers him that I don't fit the Carter family mould.

Rosanna cuts me a sidelong look that says I should tell them what I'm actually doing, but I give her a slight shake of the head. Not tonight. This is something I need to build up to.

"Actually, Mr Carter—Harry—Ben has been talking to my father. He owns a building and property development company," Rosanna jumps in. It's true as far as it goes. I have been talking to her father. And he does own a building company. If Dad chooses to interpret this as our conversations have been about a job, that's on him.

My whole body relaxes, letting go of a tension I wasn't even aware I was holding. I'm so grateful for her support. I drop my hand to Rosanna's knee and give it a squeeze. A move not lost on Will, judging by the side eye he gives me.

Rosanna's comment has the effect of stopping Dad in his tracks. "Well, that's wonderful, wonderful. Let me know how it goes, Ben," he blusters.

Ro and I share a look that has my heart beating double time. That sense of indestructibility grows. We really are a team. I've never been part of a team before. Not like this.

As we're all clearing the table, Rosanna falls into a conversation with Greer about Lulu's wedding and the dress Rosanna designed for her. Will takes the opportunity to drag me onto the patio, away from prying ears.

"What the fuck is going on?"

"What do you mean?" I have a pretty good idea what he means, but he's going to have to push me into the fire. I'm not going to jump.

"Rosanna is what I mean. She's not one of your one-and-dones. Or a fuckbuddy. She's practically family." There's another misconception my family continues to believe, the idea I'm a manwhore. I could count on one hand the number of hookups I've had in the last year. This attitude coming from Will, who does get around—a lot—is borderline insulting. Scrub that. It *is* insulting.

"How do you figure that?"

"Apart from the fact she's friends with Greer, she's as close as it comes to Lulu's sister, and Nick is as good as part of this family. Which makes Rosanna family by extension."

"That's a very long bow. And there's nothing going on. But if there was, it would be none of your business."

"Maybe not, but Nick would string you up by your balls if you hurt her. And I'd supply the barbed wire for him to do it with." It stings that my brother thinks I have nothing more on my mind than a quick fuck. Sure, it was true once upon a time. But not anymore. That he thinks I would pull that sort of shit with someone like Rosanna shows how little he knows me. Granted, that's my fault. But it still hurts.

"I have no intention of hurting her. We're friends." My hands land on my hips and I have to force them back to my sides in a less combative stance.

Will shakes his head. "Fuck off. I have eyes in my head. I saw you put your hand on her leg. I see the way you look at her, and I see the way she looks at you. So, pull your head out of your arse and back the hell off." Okay. I had no idea I was looking at her in any 'way'. Although, it shouldn't be surprising, given my feelings. But what's more interesting is that apparently, she's looking at me in a 'way' too. My heart rate kicks up, and my damn ears start burning again. Will pounces on it. "See. Your ears are red. So you're either lying or embarrassed. Or both."

"I'm not lying. We are friends. Yes, I find her attractive. I'm not blind. But I would never do anything to hurt her. What kind of arsehole do you take me for?"

"I don't know. I guess we'll find out."

Now's the time I could tell him about what's been going on with Rosanna, but it's not my story to tell. I'm saved from my dilemma by Rosanna coming out onto the patio.

"I don't want to be rude, Ben, but would it be okay if we head off shortly? I have work tomorrow, and I have a few things to get done tonight." Ro looks pointedly at Will, and I know she doesn't want to say more in front of him.

It's a relief to have an excuse to leave early.

"Of course. I'll be right there," I tell her, and then wait till she walks away to collect her bag before turning back to Will. "Thanks for the chat. It's nice to know what you think of me, brother." I follow Rosanna before he can respond.

Despite Rosanna's support, tonight has been exhausting and has confirmed what I've been thinking. I don't want to keep up the charade any longer. Honestly, I don't know how, or why, I've managed it this long.

No doubt Rosanna could tell by the body language Will and I were having a disagreement, but I'm not ready to talk about it yet. I'm still processing the idea that she looks at me in a 'way'.

We're silent for the first half of the drive back to her place.

"Thanks for stepping in with Dad at the table. I really appreciate it." This is a safe-ish topic of conversation. There's a first. It's many years since talking about my father has been safe. I know he's tough on me because he loves me and wants the best for me, but he has no idea how to show it because I'm different.

"No problem. That was my job, right? Buffer?"

"You're very good at it,"

"Why, thank you. One of my many skills. Do you want to tell me what was with you and Will on the patio?"

"Nothing to worry about. Sibling stuff. You should thank your lucky stars you're an only child." I hark back to our conversation about the merits of siblings versus singles. Although, as pissed off as I am with my brother, I wouldn't want to be without them. Will might be happy to tear me a new one himself, but I don't doubt that if anyone else tried to mess with me, he wouldn't hesitate to come to my defence.

"Yeah, well, being an only girl child isn't without problems. How do you think I ended up with Marco? Dad needed someone to leave the company to, and Marco is the son he never had."

We pull up at a red light, and I turn to face her. "Do you think that's part of why you went out with him? Why you stayed so long?"

"Probably. I was lonely. And Mum and Dad were strict. No going to parties or on dates. Until Marco. Dad was happy for me to date him because he was safe. Dad would go on and on about how he felt relieved he could leave his company and his daughter to such a good man." She pauses, clearly thinking through the development of a bad relationship. "By the time I realised how unhappy I was, Marco's dad was sick, and I couldn't break it off."

"Just promise me you won't back down this time. I know you want to wait until your dad is a bit better, but Marco is bad news. The sooner you cut him loose, the better. For you and your dad's company."

Before Ro can ask any more questions, we pull up outside her apartment. It only takes a few minutes for her to pack a proper suitcase while I empty the perishables out of the fridge and throw out the rubbish. She doesn't even mention moving back here, which is a good indication she was rattled by what happened with Marco earlier, despite playing it off as nothing.

I've never lived with anyone. It allows me to keep up my façade. People think I'm an extrovert because I love to party, but really, it's simply another mask I wear. I like my space. And other people start to aggravate me in very short order. But rather than being irritated by the thought of Rosanna staying for an extended time, I feel relief. And anticipation. And a weird kind of hope.

CHAPTER FIFTEEN

ROSANNA

In the end, Dad stays in hospital most of the week, thanks to a collection of niggling little setbacks. Ben and I settle into a routine that, to my inexperienced self, seems like more than friends, although less than a relationship. It's a kind of weird hybrid situationship, and I'm not sure what to make of it.

Everything Ben does has an effect on me. Specifically, on my lady parts. And, somewhat disturbingly, on my heart.

When he comes back sweaty and heaving from his run each morning, his T-shirt clinging to all those beautiful muscles, the red-gold hair on his long, lean thighs glistening, I can barely speak. And always, he brings me a coffee.

When he picks me up from work each evening and takes me to the hospital to visit Dad, I can't take my eyes off his long, elegant fingers on the steering wheel. And I gulp in the smell of his cologne in the enclosed space.

When he takes me to dinner at my favourite restaurants or arranges for me to have a facial and a massage, I'm mesmerised by his almost shy concern for my welfare.

Twice, I've caught him at two in the morning in his boxer briefs, backlit by the light from the fridge, chugging milk, of all things. And I wouldn't be human if I didn't notice the thick bulge behind the stretchy fabric.

I wake up in the middle of the night, my nipples tight, my thighs damp and a restlessness in my limbs I can't quiet, knowing I've had another one of *those* dreams.

I've never felt desire like it. I don't know if he's feeling it too, but by the end of the week, I'm almost a puddle on the floor at the thought of him, never mind the sight.

He couldn't be kinder or more attentive. Yet, not once has he said or done anything I could say unequivocally is a pass. It would be mortifying if I assumed and he shut me down. I wish I had more experience. Wish I knew for sure if he was interested in me. There's nobody I can ask. Lulu would go crazy. And Greer, well, you can't talk to a man's sister about stuff like this.

Overlaid on all this is the knowledge I have to tell my parents about Marco, which keeps getting derailed by Dad's health. And a vague sense of guilt at feeling these things so soon after a breakup. Shouldn't there be a mourning period? Even if the relationship was a farce. And the—I can't say man because he's not that—lowlife I was with doesn't deserve a second of my time.

The reality is, though, I have the hots for Ben Carter. Bad. And it's getting stronger every day.

On Friday, I take the afternoon off work to help Lulu set up for her father's farewell party. He's going back to Scotland tomorrow, and we won't see him again any time soon.

Before any of this Marco stuff happened, Ben arranged for a private function room in what, I now know, is one of his pubs. He told Lulu a friend owns the pub and swore me to secrecy.

"The staff here are fantastic. I can't believe how helpful they've been. Ben must be really good friends with the owner to have this much pull," she says, as we tinker with the arrangements of flowers and balloons the staff have already set up.

"Yeah, Ben has some pretty sweet connections. It doesn't hurt that he could charm a rattlesnake either," Greer adds, holding a vase steady while I add a couple more enormous lilies. It amazes me that neither Lulu nor Greer question the situation.

They seem happy to think Ben has used his connections to arrange a good deal without questioning any of it.

"I think we're done," Lulu declares, dusting her hands off and flopping down on the plush leather couch by the enormous windows overlooking the harbour. "How about we reward ourselves with a bottle of bubbles before we go home to change?"

"Ooh, that sounds perfect." Greer nips behind the bar and rummages for a bottle and glasses.

"So, how are you enjoying living with Ben?" Lulu directs a laser stare at me.

"Yes," Greer squeals. "I can't believe he asked you to move in with him. Even the family don't get an invitation to the Sanctum Sanctorum."

I'm so not good at keeping secrets. At not saying what's on my mind.

I take a gulp of sparkling wine to buy myself a second or two to think. Which gives Lulu the chance to jump in.

"I just hope all this helping you out is above board. I'm sorry, Greer, I know he's your brother, but I can't help thinking there's more to this story. What's in it for him?"

Greer's mouth flies open, presumably to defend her brother, because I know they're close, but I get in first.

"What? You think he's hitting on me?"

Lulu shrugs and raises her eyebrows in question.

"It's not like that. He's been nothing but kind. And respectful. I don't know what I would've done without him, to be honest. Marco really scared me the night he came to my apartment."

Lulu puts her glass down and launches herself at me, wrapping her arms around me and pulling my head onto her shoulder. "Oh, Ro. I'm sorry. I can't imagine how scary it must have been. You're right. Ben has been kind and very protective. I shouldn't judge him based on all the stories I've heard about his wild ways."

"Well, I've seen no evidence of wildness, to be honest."

"I know Ben has a reputation as a bit of a party boy, Lulu." Greer interjects. There's a gentle but clear rebuke in her tone. "But of all my brothers, he's the one I go to when I need support. He was the one who took care of me when I thought there was no hope for me and Josh. I'd trust him with my life, Rosanna. I think you can too."

I'm so happy Greer is stepping in and standing up for her brother.

"You know what, I do. I know we hardly know one another, but I've never felt anything but safe with Ben."

"Okay. Well, if you two think he's alright, I trust your judgement," Lulu concedes. "But I can't help wondering about all these connections he seems to have. All his strange comings and goings."

I laugh. "You just can't stand not knowing everything that's going on. Admit it." I give Lu a push and pick my drink up again.

"I think he feels like the less people know about his life, the less judgement he'll face. It may not seem like it, but sometimes it's tough being a Carter. Mum and Dad have expectations, and I think Ben believes he's let them down, although they've never said as much. To me anyway."

Greer doesn't know how close she's come to the truth there. Nor does she realise how much impact those expectations have had on Ben's self-image. But I do. I hope I can repay his kindness to me by helping him talk to his family and break the cycle he's stuck in. Soon.

"Yeah, I know all about parental expectations. If it wasn't for my parents, I would've kicked Marco to the curb years ago." I'm trying not to be bitter or resentful about the wasted years, but sometimes it sneaks through. At least now, the focus is on me and not Ben, so I don't have to watch my mouth so carefully.

Greer and I finish most of the bottle since Lulu is still breast-feeding and only has a couple of mouthfuls. Then we all go our separate ways, me with my ever-present shadow, to get ready for tonight's party.

I let myself into the apartment and am brought up short by the sight of Ben in the kitchen. Naked. Gulping water from a massive glass.

Well, that's how it looks from the hallway. In reality, he's wearing a tiny pair of flimsy running shorts, sitting low on his hips, hidden by the island bench.

What isn't hidden is his chest. Or his arms. Or the way his throat ripples as he swallows the water. Not to mention the vee of muscle above his hips that disappears enticingly into the shorts.

He's covered in a fine sheen of sweat, and every long, lean muscle is highlighted by the late-afternoon light coming in through the floor-to-ceiling windows. Clearly, he's come straight from a workout in the gym downstairs.

It takes me a moment to wind my tongue back into my mouth from where it's fallen on the floor.

"Hey," I croak.

"Hey. Did you and the girls get everything ready to Lulu's satisfaction?" Ben responds, a sly grin on his face as though he knows exactly what's going through my mind. I guess with his experience, he would.

I nod and wave my hand towards the bedrooms. "I might go and, um, have a quick nap. Before I have to ... you know, get ready." If I stand around gawping at him, the sparkling wine I guzzled might loosen my tongue enough for something embarrassing to come tumbling out.

"Good idea. It will probably be a late night. I might do the same."

Gah. The idea of Ben, all sweaty and naked, no more than a couple of metres away, is not conducive to sleep.

I scuttle off to my room without another word. Leaning against the closed door, I eye off the drawer where I've put my underwear. I've made it all week, but I can't hold out any longer.

Hiding under all the silk, satin and lace is my vibrator. I don't know why I packed it. I haven't been able to bring myself to use it since I've been here, although there have been many times when I've been sorely tempted. I can't help worrying Ben might hear the buzzing or my moans. That would be way too embarrassing. But after a week of temptation, a little too much alcohol, and what I just saw in the kitchen, I know I won't get a second of sleep. So I twist the lock on the door, synch my phone up to my little mobile speaker, and close myself in the bathroom with my BOB. Two closed doors, the music and the running water, ought to drown out any noise. I hope.

Just because I'm a virgin, doesn't mean I don't have needs. Since I've had no other option, I'm pretty handy—excuse the pun—with self-care.

There's a helpful bench seat in the enormous shower in my bathroom, so I turn on the hot water and my vibrator and settle in. One thing I've never been able to do is orgasm while standing up. Maybe it's a guy thing? I don't know.

With the visual of Ben in the kitchen forever burned into my memory, I make it to the end in record time, biting hard on my lower lip to keep as quiet as possible.

I feel so much better. This need has been building since I moved in here. No. That's not right. It's been building since I first laid eyes on Ben at Nick and Lulu's wedding.

I tried to ignore it. I had a boyfriend at the time. But since the whole clusterfuck with Marco, and spending the last week getting to know Ben, being nurtured by him, seeing him half naked at all hours? I'm only human. The problem is a complication like Ben is the last thing I need. Then it occurs to me.

Maybe the simplicity of Ben is exactly what I need.

Because the fact is, I'm a twenty-six-year-old virgin. How is that even a thing? How do I go on a date, meet a man I like, and explain that, whilst I have plenty of experience pleasing myself, I have no clue how to actually please a man? Or be pleased by one. It's humiliating.

Ben has lots of experience pleasing women, I hear. Lots of women. With no strings attached. What's one more?

CHAPTER SIXTEEN

BENEDICT

I'm never going to get any rest now. The look on Rosanna's face when she noticed me in the kitchen went straight to my running shorts, so I have to wait until she's in her bedroom with the door closed before I venture out from behind the kitchen island.

I'm in the shower, soaping my hard-on in no time. It's becoming a habit. I wonder if Ro's in her room doing the equivalent. Fuuuck. This won't take long.

I should feel guilty, but I don't. Because the alternative is leaping on her and begging her to let me fuck her. And I can't do that, despite the unmistakable look of craving she gave me today. I'm not ashamed to say I've done a fair bit of hanging about the apartment in my running shorts since Rosanna moved in. I won't hit on her. But there's nothing wrong with putting temptation in her way. Judging from how fidgety she gets when she sees me like that, it might be working. And I'm ready when—if—she is.

But I have to keep the long game in mind here because I want more from Rosanna than a quick release. Right now, she's got enough on her plate. So my right hand and I will need to stay good friends for the foreseeable future.

Once I've taken care of business, so to speak, I lay down on the bed and close my eyes, mentally running over the Marco situation.

I've tried not to scare Rosanna with what I know because I understand how worried she is about her dad. But time is running out. Marco is dangerous. To both Rosanna and her father.

Andrea has given The Cockhead too much control and not enough oversight. There's some dodgy stuff going on at Moretti & Co and I would bet this apartment Rosanna's dad knows nothing about any of it.

With two minutes to spare before we need to leave, Rosanna comes out of her room looking like something out of a sex dream.

Her hair is in a messy up-do, with a few big curls falling along her neck. The satin of her dress—which she tells me is char-treuse but which looks like a cross between yellow and green to me—clings to her wet-dream curves almost to her knees where it kicks out in a flare that flicks as she walks, emphasising the sway of those hips.

All this makes me glad I put an extra handkerchief in my pocket. To mop up the inevitable drool. Yes, I'm a guy who carries handkerchiefs. You wouldn't believe how many times the wielding of a little square of white linen has gotten me into a woman's ... well, you know.

I lift my hand in a twirl motion, and Rosanna complies with a shy smile. My wolf whistle turns it into a grin.

"You look amazing. Wait there. I think I might need to take my cricket bat with us. To beat off all the men." I make to head into the laundry where my sports gear is stored.

"Haha. I'm pretty sure I know most of the men who will be there anyway."

"Yes. But now you're single, the game has changed. Be prepared, honey." I sweep my arm towards the door.

In the lift, I take a few surreptitious deep breaths. I love the way Rosanna smells. Kind of woody and leathery and smoky and spicy, with an overlay of something sweet. Scents you would normally associate as masculine, but on her, they scream sexy woman.

I guess I'm not surreptitious enough.

"Did you just sniff me?" she asks.

"Maybe." I shrug. "You smell delicious. What is it?"

"Oud." Rosanna shifts closer and tilts her head so I can sniff at the side of her neck. Jesus. It takes all my willpower not to sink my teeth into her creamy flesh. If I don't have to excuse myself and take care of business sometime during this evening, it will be a miracle.

"What's oud?" Rosanna won't know this, but that right there was my sex voice.

"It's a Middle Eastern scent. Made from a particular type of wood. You like it?" Sadly, she straightens and shifts back.

"Love it. Very sexy." This is going to be a long night.

My team have outdone themselves. The decorations are beautiful, the food is out of this world, and the service is spot-on.

The night is going brilliantly. Until it's not.

I look across the room at Tama, who is stationed by the door and don't miss the tip of his head. Towards the last person I want to see. Marco. Who is shouldering his way through the crowd, a glass of what I know is expensive champagne in his hand.

I have the advantage because Rosanna has never been far from my line of sight all night, since I can't seem to take my eyes off her. Which, now that Marco has arrived, is probably a good thing.

Excusing myself from the conversation I'm in, I beeline right for her, making it to her side in time to take her arm before she registers Marco's presence.

"Sorry I'm late, folks," Marco says, leaning in to attempt a cheek kiss on Rosanna, who flinches before drawing closer to me. I mentally kick myself for not making sure someone had remembered to take him off the guest list.

From the corner of my eye, I notice Tama circumnavigating the room, manoeuvring himself into a position to act quickly should shit get ugly.

"What are you doing here, Marco?" Rosanna's whispered tone conveys her level of irritation.

"I was invited. Remember? As your partner." Marco is an oily piece of shit. I have no idea how he fooled Rosanna and her parents all these years. But as I know all too well, people see what they want to see. What they expect to see.

"We broke up. You're not welcome here."

"And yet, my name was on the guest list." He's not entirely steady on his feet, and his cheeks are flushed an angry red.

"An oversight. I'd appreciate it if you left." Rosanna is quivering, whether with fear or anger, I'm not sure. Possibly both.

"And miss this wonderful party? This expensive champagne? Why would I do that?" Marco lurches a step closer to Ro.

I notice Lulu has clocked Marco's arrival, and Nick and Will are making their way over, as is Josh, with Greer not far behind.

I don't want to escalate the situation, but it looks like Marco won't go quietly.

"The lady would like you to leave, Marco. So how about you finish your glass and find somewhere else to be." My tone is pleasant and friendly, but the message is clear.

"And who the fuck are you to tell me what to do, you piece of shit?" he asks, turning bloodshot eyes on me. Even accounting for the dim lighting, his pupils are unnaturally dilated, and I notice a faint white smear under his left nostril. Great. He's high.

I put my arm around Rosanna, turning her into Greer's arms and nodding for her to step back while at the same time giving Tama the signal to move forward. Nick, Will and Josh stand close behind me, and I'm grateful for their support. But Tama and I have got this.

"I'm the guy who will make sure you leave. Now. And if you continue to bother Rosanna, I'm the guy you'll have a problem with. A big problem." I'm cool and calm, and I can see Marco thinks he's going to get the best of this situation. What he doesn't know is that Tama is right behind him.

Marco reaches out to give me a shove, but almost before his hands have left his side, Tama has them in his iron grip, twisting them up behind Marco's back. What's left of the champagne in his glass arcs across the space, splattering Will's trousers.

"Time to go, little man," Tama says. Insulting but accurate. He has a good thirty centimetres and twenty kilos on Marco.

"You'll be sorry," Marco yelps at Rosanna, spittle flying from his mouth and hitting her face, as Tama pushes him towards the door.

I can see how frightened she is. She's not used to this kind of confrontation. But she's also one strong woman.

"You don't scare me, you piece of filth," she snaps back.

As Tama shoves him out the door, Marco gets the last word.

"Yeah, we'll see about that."

"Jesus Christ."

"What a dickhead."

"Fucker."

I hear muttered behind me. Will drops a heavy hand on my shoulder, and, without words, manages to convey his message—*Good job, but I warned you. Keep your hands to yourself.* Too bad for him, I only have eyes for Rosanna. I open my arms, and she's in them in an instant. Her earlier quivering has turned to shaking.

"Shhh. It's okay. He's gone. Tama will make sure he doesn't get back in."

I stroke her hair for a moment, then shift and take one of my handkerchiefs out of my pocket, gently wiping at the spit Marco left on her beautiful face. Her eyes are glittering, and her cheeks are the most glorious pink. I run a finger over the blush.

"Look at you, living up to your name with those rosie cheeks."

Somehow, despite how scared she must be, Rosanna manages a smile.

"Thank you. I don't know what I'd have done without you."

"You'd probably have kneed him in the balls. But why risk tearing your beautiful dress when there's no need?" I stuff the hanky back in my pocket. "Now, how about a dance?"

CHAPTER SEVENTEEN

ROSANNA

A gainst all odds, after Marco is escorted from the party, I have a great time.

Ben leads me out onto the dance floor and is spinning me, dipping me and making me laugh before I even realise what's happening. I don't worry that Marco will come back. Ben and Tama have got this. It was me who messed up by forgetting to take his name off the guest list at the door downstairs. And yet again, Ben came to my rescue.

As the song comes to an end, Lulu drags me off the little dance floor and onto the enclosed verandah where Isla is letting out little baby snores in her pram under the watchful eye of the professional babysitter Nick finally approved, having interrogated—and I do mean interrogated—half a dozen poor souls for the job.

"What the actual hell was he thinking?" Lulu whispers as Greer and Claire join us.

"Thinking is not something Marco is doing much of these days. If he ever did."

"Agreed. Hard to think straight when you're high as a kite. I guess." Claire hands me a fresh glass of champagne.

"High? Seriously?" It hadn't occurred to me Marco was taking drugs, but now I think about it, it makes a lot of sense.

"For sure. Josh was worried we were in for a full-on fight. Thank God security were on it." Greer leans against the wall, lifting a foot and rotating it. "Whoever invented high heels?" she groans.

"Here's to Ben." Lulu lifts her glass in a toast. Which makes me happy. Her attitude to him seems to have shifted from distrust to wary to something approaching appreciation.

"Let's hope that's the last we see of Marco until he's packing up his desk at Moretti's," I add, and we clink glasses.

I'm not left to think or fret for even a moment for the rest of the night. Lulu, Claire, Greer and Jessie, Greer's soon-to-be sister-in-law, ply me with drinks and stuff me with the delicious finger food that's doing the rounds. Nick, Josh, Will, and even Lulu's dad, Duncan, drag me onto the floor for dance after dance until my feet ache and I beg for a break. All the while, I know Ben is never far away. Keeping an eye on me. If it was anyone else, it would creep me out and, probably, piss me off. Coming from Ben, it's entirely natural. Comfortable. Or rather, comforting.

The last song of the night is a slow dance, and as our friends come together on the dance floor, Ben appears and gathers me up in his arms. Apart from the time we ended up accidentally sleeping together on the couch, we've never been this physically close for this long. My pulse picks up and heat builds low in my belly as we sway together.

"Thank you," I mumble against his crisp white shirt where my head is cradled.

"You already said that. And it was my pleasure. Not much I enjoy more than seeing a cockhead like Marco get his arse handed to him."

"Did ... Do you think Tama ..." I can't quite get the words out.

"Beat him up?" Ben seems to have no trouble. "No. Maybe a shove or two, just to scare him. Let him know what will happen if he tries it again."

"Okay. Although, he kind of deserved a bit of a belting. Not that I condone violence or anything."

"Of course not." I can hear the smile in Ben's voice. "He does deserve a belting, though. Let's hope he got the message and we won't have to deal with him anymore."

"I have to tell my father."

Ben sighs. I'm aware this conversation is becoming repetitive.

"Yes, Rosie, you do. All of it. Sooner rather than later." Rosie. He called me that earlier. Everyone else calls me Rosanna or Ro. I like that he calls me something different. Something special.

"I'm having dinner with them on Sunday. I'll tell them then."

"Good. Until then, let's enjoy this dance."

And we do, circling the floor amongst our closest friends, my hand in his, his other hand on the small of my back. I'm relaxed, and at the same time, electrified by the touch of his hands, the citrussy smell of his aftershave, the beat of his heart, too fast for the slow dance we're doing, yet perfectly in time with my own.

The goodbyes seem to take forever, all of us kissing and hugging. Duncan is pretending he's not crying at the prospect of leaving Lulu and Isla, who, having been the star attraction for a while, is again asleep in her pram.

Ben and I finally extricate ourselves and hop in an Uber. Despite the extended goodbyes, the electric energy from the dance floor follows us into the close confines of the car. I'm hyper-aware of the heat of his body. His breathing. His scent. All of which seem to call to my lady parts.

The thought I had earlier about asking Ben to take care of my virginity rears its head again. The problem is, I don't have enough experience with men to know for sure if what I'm feeling is reciprocated or if I'm projecting my attraction onto him. Then again, he's a guy. A guy who clearly enjoys sex. What's the likelihood he would turn me down? I may not be a supermodel, but I'm not Frankenstein's daughter either. Then again, our relationship, our friendship, or whatever this is, has become essential to me, despite the short timeframe. Do I want to risk ruining what we have by making a pass? Could asking him to take my virginity even be termed a 'pass'? I'm a long way from drunk, but I've had a little too much champagne to puzzle this out tonight.

Ben interrupts my hamster wheel of thoughts.

"You're quiet. Are you okay?"

"Oh. Yeah. I'm fine." I toss off, waving my hand as though my thoughts are nothing. Ben snorts out a laugh.

"Right. I know enough to know when a woman says she's *fine*, she's anything but. And after what happened earlier, I'd be surprised if you were. Don't forget, I'm here for you, whatever you need. Whenever you need it." If he only knew.

He takes my hand, his thumb stroking the back of my wrist, and opens his mouth to say more, but the Uber is pulling to a stop outside his building.

I barely make it inside the apartment door before I lean against the wall and unbuckle the torture devices from my feet with a moan-sigh.

"I felt that," Ben says with a laugh. "I think I could use a cuppa before bed. What about you?"

"Yes, please. A green tea would be great." Dropping my shoes, I hobble to the couch and flop down inelegantly, hampered as I am by my dress, which Lulu said made me walk like Morticia Addams. Bitch.

Ben puts our teas on the coffee table, sits beside me, and lifts my legs onto his lap. Taking one of my feet in his hands, he starts to massage my cramped toes and aching arch.

In seconds I'm belting out porn-worthy moans.

"Oh my God, that is sooo good. Yes. There. Right there," I say, as his thumb digs deep into my flesh. My head falls back against the arm of the sofa, and my eyes drift closed as his hands move to my other foot.

"Better?" he asks, and even with my eyes closed, I can hear the smirk on his face. Do I imagine his hands lingering on my ankles? Skimming lightly up my calves?

"Your hands are magical. Like unicorns with thumbs." I sigh, disappointed that he's finished his massage, spun me around and placed my feet on the table. Although he does hand me my tea, so it's not all bad news.

We drink in silence for a while, the peace and quiet of the apartment a welcome relief after the drama and noise of the party. All the while, I'm pondering exactly how to go about propositioning Ben. Or any man, for that matter.

"Well, Rosie, I think it might be time for this unicorn to hit the hay. You coming?" He stands and offers a hand to help me up from the couch. Which I need. I have no idea how Morticia managed to run a household in that dress of hers. Sitting is a real punishment. Lucky for her, she had Lurch and Thing, I guess.

As Ben pulls me up from the sofa, we come chest to chest, and the tension I felt on the dance floor, and in the car, is back in full force. Neither of us moves or speaks, our hands clasped, my breasts brushing his shirt front.

I think he's going to kiss me. Surely, he's going to kiss me …

As my eyes start to drift shut, he clears his throat. "Well. Goodnight. Sleep well."

And without another word, he turns on his heel and disappears up the hall and into his bedroom, the door closing with a quiet click that carries the weight of a bucket of cold water.

There was a spark. I didn't imagine it. A definite spark. And I'm back on the hamster wheel. Should I ask him? Should I not? Would he agree? Would it ruin our friendship? Round and round and round.

When the question I should be asking myself is, if I ask, and if he agrees, will I be able to walk away unscathed?

CHAPTER EIGHTEEN

BENEDICT

She's in the next room. One wall away. I picture her in those cute cotton, sexy-librarian pyjamas, dark hair spread across the white linen, and my cock throbs to life. Like it has every night since she's come to stay with me. Only tonight, it's worse. Because I nearly kissed her.

Rolling onto my back, I push the covers aside and begin to stroke the thick flesh, remembering the sight of her as she stood from the bath, droplets of water sparkling in the dark curls between her legs. Fuck. It's been forever since I've had a woman with hair down there. These days, they're all smooth and hairless. And while there's nothing wrong with that—a pussy is a beautiful thing however it's presented—her natural beauty is overpowering.

If her pussy is as lush as the rest of her, it would be like finding yourself in the Garden of Eden before everything went wrong for Adam and Eve. The version by Jan Brueghel with peacocks and rabbits and swans. Fuck.

My hand begins to move faster. Precum is dripping from the tip, and I can't hold back a quiet moan. I'm about to reach for the lube in the bedside drawer when I hear it. A quiet knocking. Three tiny taps.

"Yes?" I manage to choke out as I struggle to sit up, pulling the covers back over my lap.

"Ben? Are you okay? I thought I heard ..."

"I'm fine." Although I don't sound fine, even to my own ears.

"Can I ... can I come in for a minute?"

"Sure. Yeah. Of course." I pull my knees up and fluff the covers, making sure the erection that's still throbbing, knocking against my belly for attention, is covered.

Soft light from the hall surrounds Rosanna, silhouetting her bare legs as she comes into the room. I was right. The sexy-librarian pyjamas.

"What's up? You okay?" I ask.

"I was wondering if I could talk to you about something." She's uncharacteristically subdued. Almost nervous.

"Always. You know that." I slide up the bed and rest against the headboard as she perches on the bed next to me. Too close. The tapping of my neglected cock continues. I'm surprised she can't hear it screaming her name. Maybe it's spelling out 'Ro' in precum on my stomach.

"So. Um. Lulu says you've slept with lots of women," Rosanna starts. I have no idea what to say, so I remain silent and watch the emotions flying across her face.

"You know Marco had always insisted we wait. So, I've never ..." Her gaze is firmly glued to the carpet beside the bed.

"Yeah ..." I'm not sure where she's going with this, but if it's where I think she's going, I might be in imminent danger of a stroke. Or an aneurysm. But definitely a stroke. Just not necessarily the medical kind.

"I'm twenty-six years old, Ben, and I have no idea what to do. So I was thinking maybe you could ..." She looks up then, our gazes connecting. She must see the dawning horror in mine. Not surprisingly, she misinterprets it. "You know what, don't worry. It was a silly idea. Of course, you wouldn't want to. With me. It's only, I thought, earlier, you ... we ..."

She leaps from the bed as though it's on fire, her cheeks red and eyes glassy. I can't let her go like this. Thinking the idea of fucking her horrifies me. Because the opposite is true.

I reach out and catch her wrist before she has time to get away.

"No. Wait. I think you might be jumping to conclusions." I need a deep breath before I can continue. "Am I right in thinking you were going to ask me to be your first?"

Those cheeks get even redder as she nods, her gaze fixed on the floor again. My cock is now thumping like a Labrador's tail at feeding time.

"Yes. I'm sorry. I should never have put you in this position."

I tug on her wrist, and she sinks back onto the bed.

"Why me, Rosanna? Don't you want your first to be someone you love?" If that could be me, even for a minute, I would die a happy man.

"That's the thing, there is no one I love. And I don't know when—or if—there ever will be. And I want my first time to be with someone who ..." She stutters to a halt.

"Knows what he's doing?"

"Yes," she whispers. "I thought maybe there was a bit of a spark. With us."

Spark. She has no idea. None.

I take my time to work through what I need to say in my head, although the head under the covers is now screaming *pick me, pick me*.

"Rosie, this is a huge decision. You've waited so long. You need to think this through."

"I did think it through," she whispers. If I didn't already hate Marco, I would hate him purely for the self-doubt I see on this beautiful woman's face. One day, I will make him regret it.

"Rosanna, I don't want you to think for a second that I'm not interested. Any man in his right mind would jump at the chance. Including me." I lift her face with a finger under her chin so she can see the sincerity in my eyes. "But I want you to be sure this is what you really want. There's no rush. Why don't you take a day or two to think about it before you make any decisions?"

"Okay. And if I decide yes, you'd consider it?" Between the grinding of my back teeth over Marco and the screaming of *now, do it now, before she changes her mind you idiot,* from my dick, I can only nod in response.

"Thank you, Ben. And you don't have to worry. I won't expect anything afterwards. I just want to know what it's like. To feel wanted. Even if it's only for a moment."

Jesus. This woman. If only she knew.

I run my hand around the back of her head and pull her towards me, pressing my lips to her forehead. If I open my mouth, it will all come pouring out. How I've loved her since the moment I laid eyes on her. How I would move heaven and earth to make her happy. How Marco is the stupidest arsehole in the world to have done what he did. How I will be eternally grateful to him if it gives me even a slim chance to be what she wants.

But she's not ready to hear all that yet. And I don't want to be her rebound. Or a rescuer romance. I want to be chosen. Free and clear. For me. So I say nothing.

That doesn't mean I won't take her up on her offer. I want her to be sure, though.

Rosanna climbs off the bed and moves to the door.

"See you in the morning then. And thank you, Ben," she says as she reaches the hallway.

"No thanks necessary, Rosie. It should be me thanking you."

She smiles, still shy but less embarrassed, and closes the door quietly behind her.

I lie back down, knowing I won't get a second of sleep unless I finish what I started before she came into the room. I'm done in about three seconds, thanks to Rosanna's request. Fuck. I'm fucked.

CHAPTER NINETEEN

ROSANNA

I don't know if I'll ever be able to leave this room. I can't believe I propositioned Ben last night. Maybe it was the champagne. Or the dancing. Or the foot rub. But something possessed me.

I tried to shake the crazy idea, but by the time I had struggled out of my straight-jacket dress, showered, and put on my pyjamas, the thought was firmly planted and I couldn't let it go.

The dress. It must have been the dress. It cut off the blood supply to my brain. It's the only plausible explanation for why I had the audacity to go into Ben's room and hit him with my crazy idea.

And he was so lovely about it. So kind and compassionate.

The problem is, even though I can't believe I did it, and I'm mortified at my boldness, I meant every word I said. And if he didn't hate the idea, if he thought it might be something he would be happy to do, I would do it in a heartbeat.

The more pressing problem, however, is how I gather the courage to leave my room and face him. Because at the moment, my plan is Schrodinger's cat. It may or may not be possible. When I leave this room, I'll know. One way or the other. If it's a no, I don't know how we'll move forward. Oh, yeah, there's also the small point that I'll be crushed.

I hear Ben's door open and close. He's going for his morning run. I have about half an hour to put my big girl panties on and decide how to handle this.

I could go with the 'oh, don't take any notice of me, I was drunk' defence. Which I wasn't. I was no more than slightly mellow.

Or there's the complete amnesia angle: 'I have no recollection of such a conversation'. But my friendship with Ben means too much to me to lie.

There really is only one option. Honesty.

I must drift off—I didn't get much sleep last night, for obvious reasons—because the next thing I know, there's a knock at my door. Oh, God.

"Yes?" I struggle to sit up, pushing my hair out of my face and pulling the covers up my chest. Which is ridiculous, given he's seen me naked. But still.

Ben's head appears around the door. My cheeks burn.

"Thought you might like some breakfast." He comes into the room, still sweaty from his run, with a keep-it cup of coffee and a brown bag containing, I'm pretty sure, my favourite herb and cheese muffin. He really is too good to be true.

"Thank you." I can't even look him in the eye. So how are we going to ... ugh.

He hands them over and retreats but turns when he gets to the door.

"I need a shower. When I'm done, I thought we could talk about what happened last night. No pressure from me. If you've changed your mind, that's totally fine. I figured you might have questions or whatever."

Before I can answer, he's out the door. Well. I guess Schrodinger's cat is alive.

Ben is in his office on the phone when I finally emerge, having scoffed down the muffin and coffee and taken a long, thinking-time shower. Which, of course, involved shaving my legs, exfoliating, moisturising, and any other beauty treatment I could think of.

It was sweet of Ben to give me an out, time to rethink things. But despite my terror of rejection—or worse, having it go horribly, uninspiringly wrong—I have no intention of changing my mind. And leaving it a day or two is going to send me crazy with self-doubt and second-guessing. Now that the cat is out of the bag, or more accurately, the box, I want to get this plan moving.

I drift around the living room, unable to settle, listening to the rise and fall of his voice, his deep chuckle, which hits me right between the legs. Finally, the tone of his voice indicates he's ending the call. Before I even have time to compose myself, he's standing in front of me, looking delicious in worn jeans and a white T-shirt, feet bare, his hair still slightly damp from his shower. And the smell. Ohhh, the smell. I could orgasm on his scent alone.

"How are you this morning?" His rich blue eyes search my face, drawing heat to my cheeks.

"Good. Great. I'm great." Gotta love a good nervous babble. So sexy. I realise I'm holding my breath like some kind of romance novel heroine. Waiting for his next words. Waiting for him to say he'd rather not. Or let's do this. I don't know which is scarier. But he surprises me.

"It's a beautiful morning. How about we go for a walk?"

"Sure." My voice is a squeak compared to his deep rumble. *A walk?* What the hell does that mean? Is he trying to let me down gently? In a public place where I won't cause a scene? The one thing keeping me calm-ish is that whatever Ben is planning to do, he'll be kind about it.

Ray greets us with his usual bright 'good morning' as we exit the lift. I wonder what he thinks of me staying here. Does he assume we're lovers? My cheeks heat. Maybe we soon will be. Or maybe I'll be taking Lulu up on her offer to stay at Nick's old apartment. I suck in a deep breath as we hit the pavement. I'm going to have a stroke if I don't calm down. I hope the carnival of emotions I'm experiencing aren't painted on my face. And I hope Ben says yes. I think.

He's right. It is a beautiful morning. As we cross the road towards the Botanic Gardens, Ben takes my hand, and it feels like the most natural thing in the world, while at the same time sending every nerve and synapse in my body into overdrive.

His thumb gently brushes the back of my hand as we walk, but he says nothing. Oh, he's good at this. At building the tension. I'm a mouse trap about to spring by the time we've wandered through the gardens and reached the water. We lean side by side on the sandstone wall. I can't keep quiet for another second.

"I've thought about it. All night. I haven't changed my mind. I won't change my mind. So if you're not disgusted by the idea, I want to do ... what we talked about," I blurt, my whole body vibrating with nerves. And excitement. And *nerves*.

He smiles but doesn't look at me, his attention on the boats in the distance.

"Oh, I'm far from disgusted. I know you're a virgin, Rosie, but can I ask, did you and Marco ever do anything at all?" His question makes me glad he's looking at the boats and not me. This is embarrassing. Not the talking about sex so much, but the admitting to my failures in that department.

"We went to third base a couple of times. But Marco never seemed interested. It wasn't great. So we ... stopped bothering."

"When you say third base, do you mean oral? Hands?" He turns and leans his hip against the stone wall. Now, it's me gazing out at the boats, too ashamed to look at him.

An embarrassed groan escapes before I manage a strangled, "Just hands. Neither of us ever ... came."

"But you have had an orgasm? On your own?" As if to emphasise the point, he takes my hand in his.

"Yes. Maybe it was all my fault. I don't know." I curl my fingers around his to stop their shaking. "If you don't want to do this, I understand."

"Oh, I want to. More than you can imagine. I asked because I wanted to understand your experience. I want you to be sure. I don't want to push you."

"I am. And you're not. So, we're going to do this? When?"

Again, he surprises me.

"How about an ice-cream?" He tilts his head towards a gelato truck a couple of hundred metres away. I could scream with frustration. What is he doing? Eating ice-cream at a time like this? I thought we would go straight back to his apartment and, well, get it done.

I'm scared to open my mouth for fear of what I might say. Ben takes my silence as agreement, and we amble over.

"Oooh. It's real gelato. Proper Italian flavours." I'm momentarily distracted from my fears and the momentous nature of our decision by the joy of such a find. Well played, Ben. I guess he could see the anxiety on my face. I shouldn't be surprised.

"What would you suggest?" Ben asks, not even looking at the flavour list. I'm not sure if that's because of his dyslexia or inability to read Italian, but I'm happy to make a recommendation.

"*Due coni per favore, uno di ciocalato fondente e fior di latte e uno di biscotti e zabaglione. Grazie.*"

"*Un momento, tesoro.*" The little old guy in the truck smiles as he starts to build cones the size of our heads.

"Do you want to know what you're getting?" I ask Ben as he leans on a nearby bench.

"Nope. I trust you." He grins, totally relaxed, in direct contrast to the nervous wreck standing next to him, jumping out of her skin.

I take the cones, that are so loaded up with deliciousness they're in danger of over-balancing, while Ben pays.

"*Grazie mille,*" Ben says to the server in a more than passable Italian accent. I raise my eyebrows in question as I hand over his cone.

"What? I've spent a bit of time in Italy over the years. I can break out the occasional basic phrase." He laughs at my expression. Thank God Mum didn't say anything embarrassing at the hospital.

We wander deeper into the gardens and find a shaded bench. Our legs are pressed together. The hard muscle of his thigh rubbing against mine brings a rush of heat to my cheeks and somewhere a good bit lower. The air between us seems denser than normal. Like extra sound and light waves have been packed in, until it's bursting with invisible energy.

As if Ben can sense my growing arousal, he reaches out and gently guides the hand holding my gelato to his mouth. I expect him to lick it. But instead, as he locks his gaze with mine, he clamps his mouth across the top and sucks gently. Oooh. I can feel it all the way to my toes. His eyes let me know he's imagining sucking my nipple as he lets out a quiet hum of pleasure and his lips slide across the surface of the chocolate ice-cream before lifting, leaving behind a tight peak that matches the ones in my bra. I'm melting faster than the ice-cream.

There's a whole other level of gravel in his voice as he says, "Shall we?" He stands, trailing his fingers down the arm of the hand holding my gelato without breaking contact with my eyes.

As we walk, I'm conscious of every long, slow lap of his tongue across his steadily melting ice-cream. The way his lips rub together. The occasional hum of pleasure. All the way back to his building. Up in the lift. Into the apartment.

Until we're both standing in the entry hall. Hands sticky. Hearts pounding. Breaths catching.

CHAPTER TWENTY

BENEDICT

Both of us are covered in sticky sweetness, and if I don't miss my guess, it won't be too long until we're covered in another sort of sticky.

Our breathing is in sync. Our heartbeats are in sync. The anticipation has every cell in my body vibrating at a frequency I've never felt before.

I don't give myself time to think as the front door swings shut behind us. Oblivious to my messy hands, I slide my fingers into her lush hair and tilt her face towards mine. I take a moment to enjoy the view before I lower my mouth to her full lips. Slowly. Giving her the chance to change her mind if she wants to. But if she's feeling half of what I am, that's not going to happen.

Which doesn't mean I'm going to rush her. Or me. This will be no quickie. No hit and run. By the time I'm finished with her, we'll both be limp with satisfaction and exhaustion.

Her lips are sweet when mine touch down on them, clinging slightly open, but forcing nothing. Luxuriating in the moment. Our first kiss. The first of many, if I have my way.

A breath shudders from her and across my lips, milky from the gelato. I gather her closer, my fingers tightening slightly in her hair. It takes everything I have not to dive in when her tongue touches my bottom lip, gliding across it and into my mouth. That's all the invitation I need. My lips slide open, and my tongue slips into her mouth.

Ro lets out a tiny sound. Too high to be a moan, too warm to be a squeak. Suddenly her hands are fisting in my shirt, pulling me closer.

Walking backwards, I lead her into my bedroom, never letting go of her lips or her hair. I don't think I could, even if I wanted to.

The back of my legs bump the bed. I spin us around and lower her to the mattress. The intensity of our kiss builds to nipping, sucking, dragging, before my lips slide across her cheek, down the angle of her jaw, onto the warm column of her neck as it arches, her head thrown back.

Her hands come up to unbutton her linen shirt, but I catch them, holding them against the bed high above her head.

"Not this time, honey. This is my job."

I want her to not have to move. Or to think. I want her to soak up the sensation of being undressed. Being admired. Being touched. Being worshipped. Because God knows she deserves it.

Her eyes are wide as I rise onto my knees and straddle her thighs, my hands going to the buttons of her sleeveless shirt, slipping them one by one until the white fabric is open to the waist. Bracketing the lush flesh of her breasts encased in sheer, creamy lace. The soft skin of her belly. I can't resist resting my fingers in the hollow of her throat before drawing them down slowly to pop the button and slide the zipper of her crazy zebra print pants.

I shift down on the bed, giving myself room to draw her pants down her long legs. All the while trailing my fingers along her warm, silky flesh.

The ballet flats she was wearing have disappeared somewhere between the front door and here, and as her feet slide free of the trousers, I toss them to the floor. I lift her to sitting and slide the shirt off before unclipping her bra, brushing the straps from her shoulders, watching as the cups drop from her breasts, exposing the tight raspberry of her nipples.

Her body is full and sumptuous. I want to run my eyes over every inch of her. Then my fingers. Then my tongue.

She lifts her hips for me to slide off her sheer lace panties, but I shake my head.

"I think we'll leave those on for now," I whisper as I shift again to between her thighs, giving me a glorious view of the wet patch her arousal has created on the silk and lace that match her bra.

I run a finger back and forth across the fabric, pausing at the top with each pass to press the slightly rough lace gently on her hidden clit. Her breaths become pants, and her hands grip tight on the sheets at her sides.

"Are we okay here? You enjoying this so far, Rosie?" I ask. Her answer is a whimper as her knees pull up and out, creating a cradle for my body of their own accord. But there's something I need to do first.

I lift her hips and slide a pillow underneath to give me the right angle before I lie down, latch onto that wet patch with my lips, and suck. Her back arches off the bed, her breath an indrawn hiss.

The way she looks. The way she smells. The way she tastes. It all makes me impossibly hard. The precum leaking into my boxer briefs is creating a wet patch to rival hers.

Her feet start to scrabble for purchase on the bed, and I know it's time to stop the teasing and lose the panties. My lips follow the progress of lace down her legs until they fall off her ankles. I work my way up the inside of one leg, my hands following on the outside, raising goosebumps as they go.

And then I'm there. Face to face with her lush pussy. She's so overwrought with need I can see the moisture dripping from her folds. The whimpering has turned to moans, and the message is clear. Now. Now. Now.

I circle my index finger around her entrance, gathering moisture, and as I latch tight on her swollen clit with my mouth, I surge my finger inside her tightness. Which is all it takes. Her thighs stiffen, her breath breaks on a strangled gasp, and her muscles clench on my finger.

I keep working her through her orgasm. Sucking rhythmically on her clit, in time with the thrust of my finger until her body relaxes, subsiding onto the bed with tiny tremors.

Giving her a moment to catch her breath, I climb off the bed and shed my clothes before grabbing a condom from the bedside table.

When I look back at her, I expect her eyes to be closed, but she's watching me, her dark gaze intent in contrast to the relaxed line of her body.

She's spectacular. The angle of the sun is lining her curves, highlighting a soft sheen of sweat. Her mass of dark hair is tangled around her face and spread across the white of my pillows like I've imagined a hundred times. Better than I've imagined. Her smile is pure feminine satisfaction. Rosanna is sex and desire and passion personified.

I wait, giving her time to look her fill, and judging by the way her nipples tighten again and her thighs shift restlessly on the covers, I think she might like what she sees. I've never been shy about my body, and I've never had trouble attracting women. I'm no Chris Hemsworth, but I'm tall and lean, and I've been told I have skills. I hope my skills and Rosanna's needs align. Because whilst I've always prided myself on making sure the woman I'm with is satisfied, for the first time in my life, how this woman feels about *me* matters.

CHAPTER TWENTY-ONE

ROSANNA

I figured there would be a difference in quality between a self-induced orgasm and one provided by a skilled craftsman. I just didn't realise how *much* of a difference there would be.

Ben hasn't even taken my virginity yet and I'm splayed out on his bed, crumpled and sweaty like gym gear on the bathroom floor. I must look a mess. But the heat in Ben's eye tells me it's a mess he's liking a lot.

"You ready?" he asks, standing naked and unashamed by the bed. And so he should. His body looks like something Michelangelo or Leonardo might have sculpted. Except for the important bit. That looks more like something from a porn video. Because his cock is long and thick and pointing straight at the ceiling. I can see the veins throbbing from here. I can't wait to get my hands on it. And other things. Mostly other things.

"Yes," I answer, and I almost don't recognise my own voice. It's all soft and whispery and breathy.

I watch as he rolls the condom down his length before giving himself a couple of sharp tugs. He kneels on the end of the bed and drops to all fours between my knees. I can't stop my eyes from rolling back in my head as he starts to kiss his way up the inside of my leg, inching closer to where I need him. I'm fully expecting that accomplished mouth to land on my clit again—yes, please—but he bypasses and works his way around my mound, over my belly and up the centre of my body. His hands slide up my sides until his thumbs are brushing my nipples and his mouth is gliding across my neck, over my jaw and clamping with determination on my bottom lip.

The hard head of his cock nudges at my entrance. Teasing. Slipping. Sliding. And oh, I want him inside. So badly.

"Have you ever used a vibrator or a dildo, honey?" he murmurs into my mouth.

"Yes," I choke out.

"Hmmm. Good. You're prepared then." His voice is low and warm and dirty.

My hips lift off the pillow he shoved under them of their own accord, instinctively searching for the satisfaction his body will bring. He drops one hand to his cock and lines himself up. Then he's there. He's thrusting. And filling. And stretching. And I've never felt anything like it.

Three long, hard thrusts. Then he holds still.

"Okay?" he asks, eyes on mine. Serious and kind but tinged with a look of desperation.

"Oh, yes." It's husky and faint. "Please don't stop."

He doesn't. With a roll of his hips, he sets up a rhythm. Slow at first, but building speed until he rears back, pulling my hips with him so that my arse is propped on his thighs, my legs splayed to the sides. One hand roams across my belly, up my chest, rolling first one nipple, then the other between his fingers while the other hand holds my hips steady. And then his thumb reaches over and finds my clit.

I can't control the reaction of my body. My heels dig into the bed. My toes curl. My thighs tense, and a strangled half scream, half shout bursts from somewhere deep inside me. Somewhere I didn't even know existed.

"Yes," Ben moans, his head thrown back. The muscles in his belly tighten, and I can feel pulse after pulse of his cock inside me. Still he keeps thrusting. Working us both through this life-altering orgasm.

Ben falls forward and rolls us to the side without withdrawing from my body, wrapping his arms around my shoulders as my legs are wrapped around his hips. Having him remain inside me is the weirdest kind of comfort.

"Is it okay if I stay inside you a little longer?" he asks, somehow unconsciously echoing my thoughts.

I sigh and manage a nod, still trying to catch my breath. Again, he seems to understand.

"You good? Blink once for yes, twice for no."

I blink once before I finally find my voice. "What do I do if I'm more good than I've ever been in my life?"

"You kiss me, of course."

So I do. We kiss and kiss like a couple of teenagers making out. His cock starts to swell inside me. Again. Already. I always thought it took about half an hour for men to be able to perform again. Apparently, I was wrong.

"Are you sore?" Ben asks, flexing his hips against mine. "Too sore to go again?"

I am a little sore, but not enough to stop me from wanting to experience that high again.

"I'm good if you are."

That's all the invitation he needs. Pulling out, he peels the condom off, ties it up and reaches into the drawer behind him, grabbing another and sliding it down his length before rolling onto his back.

"Climb aboard, Rosie." Ben grins, grabbing me by the hips and dragging me on top of him, settling my pussy over the length of his cock and sliding me back and forth.

"So juicy and wet," he says, his voice bursting with satisfaction.

And he's right. I'm so wet we can hear it. If it wasn't so obvious he was loving it, I might think to be embarrassed, but his pleasure only increases mine. My hips start to move of their own accord, gliding back and forth along the length of his cock, my pussy lips parted around him, my clit bumping against the rim of his head over and over.

"That's it, honey. I could lie here all day while you work my cock like this," Ben moans while his hands work my breasts, pinching and flicking my nipples. "But you slip me inside whenever you're ready."

The way he talks to me. The desire I hear in his deep voice. It draws me in. Draws me down. Until I think I'll go crazy if I have to last another minute without him inside me.

I pause, unsure what to do.

"You've got this. Just lift up and sink down on me." His hands urge me up and hold me steady. His eyes give me courage. The head of his cock nudges at my entrance before I sink. Slowing. Savouring every inch until I'm flush with his belly and he's buried to the hilt.

"Now what?" I ask. Because this time, I'm fucking him.

"Roll your hips. You'll find a rhythm that pleases you."

"But I want to find a rhythm that pleases you."

"Just being inside you, watching you ride my cock, is enough pleasure for me." Coming from anyone else, I would call bullshit. But Ben doesn't say what he doesn't mean. So I start to move. Rolling my hips. Sliding my hips. Rising and falling. Until I learn what pleases me the most. All the while watching his face. So I can see what pleases him the most.

I come with a spine-stiffening, muscle-spasming rush. Ben holds me upright when I would've collapsed, pistoning his hips until he follows right behind me. And then we're tangled together, a mass of sweating limbs and pounding hearts before we both drift off. Clinging.

Afternoon shadows are starting to creep across the room by the time I finally wake up, alone. Naked and sprawled inelegantly all over Ben's bed. The unfamiliar yet intoxicating smell of sex is heavy in the air. Almost as heavy as my arms and legs, which, despite my less-than-alluring position, don't seem to want to move. I give myself a moment to wallow in the embarrassment of Ben having seen me like this before I sit up.

I can hear water running. Perhaps he's in the shower. I wrap the sheet around me and creep to the ensuite door. No, he's not in the shower. He's running a bath. Pouring delicious-smelling crystals into the running water.

"I'm sorry. Did I wake you?" He grins in his normal, unaffected Ben way.

"No," I croak.

"I wanted to leave you to sleep until your bath was ready. I thought you might like a soak."

I thought he would leave me to my bath, but he helps me in, then climbs into the giant tub and slides down behind me, bracketing my hips with his legs, gently urging me back against his chest. His hands come to rest where my neck meets my shoulders, and he starts to knead. Once he's satisfied I'm fully relaxed, his hands move down, over my breasts, plucking at my nipples before disappearing beneath the water to gently work on the tender flesh between my legs. I can't contain the arch of my back, and Ben chuckles.

"You want more?"

"Yes," I whisper, putting my hands on his forearms, letting him know what I want. And it turns into the best bath I've ever had.

What's left of the day passes in a haze of touching and kissing and talking and orgasms. I can't believe what I've been missing all these years, and I don't want to waste a second of the time we have together.

The sun has almost disappeared when Ben rouses me from a doze by kissing his way up my exposed back and across my shoulder.

"Do you think you have the energy to get up and get dressed?" he asks, in a voice seriously designed to encourage the exact opposite.

"Why do I need to get up?" I roll over and slide my arms around his neck.

"Because I have a surprise for you. Can you be ready in, say, thirty minutes?"

"I guess. Ready for what?"

Ben nips at my exposed nipple, causing a full-body shiver. "If I told you, it wouldn't be a surprise," he responds with a heavy dose of sarcasm. "I was thinking maybe you could wear that sexy black dress. The one you wore to meet Marco. If you have it with you."

That gets me sitting up. That's a fancy night out kind of dress.

"I do. But for that dress, I'm going to need forty-five." I slide out of bed with a grin and a shimmy, surprising myself with my lack of self-consciousness.

"And it will be worth every minute," Ben responds.

In the end, I'm ready in forty-two minutes. Because I love a good surprise and can't wait to see what this one involves.

Ben lets out a low whistle and checks his watch as I meet him in the lounge room with a deliberate sway to my hips.

"You're stunning. And early."

"A surprise is a good incentive. Are you going to tell me now?" I slide my hands down the lapels of his trendy and clearly expensive suit, finishing at the buckle of his belt, my fingers lingering. Ben laughs and takes hold of my hands, leading me to the front door.

"Nice try, but no."

We sail through the foyer and straight into a waiting car.

Last time we were in a car together, the air was fraught with unresolved tension. This time there's nothing unresolved about it, but there's no less tension. Our bodies seem to gravitate towards each other, unable to tolerate any space between.

Ben's hand lands on my bare knee, fingers slipping under and circling the tender skin at the back of my thigh, thumb stroking, moving up under the silk of my dress.

"Why did you ask me to wear this dress?" I ask the question that's been circling in my mind since he requested it. He takes a moment to answer.

"Two reasons. Firstly, it's a gorgeous dress and you look stunning in it. Secondly, I imagine there are some bad memories associated with it, and I wanted to erase them. Replace them with something more pleasant. Actually, there are three reasons. Third, and least important, because it's appropriate for where we're going."

I don't know what to say. He wanted me to reframe my relationship with a dress? Why would he care? Because he's Ben. He understands how much my meeting with Marco took out of me. And he also understands my relationship with clothing.

Clothing is not simply a fashion statement, it's a form of self-expression that goes beyond what's in fashion. For me, clothing is art. And I think maybe Ben is the first person I've met—outside Lulu and other designers—who gets it. Gets me.

I lean over and drop a lingering kiss on his cheek, hoping the simple act conveys how I feel about his gesture. Because I can't get words past the lump in my throat.

The car glides to a stop in a dingy, narrow street in Surry Hills where there's a mix of run-down terrace houses, a strange collection of random restaurants and a very noisy pub. But nothing that looks remotely like the kind of place where a skin-tight black silk dress would fit in.

We get out in front of a shiny black door adorned with a massive brass knocker, which opens seemingly by magic without us having to knock.

"Welcome to La Goulue." An enormous man with slicked-back hair, a handlebar moustache and wearing a red velvet suit sweeps his arm back for us to enter a short hall.

I can hear muffled music and chatter, but the walls, ceiling and floor are all black with dim strip lighting running down steep stairs.

Ben murmurs his name and receives nothing more than an inclination of the head.

At the bottom of the stairs is a thick velvet curtain which, much like the door above, sweeps to the side as we approach. This time we're met by a stunning woman in a red silk corset and stockings, her breasts almost spilling out of the top, a good few centimetres of creamy thigh showing between the top of the stocking and the bottom of the full-body corset. My mind takes a quick trip to the dark and dirty.

"Is this a bro—" I start before Ben places his finger across my lips and shakes his head.

"No. It's not. Just wait."

Another corridor, and we turn the corner into something I had no idea existed in Sydney. It's a burlesque club. And it's spectacular.

CHAPTER TWENTY-TWO

BENEDICT

Despite the wildly extravagant sight in front of me, I can't take my eyes off Rosanna's face. Her lush red mouth, which matches perfectly with the décor, has fallen open and her wide eyes are dancing. Darting around the room. Soaking in the magnificence of the massive space.

"Your table," the hostess says in a heavy French accent, showing us to a secluded booth. Before I even ask, a small platter of hors d'oeuvres, a bottle of champagne and two glasses arrive at the table, delivered by another stunning woman, this time in a black velvet corset and stockings. "This is Mignon. She will be your server tonight. Please let her know if there is anything at all you would like."

The opulence is over the top. The tables are packed. The music is loud. Based on Rosanna's expression, I couldn't have picked a better surprise.

"I had no idea this even existed," she whisper-shouts over the noise, her head swivelling almost three sixty degrees as she tries to take everything in at once.

The room is enormous and dimly lit. Tiny two person tables fill the centre of the room while around the perimeter are two rows of low booths with black velvet benches; each row stepped up to ensure a clear view of the stage. Small flickering lamps with red silk shades provide scarcely enough light for patrons to see the menu if they need to. Everything is black or red or aged and burnished gold. The fabrics are all velvet and satin and silk.

A potent mix of anticipation, arousal and something that re-minds me a little of Rosie's perfume—dark and sensual—scents the air.

We have a clear view of the stage, which is empty but for a single old-fashioned microphone standing in a spotlight in front of a gold-tasselled red velvet curtain.

To the right is a shallow orchestra pit where a dozen or more musicians, all dressed in dinner suits, are settling into position with their instruments. Looks like we're right on time.

The room goes suddenly black for a second, causing the crowd to roar, before the single spotlight returns, illuminating a guy in nothing but gold lamé hotpants and a great deal of body oil and glitter.

"Welcome to La Goulue. Come with us as we unearth your hidden sensuality. Titillate your erotic desires. Arouse your in-nermost sensual secrets." The way he says it, the teasing tone in his voice, has my cock swelling. This guy is sex on legs no matter which way you swing. I shift closer to Rosie on the booth seat, sliding my arm across her shoulder to circle my fingers on the bare flesh of her upper arm and pressing our thighs together. We're close enough that I can feel the muscles in her legs squeezing together.

She turns glittering eyes on me as the stage lights drop and the music starts.

"I can't believe ..." she says before cutting herself off and turning back to the stage where the show is beginning.

The stage explodes with dancers. Their costumes are rich with colour and tassels and glittering trims, exposing more flesh than they cover. Lush bodies, male and female, come togeth-er, part, come together again. Their movements sensual and unabashed. The music creates rhythms alternately sensual and driving. It's impossible not to be aroused.

I've been to one or two burlesque shows in my life, but none have compared to this. Not because the singers, the dancers, the costumes, the music and the choreography are all superb, although they are. But because I'm here with Rosanna. I'm aware of the awakening coursing through her veins. I see it in the way she catches her breath, flexes her hips, shifts her legs, flutters her hands. She's beyond aroused. So am I.

Finally, the curtain drops with dramatic speed.

"That was ... I'm speechless," Rosie gasps, turning to me with a glazed expression not dissimilar to her post-orgasm face.

"I'm glad you're enjoying it." I can't help myself. I slide my fingers into the hair at the nape of her neck and bring her closer. Our lips are almost touching. "That was only the first act. There are two more." Even in the dim lighting, I can see the blush on her cheeks.

"Oooh." She takes a deep breath. "I might need a ... phew ... a drink." She throws back the champagne that has sat untouched since the start of the show.

"I thought you'd like it. When I saw your drag queen costumes, I knew I wanted to bring you here." And now I'm thinking about buying the place. So we can enjoy it whenever we want.

"Oh, yes. The costumes are, wow. They're superb. But it's the, oh, um, it's the *sensuality* of it. I can *feel* the desire. You know?" She presses an olive onto her lips and sucks it into her mouth without taking her eyes off my face. Fuck me.

This was the other reason for bringing Rosie here. She's a sensual woman, and it's a crime she's had to wait this long to explore that side of herself. She may have presented this arrangement as me taking care of a perceived obstacle for her, but there is no way I'm going to half-arse this. I'm hoping by the time I'm finished with her, it will be to death do us part. If not, she's leaving my bed with all the experience, satisfaction and confidence I can pack into whatever time we have.

"Has it unearthed your hidden sensuality, Rosie?" My voice is barely more than a rasp of air. She nods, sucking another olive into her mouth.

"Are you swollen and wet and ready?" I know the answer.

"Yes." It's barely more than a breath.

"Hold that feeling," I say, refilling her glass.

We order some share plates of food. And share we do. There's no conversation, just looks and touches and feeding each other morsels of I don't even know what, fingers lingering on each other's lips until the lights drop, and we're again plunged into the erotic moves of the dancers.

The lights are low. The tablecloth is long. I can't resist. We're minutes into the second act, and my hand is sliding up the inside of Rosie's leg. Her thighs shift, parting, allowing me better access until my fingers brush gently across the wet lace of her knickers. She lets out a quiet whimper that only I could possibly have heard but which reverberates in my skull. I nearly jump out of my skin when her hand lands on my leg mid-thigh and slowly traces upwards, finally coming to a stop on the hard bulge of my cock, lightly kneading my flesh.

Her body stiffens as my fingers slip under the lace.

"Nobody can see," I whisper against her ear, raising a shiver across her skin.

For a brief moment, she tears her gaze from the stage. I can't hear what she says, but the message is clear. "Please don't stop."

"Watch the show. Don't take your eyes off that stage." I turn her chin gently with my free hand.

The angle is a little awkward, but wild horses couldn't stop me from giving Rosie what she needs. My fingers slip and slide into her dripping folds, finally finding the perfect position. Her breasts are rising and falling fast. A deep blush rising from the neckline of her dress and up onto her cheeks. Her breath catches. Her hand spasms on my cock. With a low whimper her muscles contract. There's a rush of moisture and a release of tension in her thighs. Not once does she take her eyes off the stage.

CHAPTER TWENTY-THREE

ROSANNA

I have absolutely no idea who I am. I just allowed Benedict Carter to finger me to orgasm in public. It was far and away the best thing that's ever happened to me. Well, since this afternoon anyway.

The second act comes to a close and I don't think I can take any more. Because that orgasm was delicious and delightful. But what I really need is him naked. Inside me.

"Could we maybe ... Is it time we went ..."

"Home? My thoughts exactly." Ben removes my hand from his pants. I hadn't even realised it was still there.

Like magic Mignon, our server appears. Ben takes care of the bill, and as we stand, he drapes his suit jacket over my shoulders. He grins when I give him a questioning look.

"You have a little wet patch." The burn I've felt in my cheeks since we walked into this incredible place intensifies. I've turned into someone else. But it feels like this is the me I was always meant to be.

It seems Ben is not embarrassed by the bulge in his pants as we make our way out onto the street.

The short trip home in a taxi Ben hails on the street passes in a blur of loaded looks and barely there touches. I'm so close to the edge; it won't take much to push me over into another orgasm, and I want Ben with me for this one.

The sheets are still rumpled and smelling of sex from this afternoon when we walk into the bedroom, and there's a rush of heat to the flesh that's still post-orgasm swollen and wet. I don't know how it happens, but it's as though our clothes melt off without any help from us. And then we're standing naked. Facing one another.

Ben's cock is hard, pointing skyward and dripping precum. My nipples are tight and aching, and I can smell my earlier orgasm. As though he hears my thoughts, he raises the hand that did so much damage to my panties and my dress to his lips and sucks his finger into his mouth with a sound somewhere between a moan and a sigh.

"Jesus, you taste good."

I reach out and swipe a pillow from the bed, and dropping it to the floor in front of him, I fall to my knees.

"You, coming on my hand in that club, was the sexiest thing I've ever seen. Until now." He hisses out a breath as I run my tongue from base to tip, then suck the head the way he sucked my gelato in the park this morning. Not even twenty-four hours ago.

"Touch yourself while you suck me, honey." His hips flex, pressing his cock further into my mouth.

His words give me an idea, and I scramble to my feet, holding up a finger for him to wait. In seconds, I'm back from my room, my trusty BOB in my hand.

I don't need lube. I'm already more than wet enough. I fall to my knees, take him into my mouth again and, flicking the vibrator on, rub it over my clit and slip it inside me while his hand cradles my head.

Looks like I'll have to wait to have Ben inside me because right now, all I want to do is suck until he comes. Doesn't matter. Because I know this is only round one. Well, round two, I guess. The point is, there'll be plenty more where this came from.

By Sunday afternoon, we've barely made it out of bed, except to shower or accept a much-needed food delivery. Ben has a seemingly never-ending supply of stamina and a treasure trove of skills he has no hesitation in teaching me.

But all good things must come to an end.

"I'll have to get up and dress soon. I promised Mum and Dad I would call in for dinner tonight." Even I can hear the regret in my voice. It's not only reluctance to leave our cocoon but also to face my parents and tell them what's happened.

"You're going to tell them about Marco?"

I know I have to. I wish I could avoid it.

Ben picks up on my hesitation.

"Rosanna, you really have to tell them. It's only going to get harder the longer you leave it. Who knows what shit Marco might pull in the meantime?"

"It's not that simple. Dad is in no state to take over the business again. There's nobody else. This is not just about me, Ben." Knowing what you need to do and being told are not always comfortable bedfellows.

"I understand the problem. But is worrying about who runs the business worth risking your welfare?" Ben makes a sensible point. Except, his main concern is for me. Mine is for Dad.

"My father's welfare, yes." I snap. "And if we're talking about 'fessing up to parents, isn't it about time you did some talking? It's very easy to lecture me."

"That's different," Ben responds in a similar tone, his drawn eyebrows letting me know my dart hit the target. "There's no rush for me. Marco could be dangerous. You need to get him out of your lives. And quickly."

He's right, it is different. The indignation filling my chest deflates. Our sharp words, however brief, have caused a crack in the soft space we've created for ourselves in the last few days, and regret washes through me.

"I can't believe this. I've known him all my life. Our parents are best friends." Despite all the evidence Marco has provided, it's hard to digest the idea that someone you thought loved—or at least liked—you could wish you harm. I wish I could articulate how confronting the past few days have been.

It's clear Ben thinks Marco wouldn't think twice about hurting me, and based on his recent behaviour, I can't dismiss the possibility. As much as I've been unhappy in the relationship, this is an unexpected plot twist to my life.

"He threatened you. More than once. As recently as two days ago. And a week ago you were rattled enough that you were fearful of staying in your own apartment," he reminds me.

"I know. But he's a bully, so maybe it's all bluster?" Although, even as I say it, I know it's unlikely. Nothing more than wishful thinking.

"I hope you're right, but it's not a chance I'm comfortable taking." Ben follows me into the bathroom where we start the routine that has become second nature in less than forty-eight hours. He turns on the shower, while I pile my hair on my head. We step into the shower stall together and silently soap each other up.

Last time we did this, it quickly turned into shower sex. This time, the vibe is different. This time, our hands are soothing and comforting. Apologising for our harsh words, giving each other reassurance. Whether it's reassurance about what's to come with Marco or what's to come between us, I have no idea.

"I'm sorry I snapped." I wrap a towel around me, grabbing my body lotion from the counter. "I'm just anxious about telling them."

"That's okay. I understand. Would you like me to come with you? Would that help?" he asks as I slick the lotion over my legs and arms.

"No, I don't think that's a good idea. There'll be yelling. Lots of yelling. In Italian. And you being there might raise questions. But thanks for offering."

While I go into my bedroom to dress, Ben does the same, giving us both time to think.

When I finally emerge in a flowing sundress with my hair out and styled in big waves, I don't miss the look of appreciation Ben runs up and down my body.

"I'm going to dinner at my parents' place too, so I might not be home when you get back. One of Tama's boys is downstairs waiting for you."

"You think I still need Tama? You don't think what happened on Friday night was enough to scare him off?" Ben's concern makes me nervous. For me and my parents.

"Maybe. Humour me anyway. And please, promise me you'll tell them tonight?"

"I'll tell them."

He folds me up in his arms and kisses my forehead. He seems reluctant to let me go when I start to pull away.

"Good luck. Call me anytime if you need me."

I reach up and kiss his cheek with a smile.

This man. He's nothing like I imagined him from everything I've been told. And exactly like everything I would wish for if things were different.

It scares me a little. Or a lot.

CHAPTER TWENTY-FOUR

BENEDICT

As the door swings shut behind Rosanna, I have an over-whelming sense of impending doom. Like that was goodbye. At least goodbye to what we've been doing all week-end. I'm not ready for that, but more worrying is the fact I'm not sure I'll survive it.

I get why she's been reluctant to tell her parents, but it needs doing. If she keeps putting it off, I'm going to have to tell her about my suspicions. I was hoping to wait until I had a better handle on the extent of the problem, some concrete proof, and more importantly, a plan for a solution.

Her hesitation is telling. It also hurts. Because despite what she says, there's a tiny, insecure corner of me that wonders if she's having trouble letting go of Marco because of unresolved feelings for him. Women fall for the wrong man all the time. She wouldn't be the first.

I know it's irrational, and I should take her at her word, but when you've lived with imposter syndrome as long as I have, when you've had to hide who you are, it's sometimes impossible to tease out the rational from the irrational.

There's no denying things are coming to a head, and I know the time has come for me to shit or get off the pot. If I'm going to bring Marco down and make sure he can't hurt Rosanna or her father, I can't do it alone. Which means I'm going to have to come clean to my family. Well, to Will, at least. Because having the advice of a lawyer—and a damn good one—is going to be essential if I'm going to pull off the vague idea I have forming. I have business lawyers I could talk to. But this is personal. I can't take risks with Rosanna. His arseholery in relation to me notwithstanding, there's nobody I trust more than Will.

Dinner with the family is the usual three-ring circus. Ethan and Jessie's wedding is coming up fast, and Josh's brother Ty is about to start his HSC exams, so there's lots going on. By far, the biggest topic of conversation, though, is Duncan's farewell party and the performance Marco put on. Which does nothing for my anxiety over Rosanna's conversation with her parents and my looming conversation with Will.

It's hard to believe the party was only two nights ago. I feel like I've lived a lifetime in those few days. I've had a glimpse of what life with Rosanna could be, and I'll do what needs to be done to ensure it happens.

By the time dinner is finished, I'm practically jumping out of my seat. I use the pandemonium of the table being cleared as cover to pull Will aside. I've been over and over this in my head. I know Mum and Dad and the rest of the family will need to be read in at some point. I'm not quite ready for that yet, though. It's going to be hard enough to tell Will. But I don't have the luxury of waiting if I want to bring Marco down and protect Rosanna.

It doesn't escape my notice that after all these years, what has me facing up to my family is not my own needs but those of someone else. Maybe I needed to be backed into this corner. I just wish it didn't involve Rosanna's safety.

"Hey, bro, do you have any plans tonight?"

Will looks understandably confused. There's a little lingering tension from our last conversation. But this can't be put off.

"I was going to maybe go old school with some Mario Kart. Why?" Traditionally, after Sunday night dinner, we blow some brain cells killing zombies or racing cars.

I have to clear my throat before I can get another word out.

"I was wondering if we could go and grab a drink? Somewhere quiet, maybe?"

Will is a sharp operator despite the jokey and somewhat vague persona he projects. His eyes narrow.

"Everything okay? Is this a five-alarm fire?" he asks.

"Yeah. No. Everything's okay. I need some advice, that's all."

"Do we need Dad? Or Ethan? Josh?"

I don't know if I can do this with a full-theatre audience. And definitely not with Dad. But Josh is cool. And maybe a second opinion would be helpful. Also, Josh might be able to keep Will from going nuclear when he finds out how much I've been hiding all these years.

"Yeah, maybe Josh."

"Done." Will claps me on the back and wanders over to murmur something in Josh's ear. I've never been more grateful for my protective oldest brother. Maybe this won't be so bad after all. Because for the first time, mixed with the dread and fear of coming clean about my life, there's a tremor of anticipation, that maybe, just maybe, things will work out.

The three of us settle into a back corner table at the same café at Neutral Bay we used to come to for coffee and cake when we needed to get sober before heading home back in the day. It's open till three am, and they still have the best chocolate cake I've ever eaten. If only it went with beer. Because to tell this story, I'm going to need a drink.

"Before you say anything, I need to ask, is any of this illegal? Because if I'm going to represent you, we need to be careful about what you tell me," Will says after a gulp of his beer. I'm simultaneously annoyed he might think I'd be doing something illegal and grateful there's no tone of judgement in what he says.

"Nothing illegal." I watch Will stuff some chips into his mouth. He's a bottomless pit. "Well, *I* haven't done anything illegal," I clarify.

Josh and Will wait patiently while I work out how to start. It takes a couple of goes before I get any words out.

"First, I need you to promise this stays between us. At least until it can't." They nod, exchanging a look loaded with curiosity. "It's Marco. You know about the cheating, which goes much deeper than you might think, and is a story for another day. What you don't know, what nobody knows, including Rosanna, is that he's been doing dodgy deals. Through Rosanna's father's company. I need your help to take out the trash, so to speak."

"He works for Moretti's, yeah?" Josh asks for confirmation.

"Yes. He's the 2IC. Since Ro's dad has been sick, he's been handing more and more responsibility over to Marco. On the understanding Marco and Rosanna will get married."

It doesn't take Will long to ask the forty-two-dollar question.

"Hang on. Back the truck up, Sparky. How do you know about this if Rosanna doesn't?"

Josh takes a deep breath, muttering, "Oh fuck, here we go." I don't know what he's expecting, but I'm pretty sure he hasn't been entirely convinced by my Eurotrash impersonation over the years.

"I've had him watched. He's been hanging out with some pretty dodgy characters. Spending a lot of time meeting with councillors and building inspectors in dark alleys. Exchanging envelopes."

"Why are you having him watched?" Will doesn't have enough data to piece it all together yet. "I mean, I know he's a tool, but what prompted you to go all MI5? And while we're on the subject, surveillance is expensive. Where did you get the money?"

Time to fess up. I take a fortifying mouthful of my drink.

"Yeah, funny story. You know how you all think I've drunk my way through Granny's money and I'm living off friends?" Will nods. "Well, that's not quite true."

For the next half hour, I tell my brother and Josh all the things they don't know about me. Well, most of them. I'll never tell anyone about the orgy in Budapest. But I digress.

By the time I stumble to a halt on my tale of success, Will and Josh are slumped back in their chairs, mouths hanging open.

"I was not expecting that," Josh mutters, polishing off the remainder of his beer in one large gulp.

"So, the fancy fucking apartment?" Will asks.

"Mine."

"And the club we went to the other night?"

"Half mine."

"And that app everyone uses to find the best restaurant or hotel for their tastes?"

"Not mine anymore. We sold it. I was only a silent partner, but yes, at one time, it was partially mine."

"Why did you never tell us? Why let us think the worst?" Will is starting to get annoyed. I get it. I kept secrets in a family that tells each other everything.

"At first, I think, I assumed Dad wouldn't approve. What I was up to was risky. I had no idea what I was doing. It was blind luck, and I could've lost everything on that first app. Or any deal since, in all honesty. I never expected to make money. It just seemed like a cool thing to do. And then I was scared every successful deal would be my last. That somehow my luck would run out. And Dad would be all *I told you so*. It was easier to keep it to myself. If there are no expectations, you can't let people down."

"So, all those times you let us think you were going off partying?"

"Working. Mostly."

Will seems annoyed that he didn't pick up on my subterfuge. I can see the cogs turning in his head as he thinks back over the past few years.

Suddenly he sits up straight, clicking his fingers, pointing, and grinning as though he's caught me out.

"Okay, what about that time at the sailing club, huh? When Josh first came back from London. You were definitely hung over. Then you took off for a date with a fuck buddy, I seem to recall."

I remember the afternoon clearly. Josh was behaving very strangely. There was a familiar smell about him. It took me a while to work out what it was. My sister's shampoo. And then I noticed the love bite on his neck. It didn't take a rocket scientist to put two and two together.

Will is looking at me with a challenging gleam in his eye.

"Yep. I did have a hangover. Never said I was a saint. That was the morning after we sold an app for twice what any of us were expecting. So we celebrated. And I did have a date. With a guy who wanted me to invest in his new club idea. I never said it was with a woman."

"But you let me assume, you fucker," Will growls, but there's awe and pride in his tone. I grin and lift my beer in a toast.

The café continues to bustle around us, but there's silence at our table for a good few minutes while Will and Josh digest what I've told them. Meanwhile, I'm squirming in my seat, wondering where their thoughts will settle.

Finally, Will sighs and signals for another round of beers.

"I think you're selling yourself short, Ben." Will skewers me with what the family call 'the lawyer look'. "None of that was luck, bro. You're a clever fucker. I've always known it. But I get why you kept it under wraps. I know Dad's always been hard on you, and that can't have been easy."

"I'm sorry I wasn't more up-front with you." I sag back against the chair, relieved he's taken it so well.

"No. I'm sorry you felt you couldn't tell us." Will leans forward and claps me on the shoulder. "And that you kept all these money-making schemes to yourself. Share the sugar a bit from now on, yeah?"

The tension breaks as we all laugh.

Josh checks his phone, and we realise how late it is.

"Right, I have a woman to get home to and work in not too many hours, so I'd like to suggest we reconvene tomorrow to work out a plan for what to do about Marco. Sound good?" Josh slurps down the last of his beer and signals for the check. We agree to meet at my place tomorrow evening.

"I have to say, I'm looking forward to seeing the inner sanctum, bro." Josh slaps me on the back as he climbs into a passing taxi. I've never invited anyone into my apartment—other than Ro, of course—because I didn't want them asking questions, so this is a big step for me.

"You going to tell Mum and Dad about your hella successful angel investing gig anytime soon?" Will asks as we wait for my Uber on Military Road.

"Yeah. That was the plan. But I'll maybe hold off until this Rosanna thing is all sorted."

"Fair enough. They won't hear about it from me." Will mimes zipping his lips. "But don't leave it too long, yeah? You deserve to be able to live your authentic life." He wanders off down the street towards his apartment a few blocks away. Leaving me relieved that the first Band-aid has been ripped off.

I've barely buckled myself into the Uber when the alert I have set for social media activity from Marco goes off.

I check my phone. Fuck. I can't believe what I'm seeing.

CHAPTER TWENTY-FIVE

ROSANNA

Despite the unpleasant task I know is ahead of me and the lingering regret over my sharp words with Ben, I arrive at my parents' house in a fog of orgasm-induced bliss. The past couple of days have been a revelation. In more ways than one.

The second I walk in the door, my euphoria gets a bucket of cold water in the face. Marco and his mother are sitting with Mum and Dad, laughing and chatting like nothing has happened. The hairs on the back of my neck go up, and I'm grateful Ben insisted on one of the boys coming with me. I'm also grateful he's parked at a discreet distance down the road.

"Rosanna, *tesoro*," my mother croons, smothering me in a hug. There's something in her expression I can't quite place, and my trepidation ratchets up to eleven.

Marco's mother, Fernanda, hugs and kisses me, chattering on about how beautiful I am and how she's missed seeing me recently. Yeah, talk to your arsehole offspring about that, lady.

Fernanda has always idolised Marco—her youngest child and only son. But ever since her husband died, it's gotten completely out of hand. He's a demigod in her eyes. If only she knew.

Marco hangs back, a slimy smirk on his face. I can't believe I once thought he was handsome. Now all I see are lies and threats in his dark eyes.

The greetings over with, Mum drags us all to the table, which is set with the best cutlery and china, I notice. My heart rate picks up as everyone starts to eat. I push my meal around my plate. There's no way I could get a single bite past the lump of bitterness in my throat.

How am I supposed to tell my parents now?

Marco, who as usual sits next to me, presses his foot on mine—hard—an unsubtle warning for me not to speak up about what's going on. As soon as Marco lifts his foot, I return the favour. Making sure to dig in hard with my spike heel, smiling the whole time.

By the time dinner is over and we're onto coffee, Dad's breathing is laboured, and I notice how much he's relying on his oxygen. It's clear the doctors were right about him no longer being able to work.

Unfortunately, it's also clear to Marco.

"There's no need for you to worry, Andrea. As always, I have everything under control at work. You relax. Enjoy your rest and retirement. Leave the company to me," Marco says.

I'd like to wipe the arrogant smirk off his face. As if it wasn't going to be hard enough to tell Mum and Dad I've broken it off with Marco—and why—it's been delayed yet again. I can't do what I came here to do in front of him and his mother and risk causing the kind of scene that will send Dad straight back to hospital. I can only hope they go home early. But something tells me this evening is not going to go down as I'd planned.

"I am so lucky to have you to take care of my business for me. This is my legacy to my Rosanna. It is a relief to know it is in good hands. And that Rosanna is in good hands, too." Dad's words are halting, interspersed with gasps and wheezes. He pats Marco's hand where it lies on the table beside his cup. It's almost too much to bear, and I nearly blurt out the truth. But Dad's wheezing holds me back.

"Of course, I will take care of the company—and our Rosanna—in every way." Dad misses the sinister subtext of what Marco has said and gazes at him in appreciation, tears in his eyes.

Marco gets up from his chair and, grasping my hand, pulls me to my feet. His lips are smiling, but his eyes are hard. I wish

I could slap him. Push him away. But Dad's wheezing is an ever-present reminder to keep things calm.

My mother clasps her hands and gasps, and I have a sudden premonition. Before I can even get a word out, Marco drops to one knee, holding out the ugliest, gaudiest ring I have ever seen. I try to snatch my hand away, but his fingers are like a vice, digging between the bones in the back of my hand.

"Rosanna, *cara mia*," he starts in Italian. "Today, I finally asked your father for permission to marry you. I have been waiting for many years, and now Mama is settled after the loss of my beloved father, the time is right at last for us to marry." That manipulative bastard. I should've expected he'd pull something like this.

All hell breaks loose. Fernanda is crying and hugging Marco and me. Dad beams from his chair. My mother is smiling and crying, but something about her tears makes me wonder if they're tears of joy or something else altogether. Marco shoves the ring roughly on my finger without waiting for a response. It's sharp and heavy, like handcuffs on my finger. I want to rip it off. Tell him no. He's crazy if he thinks I'm going to marry him. But I'm frozen. It's all happening too fast. Panic claws at my throat.

Strangely, my mind is clear enough to register that Marco has made a statement. Not asked a question. And to thank my lucky stars for my escape. Because there's no way in hell I'd marry him now. If he'd gotten around to proposing before his father got sick, I would've said yes. We'd probably have a couple of kids by now. I'd be tied to him forever, in one way or another.

"*Baciala, baciala*," cries his mother. Kiss. So he does. At least he tries. My lips remain firmly closed. I almost gag on the overpowering smell of his cologne.

"Marco—" I start, ready to tell them all the truth, despite what might follow, but Dad interrupts. He's crying and struggling for breath so hard he can barely get the words out.

"*Alla fine, alla fine. Posso morire in pace sapendo che mia figlia ha un brav'uomo che si prende cura di lei. Sono così felice.*"

That's another bucket of cold water to the face. Dad talking about dying in peace, knowing I'll have a good man to look after me. How can I tell them what Marco has done now?

I'm drowning. I think of Ben. I can't let this happen. Because that means losing Ben. Yet speaking up might put my father's health at risk. I have no choice other than to go along with it for the time being. Until I have time to think. And talk to Ben. Yes, we'll work out a plan together.

Marco pulls me closer and whispers in my ear so low that only I can hear. "Your father is so happy. It will kill him if you refuse me. Who will take care of his company? Who will take care of you? Do you want his death on your hands?" Marco knows precisely where to stick the knife for the greatest damage. I look at my father, struggling for breath, my mother fussing. My blood turns to ice water in my veins.

I hear popping. Fernanda has produced a bottle of champagne. Nobody seems to notice I haven't said yes. Or that I'm frozen to the spot. A glass of champagne is shoved in my hand, and Marco is sliding his arm around my shoulders, lifting his phone and snapping a shot of us together, the ugly ring front and centre.

Finally, I break out of my stupor and pull away from his iron grip.

"Marco, I'd like a word in private, please?" Can none of them hear the fear and disgust in my voice? See the horror on my face? Ben's right. People see what they expect to see.

"Oooh," gasps Fernanda, clapping her hands together. "The *piccioncini* want some privacy. Yes. They must have a moment to celebrate their love in private. But not too private, no?" She winks at Marco and shepherds us out onto the back verandah. Before the door closes behind us, I catch a glimpse of my mother's face. Her smile is frozen. Forced. Of course, she's worried about Dad, who's still struggling to breathe, but her eyes are on me.

Now that I'm over the shock of his absolute nerve, I don't waste any time. There is no way any of this is happening. I might not be able to break it to Dad yet, but I can sure as shit let Marco know he's deluded.

"What the hell do you think you're doing?" I try to keep my voice low enough that the parents won't hear. I probably don't need to worry; there's a loud babble of excited voices coming from inside, led by a delighted Fernanda. I move to the darkest corner of the verandah and turn my back to the windows so my parents can't see my expression.

Marco has dropped the slimy smile and looks at me with a venom I would not have thought possible.

"I'm ensuring you don't do something stupid and ruin all my plans." He leans against the verandah railing, casually crossing his legs at the ankles and folding his arms across his chest.

"If you think I'm going to marry you, you're crazy." I tug at the ring. Having it on my finger makes me sick. But it's maybe a size too small and doesn't want to come off.

"You think I *want* to marry you? To be tied to you for life? This is all your fault. You've brought this on us with your stupid, childish behaviour."

His words hit me like a slap.

"My behaviour?" I gasp. "You're the one who was cheating. And you're the one who proposed."

Marco leans in, gripping my chin tight in cruel fingers. Squeezing hard until tears well in my eyes.

"You have given me little choice. I was happy to let nature take its course, but you had to interfere."

"Let nature take its course?" It's all coming into focus now. "You never had any intention of marrying me, did you? You were waiting for my father to die."

The sudden clarity is blinding. Marco had never shown the slightest interest in me. Until I was eighteen. Until my father had a mild heart attack and was told to slow down and eat healthy. Advice he ignored. I'd never put the two events together until tonight, but Marco first asked me out only a couple of weeks after Dad came home from hospital. I remember it clearly because it was Dad's birthday, and Marco made a big show of asking permission to take me out. Idiot. I'm such a stupid, gullible idiot. Marco has been playing a very long game indeed.

The enormity of his betrayal takes my breath away. I shouldn't be shocked after his behaviour of the past couple of weeks, yet I am. My father has been a mentor to him. This is what he gets in return? No. I won't tolerate it.

"You were never interested in me. It was all an elaborate scheme."

His laugh is as cruel as his behaviour has been.

"Bravo. At last, you're seeing it. All I had to do was wait."

"You're despicable. I'll tell him. Right now." I go to push past him, but he stops me with an iron grip on my wrist and shoves me. I stumble back against the outdoor table.

"And what will that do to his health? I know what the doctors said. No stress. Imagine the stress of worrying about his company and his beloved daughter. He wouldn't survive. His death will be on your hands." I struggle to get free, but he squeezes tight.

I'm trapped. By Marco's steel grip on my wrist and by my own fears for my father. But I know Dad wouldn't want this for me. I have to tell him the truth. Now.

"You think I've tolerated you and your *stupido* father all these years for you to take everything away from me now? You'll keep quiet. You will marry me. And I will have what is owed to me."

My rage bubbles over, and I swing back my free arm, not caring if anyone sees, but he catches it before my palm can connect with his face.

"What's owed to you? We owe you nothing. Walk away, Marco."

"Even you can't be that ignorant." If I hadn't discovered what a lowlife he is, the look of contempt on his face might have hurt. Not anymore. Even the risk of Dad having another attack won't hold me back now. As soon as I get free, I'm telling everyone the whole sordid story.

My mind is racing for a solution. There must be something I can say, something I can offer, that will satisfy him.

"Just go, Marco." I hate the pleading tone in my voice. "I'll make sure he gives you a good reference. And a payout. A good one. You'll get another job. Somewhere bigger and better. And you won't have to put up with me or my father any longer."

He laughs. "Ah, so naïve. So stupid. I will be going nowhere. You will marry me. And I will have the company. Otherwise, *cara mia*, your father might find himself in hot water. It would be a shame for him to spend the final years of his life in prison."

"Prison? What are you ..." And the light goes on in my head. Marco has somehow done something illegal. And my father will be implicated.

I know with one hundred percent certainty my father knows nothing about this. Because he's never lied or cheated in his life. But Marco? I know which way his moral compass points. This makes terrifying sense of the threats he's been throwing at me since I broke up with him.

"And while we're talking about our future, you will stay away from that interfering fool Ben Carter. Starting immediately." The mention of Ben's name has my rage turning to ice. How could Marco possibly know what Ben is to me? Then I remember the party. How Ben stood up to him for me. How his kindness is now coming back to bite us both on the arse. I dare not think of what's happened between us this weekend. My poker face is not that good. "I don't know what was going on with him, but I will not tolerate disloyalty or infidelity from you."

The hypocrisy of his words takes my breath away. Ben warned me. I thought he was overreacting. Being over-protective. Turns out he was right on the money. Literally. Because this is about money. Money and power and ego. I give it one last try. Everyone has their price. Even Marco. Surely.

"How much do you want?" I ask. I don't have a lot of cash, but if I sell my apartment, maybe it will be enough. I know Ben would give me the money in a hot second, but I'd cut out my tongue before asking him to hand money over to this scum.

"How much?" Marco laughs. Long and loud. "You still don't get it, do you? I want the company. All of it. And I will have it. And you will keep your ears, eyes and mouth closed, and do exactly as you are told. Or things will not go well for poor, sick Andrea." He pulls an exaggerated sad frowny face.

"You're insane."

"No. I am in charge. And it's time you did as you are told. Now"—he starts scrolling through his phone—"I think this photo is the best. Not a bad picture of me, I think. You could have smiled, but it will do. How about we post our joyous news for all our friends and family to see, hmm?" He taps away for a moment before standing straight and moving to the back door.

"Don't forget. I expect complete loyalty. No seeing or speaking to Ben Carter. Not a word to Lulu or her hotshot husband, or anyone else. Or the Anti-Corruption Commission will hear from me about what I have *discovered*."

My blood runs cold as he goes to open the door but pauses and turns.

"By the way, perhaps you could lose some weight before the wedding? We wouldn't want you looking this fat in the wedding photos, would we?"

I imagine slapping his nasty face. But for the time being, imagining is all I can do.

Instead, I plaster on a fake smile, my mind working furiously to come up with a solution. But I'm not a businessperson. I design costumes for crying out loud. I have no idea how to untangle this mess. So I have to play along until I come up with a solution.

I can't afford to upset my father. Or Marco. Until I have a plan. Because one way or another, I *will* fix this.

Amongst all this hideousness, my heart is breaking. It might seem ridiculous, and maybe he's not even on the same page, but the past couple of days with Ben have shown me what's possible between two people. And before I've even had a chance to savour it, I have to walk away. Because I can't risk my father. Not even for Ben.

CHAPTER TWENTY-SIX

BENEDICT

To say I'm shocked by what I saw on Marco's social media would be a gross understatement. I couldn't be in more pain if someone had ripped my actual heart out.

I try to call Rosanna, but it goes to voicemail. All I can do is pace my apartment and think. Except it's not really thinking. It's feeling. Fear. Hurt. Confusion. Fear again. Spinning through my head until it feels like a cyclone has hijacked my skull.

I call again and again. Nothing. Until finally I get the message the phone is turned off or out of range. I'm going insane with worry. I'm clutching my phone so tight I'm in danger of cracking the screen, and when it rings, I stab at the accept button so hard it flies across the room and I scramble to pick it up. But it's not her. It's Tama.

"Hey, boss. Don't know what's going on, but your girl just left her parent's place with The Cockhead and an older lady. I followed and they dropped her at her apartment."

My stomach flips. I don't want to know the answer, but I ask the question.

"What then? Did they go in with her?"

"The other woman waited in the car. Cockhead took her inside, but he was only there for a minute or two. Then they took off. You want me to go in and check on her?"

It's on the tip of my tongue to say yes. But it's a fine line between protecting her and controlling her. And as long as Marco's not there, she's at least safe. I fill Tama in on what appears to have happened tonight, and he lets fly a gusty sigh along with a few choice expletives.

"Do you want the boys to stand down?"

"Fuck, no. Keep a close eye on her. I don't know yet what's really going on, but whatever it is, it's not good. Let me know if he comes back. Any time. Day or night."

"Gotcha. Don't worry. We'll stick to her like shit on a blanket."

I attempt a chuckle, although it comes out more like a choked cough.

Calming my mind enough to think straight is proving difficult. Did she let him take her home to shake him? If so, and she's now home alone, why isn't she answering my calls?

I transfer the picture Marco posted to my laptop and blow it up, focusing on Rosanna's face. Analysing every line and angle. After the weekend we spent together, I know her face. I know how it looks when she's joyous, and this is not it. There's no genuine happiness in her expression. She looks stunned.

There's only one possible conclusion. He's threatening her.

But if that's the case, why not call me? Tell me. Let me help.

Every doubt and insecurity I have about myself is screaming like a flock of cockatoos. Why would a woman like Rosanna want to get involved with someone like me? I can't even read properly, for fuck's sake. For the first time in years, my dyslexia is making me doubt my worth as a man.

The old image of a man with an angel on one shoulder and the devil on the other flashes through my mind. One whispering good, the other bad.

On the one hand, I know Rosanna. I know her heart. I trust her implicitly.

On the other, the devil is asking *was this what she wanted all along*? To push Marco into a proposal? Was that why she was so hesitant to tell her parents?

I can't believe that. I don't believe that. We spent two days wrapped up together. How could she respond to me the way she did if she still wanted Marco? If there was even a tiny flicker of affection left for him? You can't fake responses like that.

But maybe for her it was nothing more than physical? She's a passionate woman. Maybe she was so desperate for release that any man would do and I happened to be on hand.

I pace through what's left of the night. Listening for the faint sound of the elevator bringing her back to me. It never comes.

By the time the sun comes up, I'm jumping out of my skin. I throw on running shorts, go downstairs to the gym and run. And run. And run. Normally I prefer to run on the street, but the steady pounding thump of my feet on the treadmill gives a soundtrack to my pain. The circling of the running belt an echo of my circling thoughts. Never ending. Never resolving.

But I can't outrun the toxic loop of my thoughts. My fears and insecurities are in danger of getting the best of me.

When I can't run another step, I go back to my apartment and fall asleep without showering, in a disgusting, sweaty heap, clutching my phone in case she calls. But she doesn't.

By the time I wake, it's midafternoon. My face is buried in a pillow that still smells of her. My phone is silent. At least my brain has calmed enough for me to think straight.

I push down the whispering voice of doubt and insecurity. I have to trust her. Trust myself. Trust us. No promises were made. There was no talk of anything beyond what we had already shared. But I felt it. And I believe she did too.

Even if I did imagine it. Even if she doesn't feel the same. I know in my heart she wouldn't go back to Marco.

Something is wrong. And it's up to me to help her.

CHAPTER TWENTY-SEVEN

ROSANNA

An adult female is fifty-five percent water. Which explains why I feel like a piece of dried fruit. Because I've cried buckets.

I call in sick on Monday morning. For the first time in my life, I thank God for migraines. Nobody questions me. Certainly not the receptionist, Julie, who promises to tell my boss. I've always had a slightly off vibe from her, but even in this agonised state, I pick up on the contempt in her tone. When she tells me to 'get well soon' it sounds more like 'I hope you have the plague'.

I still haven't called Ben. I know he must be worried sick, based on the number of missed calls from him alone. But I can't face talking to him. I know I'm being a coward, but I'm scared if I speak to him, I'll break down and tell him the whole sorry tale. I can't afford that. For Ben's sake as well as my father's.

Lulu has been blowing up my phone too. Another person I can't face. So, it's no surprise there's a furious banging on my door before I've even managed to drag my carcass into the shower.

"What the actual F.U.C.K.?" She spells out the word, determined Isla's first word won't be worthy of a viral TikTok video, and pushes the pram into the middle of the living room.

She's furious. I get it. I'm furious too. But I can't tell her either.

"It's what Dad wants. I can't do anything to upset him." My answer sounds weak even to my ears. Her expression is priceless. If I wasn't so broken, I'd be looking for my phone to capture it.

"You really think your father, who adores you, would want you to be married to that sack of S.H.I.T?"

I want to scream, *I know*. Tell her everything. But I also know Lulu won't let Marco's threats stop her. And that puts Dad at risk. I need time. To clear my head. To think it through.

"You know how sick Dad is. How much he relies on Marco, and how much he wants this." I turn away. I can't utter such rubbish to her face. "It's the least I can do. It won't be so bad. At least I won't be shocked when he cheats. I'll be expecting it." If someone gave me that argument, they'd get a swift smack upside the head. I'm surprised when Lulu doesn't do exactly that.

Unsurprisingly, she sees straight through my pathetic attempts to excuse my decision.

"Are you *freaking* kidding me?" Hearing the anger in her mother's voice, Isla's plump bottom lip starts to quiver, and one big fat tear rolls down her baby cheek.

Scooping her out of the pram, I nuzzle her sweet little neck, making hushing noises.

"You're upsetting Isla. And me. I have a migraine. I really need quiet. And dark."

Lulu looks chastened and takes her delicious baby back, kissing her hair.

"It's alright, baby. Mumma's not mad. Just a bit upset. I love you. I'm sorry for shouting."

Isla sniffles and clings to Lulu's neck. Lulu gives me her stern mother glare. "And I love you too. Which is why I'm going to go and let you get some rest. But you have not heard the last of this. Be prepared to come up with a better reason than the one you've just given me. And soon."

She's almost out the door before she turns. "What about Ben?"

The turnaround on her attitude towards Ben nearly breaks me.

"What about Ben? This has nothing to do with him." The words are like razor wire in my throat.

Shaking her head, she leaves without another word.

Once she's gone, I run myself a bath, tears rolling unchecked down my face. I think about the last time I was in this tub, with Ben outside the door, keeping up a running commentary. It's hard to believe how much he's come to mean to me in such a short amount of time. I try and relax but there's no hope, so I put on a T-shirt and yoga pants and crawl under the covers to hide. Sadly, there's no hiding from myself.

My mind is spinning in ever-decreasing circles.

I can't marry Marco.

But I can't let him ruin my father. And as deceitful as he is, I believe him when he says he has the means to ruin Moretti's and Dad. Because he's sly and dishonest and a despicable human being.

And I can't let him potentially hurt Ben.

So I have to stay away.

But I can't marry Marco.

And Ben and Lulu are right. My father would not want me tied to that lying sack of shit if he knew.

How do I get rid of Marco without risking my father's health? His company? His freedom?

Stop the ride. I want to get off.

And I want to talk to Ben. Desperately. But I can't. Because I can't risk Marco finding out. I'm a director of Moretti's, so my phone contract is with them. I wouldn't put it past Marco to monitor my calls.

And I don't feel safe here, on my own in my apartment, like I did at Ben's. With the doorman. And Tama. And Ben.

And. And. And.

Which brings me back to the beginning again.

When my phone lights up with a call from Marco, I'm too scared to let it go to voicemail. I have to keep him thinking I've capitulated until I work out what to do.

"Have you called that loser Ben Carter and told him to back off yet?" he starts, without any preamble.

"What have you got against Ben? He's just a friend." My voice is muffled by the covers pulled up to almost over my head.

"Don't treat me like a fool. I saw the way he looked at you at that fancy party Lulu threw for her father. The way he stood up for you. Christ knows why. Call him and put an end to whatever it is. Or he's going down too. Do it now. I'll be blocking his number in one hour."

Jesus. I had no idea he could even do that.

I feel trapped.

Lulu once said she felt trapped by her own stupidity when things were going badly with Nick. I can't believe how dismissive I was of her then. Now that the shoe is on the other foot, I can relate. It's easy to give advice when it's not you in the hot seat.

Ben answers on the first ring, as though he already had his phone in his hand.

"Rosanna, where are you? What the hell happened? Why haven't you called? I've been worried sick." His words fall over the top of one another.

"I've been busy."

"Busy? You didn't come home for fuck's sake. Did you not think I'd worry?" I hear the terror in his voice, and it takes all my strength to hold my heart together. Hearing him call his apartment home? I don't know if I can do this. All I want is to get this over with so I can let the pieces of my heart fall.

"Yes. No. I mean, I am home. At my place," I whisper. "Don't shout at me, please."

"I know. Tama told me. I saw the post. Why are you at your place? What the fuck happened, Ro?" He's struggling to keep his voice level; it's sharp and bitter.

"You saw the post. He asked me to marry him, and I ..." My voice trails off. What else is there to say? I have to let Ben believe this is what I want. Because if I don't, he'll try to help. There's no knowing what Marco would do then.

"You accepted? Why? What possessed you?"

"My father ..." I can't finish my sentence.

"Don't give me that. Your father is a grown man. And he wouldn't want you tying yourself to a cheating scumbag like Marco. What really happened?"

"My father needs to feel the company is in safe hands. That I'm in safe hands. I can't risk his health right now." Even I can hear my voice is mechanical. Wooden. Like a badly rehearsed line.

"Bullshit. You expect me to believe you think Marco is safe hands? What's really going on?" He's not stupid. He knows that's not the reason.

"Just because we had sex doesn't give you the right to interrogate me."

He gasps as though I've slapped him. I might as well have done. That was a horrible thing to say. I hope one day, when it all comes out, he can forgive me.

"I'm not interrogating you, but I do want an explanation. I think I deserve that, at least. And why are you at your flat? Get Tama to bring you back home and we'll talk about it here. In person."

"Don't tell me what to do."

"I'm not telling you what to do. I'm trying to keep you safe."

There's not much courage left in me. I need to end this. I search for something unforgivable to say. Something that will make him walk away.

"I didn't swap one overbearing arsehole for another, Ben. I'm perfectly fine at home. And my reasons for"—my voice catches—"for doing what I'm doing, are none of your business. Thank you for watching out for me for the past couple of weeks, but I've got this now. I'll send Lulu over to collect my things later in the week."

He's silent for so long I wonder if he's hung up. But then he speaks, and his voice sounds so broken I nearly relent. Nearly wail and beg him to help me. But I can't do that to him. Or Dad. Or myself. So I let the tears fall silently, soaking my T-shirt.

"I'm sorry. I didn't mean to be overbearing. Please. Come home and we'll talk about it."

I can't stand another minute of his patience. I'm about to break.

"I am home. Goodbye, Ben." I end the call. It feels like the end of everything good.

CHAPTER TWENTY-EIGHT

BENEDICT

"Whoa. This is even fancier than I expected." Will whistles as I let him into my apartment a couple of hours after the worst experience of my life. "I thought my view was good, but this is incredible." He heads straight for the windows while Josh starts nosing through my record collection and checking out the art.

"I can't believe you kept all this to yourself, man. I mean, I get why you did, but fuck. What a place for a New Year's Eve party." Josh raises his eyebrows at me in question.

"You can see the fireworks from Mum and Dad's place," I argue. A party is the last thing I want to think about right now.

"Yeah, but not the bridge."

"Fine. I'll think about it. Maybe. Meanwhile, can we get down to business?" I don't have mind space for anything but Rosie right now.

They've already heard the news from Greer, so I don't need to tell them about the engagement. But I poke the bear that is my pain and disbelief by showing them Marco's post. The picture of Marco and Rosanna holding champagne glasses. A big, ugly ring on her left hand. And a drivelling caption about how he's the luckiest man alive to be marrying such a wonderful woman. It would be true if it was going to happen. But it won't if I've got anything to say about it. I don't care what she said on the phone. This is not what she wants. Nothing she said during our conversation has convinced me otherwise.

"You've got to be kidding me." Josh falls back in his chair, scrubbing his hands over his face.

"Is it just me or does she look, I don't know, shocked? And not in a good way," Will says.

"I think it's safe to say she's been blindsided by this." I look again at Rosanna's beautiful face, searching for some hint of the woman I know.

I can't think of her as Rosie in the same breath as Marco. Rosie is mine, and mine alone. I know he's forcing her somehow. My guess is it's more than her father's health. If I had to put money on it, I'd say he's threatening the business. Because the Rosie who left my apartment yesterday—I can't believe it was only yesterday—would never agree to marry this guy.

I fill them in on our conversation. When I get to the comment about swapping overbearing arseholes, they laugh.

"Yeah, that sounds like a love match right there. You think she's being coerced?" Will asks.

"Abso-fucking-lutely she's being coerced. There's no way I'm letting him get away with this."

I haven't told them what happened between me and Rosanna this weekend, but it turns out I don't really need to.

"I saw how you looked at her at Nick and Lulu's wedding, man. Are you okay?" Josh asks.

No point denying it.

"No, but not because she's engaged. Because that's a pile of steaming crap. I'm not okay because whatever's going on, he's got her scared. Which means we have to take him down. Hard and fast. In a way that won't hurt Rosanna or her father. You guys in?" I ask.

"I think we're going to need a bigger team." Will grins.

Half an hour and the better part of a bottle of tequila later, I've explained my rough plan, and we've filled in the details.

I've contacted Sabrina, who is getting to work on tracing any and all calls, transactions and contacts Marco has made in the past two years, looking for patterns or suspicious activity. Tama is calling on his security colleagues to get as much footage as we can of Marco coming and going from places he shouldn't.

Will has conferred, off the record, with a couple of criminal lawyers he knows about the legalities of what we're up to, and whilst it won't necessarily stand up in court, it should be enough to put Marco onto the radar of a serious investigation.

The pièce de résistance is a real estate developer I know, who I'm going to ask to reach out to Marco to set up a dodgy deal.

By the time we've finished with this guy, not only will he not get a job in this town again, but he won't be able to set foot in a club or pub without being shown the door. If they haven't locked him up and thrown away the key.

Sadly, Josh and Will drew the line at Sabrina hacking the police database to put him on the sex offender registry. Apparently, that's illegal. Even if he is offensive. Maybe I can convince her to add a nasty STI to his medical records. We'll put a pin in that for another day.

The whole time we're talking and planning, what I want to be doing is calling Rosie, telling her I'm sorry for shouting, asking if she's alright. But I know I can't. If there's a chance Marco is with her—God forbid—it could make things worse.

CHAPTER TWENTY-NINE

ROSANNA

The rest of the week rolls by like *Groundhog Day*. Every morning, I call in sick. I don't care if I lose my job. In the scheme of things, that's the least bad thing that could happen to me right now. After my call to the office, I soak in the bath until it goes cold. I put on yoga pants and a sweatshirt, because, despite the summer heat, I can't seem to get warm. Then I crawl back into bed where I cry myself to sleep. The only time I rouse from my stupor is when my parents call, worried about my 'migraine'.

But every minute of the day, I'm turning the problem over and over in my head. There's a way out of this. There has to be. All I have to do is find it.

Marco appears at my apartment unannounced at random times during the day as though he's trying to catch me out disobeying his orders. At least he doesn't hang around. Pretty sure he doesn't enjoy seeing me in my yoga pants and sleep shirt, sans makeup. By Thursday, he's lost patience and informs me I will be back at work on Monday. Ready to put on a show. Or else.

Lulu, whose unanswered calls have been filling up my mailbox, arrives unannounced with Isla on Friday morning, shoves me into the shower and lays out some clothes for me.

"We're going for a walk. You need some fresh air," she announces. "No arguments."

We're in the middle of the park, where we used to be tortured by a bootcamp instructor once a week, before Lulu speaks.

"Firstly, what the *fudge* is going on? Secondly, what do you need?" Seems like we've graduated from spelling to replacement words.

"Nick doesn't want the first word she learns to spell to be the f-bomb," she explains when I raise my brows. As though a six-month-old baby is close to learning to spell.

We walk in silence for a couple more minutes. "I've got all day," she says.

And I can't do this any longer. The dam bursts. Everything that's happened since the night I confronted Marco pours out of me. The threats. The revelations about his motives. My growing feelings for Ben. Along with more tears I didn't even know were still inside me.

Lulu listens with little more than shocked gasps and the occasional hand roll to keep me moving. The only thing I leave out is what I know about Ben and his business. It's not my story to tell.

I grind to a halt as we reach the shade of a giant Moreton Bay fig and we stop to stare at the boats in the bay.

"I knew that guy was scum, but I would never have even imagined ..." Lulu finally manages.

"Me either. The only one who saw him for what he is, right from the beginning, was Ben." I didn't even realise that fact until the words come out of my mouth.

Suddenly, it all clicks into place. All week I've felt like a solution was there, tantalisingly out of reach. Now I don't know how I didn't see it before. Keeping this from Ben is ridiculous. Because if there's one thing I know, it's that Ben will keep me—and my dad—safe. Whatever he has to do. I completely trust him to do what needs to be done. To help me come up with a solution. To find a way to make this right. There's not a soul I trust more.

It's as though this epiphany puts my brain into fifth gear at last. I need to talk to Ben. Without Marco getting wind of it.

Even though I blew him off on Monday night, and his number has been blocked, I know Ben won't let me down.

I start walking again, faster this time as though my brain and feet are connected.

"I need a phone. One Marco doesn't know about. The bill for mine goes through Moretti's. I need him not to know what I'm doing."

Lulu's eyes nearly pop out of her head. "Shit. Okay. I can do that. What else?"

"I need you to play along. Whatever I say, however weird it might be, just play along. Okay?"

Lulu stops walking and looks me square in the eye. "Ro, are you in danger?"

"No. Maybe. Who knows what Marco will do? But it'll be alright. All you have to do is act natural and normal, and I promise I'll fill you in when I can."

"Act natural and normal when my best friend is marrying a psycho? Tall order. But whatever you need. You know that."

We sit on the grass in the shade and lay Isla on a blanket. Lulu pretends to take photos of her, all the while ordering a new mobile phone from Amazon to be delivered to her place so Marco won't know. It's all a bit James Bond, but I can't risk him catching on to what I'm doing.

The phone arrives the following morning. Gotta love Amazon Prime. Lulu drops it in and leaves me to it. Unsure if Marco would go so far as to bug my apartment—not a thought I ever expected to have—I leave with shopping bags as if I'm going to the supermarket. Thanks to the prepaid sim card Lulu picked up for me at the corner store yesterday, I can call Ben.

He answers on the first ring because Lulu has already let him know I'd be calling.

"Are you okay?" he asks, without even a hello. I can't help it. I start to cry.

"Yes. I'm okay. I'm sorry for what I said the other night. I didn't mean it. Any of it."

"I know, Rosie, I know. Don't give it a second thought." His voice is low and rich and hearing him call me the name only he uses soothes my frantic soul. He's not mad at me. He understands. Like I knew he would.

"He's done something, Ben. I don't know what, but he's done something. He said if I didn't agree to marry him, he'd tell the NACC that Dad is doing dodgy deals. He could go to jail. And I know Dad would never do anything wrong." The words tumble out, and I'd bet Ben can hear me wringing my hands through the phone.

"No. Your dad hasn't. But Marco has."

"Marco said if I see you, he'd bring you down too."

Ben barks out a laugh. Hearing it warms me from the inside out. I sag back against the shelves in the canned soup aisle of the supermarket, lightheaded with relief.

"I'd like to see him try. Cockhead."

"I think he's dangerous. Unstable." I get a strange look from an older man who seems to be tossing up between tomato and minestrone. Maybe it's the tears running down my face.

"He is dangerous. Which is why you need to be careful."

"What should I do?"

"Do you think you can pretend to go along with him for a week or two?"

"I guess so. Why? You sound like you already know what he's been doing." The old guy settles on tomato and shuffles away with one last suspicious look.

"Yeah. I had a feeling about him from the get-go, so I looked into him. Didn't take long for some, shall we say, irregularities, to show up. He's not as smart as he thinks he is. I just need a bit of time to get some evidence and put some things in place."

For the first time in days, I laugh. Of course, Ben has a plan. I should've known all along he would, and maybe if I hadn't been so scared, I would've realised it earlier.

Knowing I have Ben beside me sorting this out, I feel invincible. My tears dry up, and I straighten my shoulders.

"I can string him along. What else?" This is starting to remind me of the first weekend we spent together, hatching the plan to catch Marco out in his cheating. I can't believe it, but I'm suddenly excited for the outcome.

"Keep your ears and eyes open. If there's anything you think seems dodgy, let me know. But don't take any risks. I'll fill you in as things come together. In the meantime, Tama and the boys will continue keeping an eye on you. I'll text a number to this phone. Save it, and if you need them for any reason at all, call. Or call me. But don't ever call any of us from your old phone." I can't believe he still had Tama watching me after what I said to him.

"Understood. Maybe we need code names. How about Max and 99?" It feels good to be making a joke.

"I don't think I like being compared to a bumbling idiot. Although, 99 was hot. So you fit the bill."

My cheeks start to burn.

"007 for you then?"

"Much better," he agrees. And we both fall silent. There's so much to say, but now isn't the right time to say it.

Ben sighs. "I'd better go. We need to keep contact to a minimum. You can't do anything to make Marco suspicious, okay?"

I laugh before I realise this could be dangerous. For both of us. "Be careful."

"Oh, I'll be fine. It's you I'm worried about. Try not to spend any time alone with him or change the way you treat him."

"Ugh. Not a chance. He knows I don't want anything to do with him. I don't need to put that on. I only need to keep up the act in front of the parents." I shudder at the thought of spending any time at all with Marco, let alone by ourselves.

"I miss you, 99," Ben whispers.

"Miss you too, Double Oh." Which is as close as we can come right now to an admission of feelings I know are too soon to be logical but exist, nonetheless.

I still look like I've been dragged through a hedge backwards by the time I return to work on Monday. I haven't even made it through the doors to the main office when the outside door opens and a delivery driver comes in carrying an old-fashioned flower box. Of course, they're for me. From Marco. Who has never sent me flowers in our entire relationship.

Our receptionist, Julie, is supposed to sign for all deliveries but holds up both hands and points to me as though touching the box might give her some sort of disease. She sneers at me as I sign for them. A vague impression of her talking to Marco at one of the few company functions he's ever bothered to attend flickers in the back of my mind. I recall her twirling her improbably blonde hair around a purple-taloned finger. Surely not. Then again ...

I don't have an office, but the shelves of trim and racks of fabric form a little cubby hole, giving me a small amount of privacy. I drop the box on my desk. When I whip off the lid, I can't hold in a horrified gasp.

Inside are twelve blood-red roses along with twelve white carnations. There is so much wrong with this arrangement. Firstly, Marco knows I hate red roses. They're so overused and pedestrian. Secondly, Marco knows I'm superstitious. He also knows red and white flowers together mean death. I pick up the card.

Glad to see you're back at work today. I will collect you at 5pm. We need to discuss wedding dates with your parents. Don't keep me waiting.

He added a smiley face to make it look like a joke or a wish to not be delayed in seeing me, but I hear the threat loud and clear. The idea we're going to be discussing wedding dates already sends a shiver up my spine. I'm learning to trust these visceral physical responses. Marco is going to try and rush this wedding.

I hope Ben can get his plan in place pronto because this is quickly becoming a runaway train.

CHAPTER THIRTY

BENEDICT

I meet with Peter White, a real estate developer I know, on Sunday at a funny little café on the beach at North Narrabeen. Far, far away from anywhere we're likely to be spotted by Marco. His loss. The coffee is exceptional. I've known Pete for a few years now. We first met when I was looking for space for a new club, and we hit it off right away. I've picked up a couple of properties from him since then. He's the perfect guy to approach Marco, and more importantly, I trust him implicitly.

"It's been way too long, mate." Pete gives my hand a hearty shake and settles his solid frame into a chair across from me. Unlike a lot of cafés, the chairs in this place are solid. Built to take their regular surfer clientele.

"Yeah, it has." We give the server our order and shoot the shit for a while, chatting about what we've been up to, where we've been and Pete's family of three out-of-control teenage girls.

"So, to what do I owe the pleasure?" he asks as our coffees are put in front of us. "I got the impression this wasn't a social call."

"No. It isn't." I take a deep breath. Despite the fact I trust Pete, it's a risk telling anyone about what's going on. "Have you ever come across Moretti & Co, in your dealings?"

A shadow passes over Pete's face, and he leans back in his chair, crossing his arms.

"I have. Why?" Most of the friendliness has drained out of his tone. Looks like he's familiar with the way Marco operates.

"What do you know of them?"

"The old guy, Andrea Moretti, was a straight shooter. But he's handed over to his son-in-law, Marco. I don't like the way he does business. To be honest, Ben, if you're wanting me to do some kind of deal with them, I'll tell you right now, I'm not interested."

My temper spikes to hear Marco referred to as Andrea's son-in-law, but I let it go. Bigger fish to fry here.

"Well, I am, and I'm not. Rosanna Moretti, Andrea's daughter, is a friend of mine. She recently got wind of Marco—who is not her husband, by the way—doing some dodgy deals. Her problem is he's threatening to set Andrea up for the fall. I've offered to help her out by taking the lowlife down."

"I see. Are you sure the old guy isn't involved?"

"He has no idea. From what I can piece together, Marco has been skimming funds for a while now, but it's only since Moretti has had to step back because of his health that the real dirty stuff has been happening."

Suddenly, Pete is leaning forward again, listening intently.

"Go on."

"I'm looking for someone to act as a lure. Offer him a deal, get him talking until he incriminates himself. It would mean meeting with him, probably a few times, getting his confidence, and wearing a wire. I don't know if you know, but my brother is a partner at Carter, Pierce and Millwood. He's going to be liaising with the fraud squad and any other squad we can think of, so there'd be no blowback on you. Just the opportunity to do some good Samaritan work."

Pete slurps his coffee, frowning.

"That little shit did the dirty on a friend of mine last year. Lost him nearly a million dollars. I would like the chance to repay the favour ..."

I watch the thoughts play across his face. I'm aware there's a small level of risk for Pete. But if the worst were to happen, I'm confident Will and Nick, who has now been read in on what we're up to, would be able to sort it out.

"You don't have to give me an answer now. Have a think about it. If you decide you can't do it, for whatever reason, absolutely no hard feelings." I'm hoping it won't come to that.

"You know what? If this gets another dodgy dealer out of the business and helps you in the process, I'm in. Might be a bit of fun." Pete grins, showing off his unnaturally straight white teeth.

We order another coffee and settle in to come up with a plan. Peter will contact Marco and set up a meeting. Ostensibly about an aboveboard project. During the conversation he'll start to lead Marco into slightly murky waters. All while wearing a wire. It may take a couple of meetings for Marco to feel bold enough to say something incriminating, but we're all prepared for that.

"I'll email him first thing tomorrow morning and suggest a meeting. Let you know how it goes." Pete climbs into his souped-up twin cab ute and waves as he tears off.

I text Rosie to let her know how it went and I've barely made it to my car before she calls me back.

"Hey, 99. What are you up to?"

"I'm going to Mum and Dad's. I thought I might try and do some digging. Marco isn't giving me much rope, but he's playing golf today. Or so he says. Is it bad to hope there's a freak lightning storm and he gets hit?"

It's good to see she hasn't lost her sense of humour. The next week or two are going to be hard on her.

"Nah, that would be doing everyone a favour. Just, if you're going to interrogate your dad, be subtle. You don't want to say anything that might get back to Marco and tip him off."

"Hey, I can be subtle." We both laugh at the untruth of that.

"Yeah. Subtlety's your signature personality trait for sure." I manoeuvre the car into the never-ending traffic on Pittwater Road and start for home.

"Anyway, is there anything I should ask about specifically?"

"Hmm. Does your dad have an office at home?"

"Yes." I hear the indicator in her car and the engine slowing.

"If you get the chance, have a poke around. Take a photo of anything you can find about the business. Bank statements. Employee lists. Contracts. Even if they look legit. Anything that might show your father was none the wiser to what's going on."

"Roger that, Double Oh. I'd better go. I just pulled up." I wish we could keep talking. I wish I could be there with her.

"Miss you, 99. Be careful."

"Miss you more." I can't wipe the smile off my face.

Things might be dire right now, but they're definitely looking up.

By Monday morning, Sabrina is starting to get data from Marco's bugged phone and cloned email account. Nothing concrete has shown up yet, although there are a couple of fishy-looking communications, so I'm confident we'll unearth plenty of useful information.

Tama and the boys are working overtime keeping an eye on Rosanna, and on Marco, who appears to think he's untouchable. He continues to meet with councillors in dark carparks and skeevey pubs and to turn up at clubs around the city, often leaving with an interchangeable version of his preferred skinny blonde women. He's oblivious to security cameras because we even find footage of him getting a blow job in a back alley. And if my eyes don't deceive me, there's a distinct dusting of white powder around his nostrils. These new high-resolution cameras are the bomb.

He's almost making this too easy. I'd be enjoying it if it wasn't for my fear for Rosanna. And her father. Because he's a bit gruff, but he seems like a nice old guy. I need to make sure we keep this stealthy and have everything locked down tight before we move on Marco. If he gets any hint he's in the crosshairs, there's no telling what he'll do.

This is one time when it's good to be underestimated. It won't have occurred to him I might be able to bring him undone, so he won't even be looking for it. Unless he connected me to the catfishing episode. Lucky for me, he's not that sharp.

I also want to try and find a way to see Rosanna. It's crazy how much I miss her after no more than a week, but there you have it.

When Nick told me Rosie asked Lulu to get her a phone and had filled her in on everything that happened—including our wild weekend of sex—my heart soared.

It hurt when she pushed me away, even though I knew full well she was scared and confused. Those hours not knowing what was going on and wondering if she might have agreed to marry Marco of her own free will, were the worst of my life. When she suggested what happened between us was nothing more than sex ... well, I'm only human. Even though, once I'd had a minute to process it, my head knew she was lying, my heart still took a hit.

We haven't talked about it, but I know our weekend together meant more than just a physical release. It sucks that exploring whatever it is will have to wait until Marco is dealt with.

What really brought me joy was her complete trust in me to be able to sort this out. It might have taken her a few days to realise it, but there was no doubt, no hesitation, no fear. Just utter confidence I would come up with a plan to keep her safe and deal with Marco. Who knew trust was such a powerful aphrodisiac.

At lunchtime Rosie sends me a screen shot of some truly ugly flowers, and a note that to the uninformed might seem benign. Rosie and I know better.

Rosie: these arrived today. Aren't they lovely?

Me: never pegged you for a red rose girl

Rosie: such a cliché

Me: exactly—you're more of a lotus kind of girl. Or peonies.

Rosie: love love love peonies

Me: Noted. Not to bring the mood down, but keep the note and a pic of those flowers

Rosie: good thinking Double Oh

Me: have a good afternoon 99 x

There's a prickle of fear that Marco will try and push this wedding through quickly. But if anyone can stall him, it's Rosanna.

A few minutes later, I get confirmation from Pete that a meeting has been set up for next Monday. Maybe we'll have this all wrapped up with a bow on it by the end of next week.

Then Rosanna and I can work out what it is we are. And where we might want it to go.

CHAPTER THIRTY-ONE

ROSANNA

It's like a bad movie. The script is so obvious. If Mum and Dad weren't so innocent and excited that their little girl is getting married, maybe they'd smell a rat. As it is, Dad plays right into Marco's hands while Mum frets about the inappropriateness of rushing. It almost seems like she's unsure. Or reluctant. But Marco pushes hard.

"Andrea, I want you to be able to walk Rosanna down the aisle. To enjoy the first dance with her at our reception. I think it would be foolish to wait," Marco says with oily insincerity. "Why wait with your health as it is? Besides, how could you expect me to wait to make this beautiful woman my wife? It's cruel." Marco's hands come up to clutch at where his heart would be if he had one. Ugh.

My poor, sick father gobbles this up. The fact that Marco wants to get married in a month, after he waited more than eight years to propose, seems lost on Dad.

"*Si, si. È molto saggio, Marco,*" Dad agrees from his recliner, which he has barely left since the night of my 'engagement', according to Mum.

"*Non possiamo organizzarlo,*" Mum argues. Of course, it's not possible to organise the kind of wedding she wants for her only child as quickly as Marco wants to move.

"Exactly. That's not enough time to organise anything. There are venues, and flowers and photographers," I add, desperate to drag this out and give Ben the time he needs, even if it means staying 'engaged' to Marco. "Papa, don't you want your little girl to have the wedding of her dreams?"

"Si, tesoro, Marco hanno ragione. Aspetteremo." Dad looks to Mum. *"Tre mesi sono sufficienti?"*

"No, no, no," Fernanda interrupts, talking over my mother, who is shaking her head. No reasonable person would think you could organise a big fat Italian wedding in three months. But Fernanda has taken the ball Marco threw and runs with it. "Who are we to stand in the way of true love? One month will be plenty of time. Marco has already done the paperwork." She looks pointedly at me.

Ever since The Engagement—she refers to it as though it's a proper noun—she's been blowing my phone up with messages and pictures of venues, flowers and bonbonnieres. She's gone from friendly and kind to Mother of Dragons. Apparently, every objection I raise is me being *difficult* and *spoilt*. If Marco himself wasn't enough to put me off, her behaviour would certainly have me running a mile. She'll be the monster-in-law from hell for some poor woman.

"I don't know," my mother sniffles. "I have to think of taking care of Andrea. It is too much to organise." Bless her.

"You leave all the organising to me, Flavia. Or should I call you Mama?" Marco folds my mother in a hug and smirks at me over her shoulder. I struggle not to gag.

"I can't make a dress that quickly," I object, knowing full well this won't provide sufficient reason.

"A woman as talented as you, *cara mia*, I have no doubt you will achieve it. My mama will, of course, help you." Just what I need. More time with Fernanda. "As will your own mama, yes?" He looks to my mother, who nods, helpless in the face of Marco's unstoppable determination to get this done.

"Then it's settled. I will locate a venue. Rosanna, you will start on the dress, and together we will choose the flowers and invitations." It isn't lost on me that Marco speaks in Italian Australian whenever he's with my parents. It's such an affectation. "Of course, Rosanna must have whatever she wishes. My only request is red roses for the flowers. To show the world my passion for my beautiful bride." He grabs my hands and kisses them with a fervour I might have welcomed once upon a time. Dad beams with pride. I hide my snort of derision behind a cough. Which, of course, doesn't fool Marco, who gives me a cutting glare before pulling out his laptop and sitting with my mother to discuss invitation styles.

Even if I were on board with this wedding, the ideas Marco is suggesting and my mother is agreeing to, under duress from Fernanda, are hideous in the extreme.

I stifle a groan. I'll have to wait till Marco and Fernanda are not around—a rare occurrence these days—to try and convince my father to wait. But I'll do it. Whatever it takes.

All I want to do is text Ben and let him know what's happening here. But I dare not while Marco is around. Even going to the bathroom to text seems like too much of a risk. It will have to wait until I get home.

As soon as I walk in the door, my new 'burner phone' as I think of it—yeah, I really need to get a grip on this spy stuff—is out of the pocket concealed in the lining of my handbag and I go straight out onto the balcony to call Ben.

Predictably, he's not surprised by the stunt Marco pulled tonight.

"He can't afford to wait, Rosie. He needs to lock you down. Because if something happens to your father, he loses his leverage." I stretch out on the sun lounger, my anxiety calmed by nothing more than Ben's voice and his confidence that we'll prevail.

"Do you think you'll be able to get what you need on him in the next few weeks? It doesn't give you much time."

"We're already well on our way. My developer mate is meeting with him on Monday. It probably won't happen overnight. He'll have to gain Marco's trust, but don't worry. You won't be marrying Marco any time soon."

Knowing Ben has a plan gives me faith this will all be over soon. That Dad and his company will be safe.

Marco is building up a head of steam. Knowing, or at least thinking, he's got me where he wants me, he's taken to texting instructions on what I can do, with whom and when.

On Thursday morning, he 'suggests' I go with Lulu to find a bridesmaid's dress since I clearly won't have time to make one before our wedding next month. He'd love to cut Lulu out of the picture but knows that would raise questions with my parents, so he allows me to see her. Lulu agrees immediately and we arrange to meet at a bridal salon in Woollarah. Where the dresses are extortionate and not nearly as lovely as anything I could design or make myself.

As soon as Lulu arrives, I can tell she's up to something.

"Why don't you try on some dresses yourself?" she suggests.

"Even if I was getting married, which I'm not, I would make my dress, so why would I do that?" I whisper, hopefully low enough that the sales staff don't overhear.

"I know. But maybe trying some on will give you some ideas. Humour me." She shoves a frilly meringue of a dress I know will look awful on me into my hands.

"You've got to be kidding." Lulu has lost her mind if she thinks I would even try this thing on.

"Take it to the dressing room right there at the back."

Dressing rooms for bridal wear are huge. Because so many of the dresses are huge. Or require an army to get you into them. The one at the back of the shop looks particularly roomy. I hesitate, and Lulu grins, giving me a shooing motion before disappearing into a dressing room with the hideous chiffon number we selected for her as a joke.

I'm confused. Until I open the curtain. Lounging on the satin-covered faux Louis XV chair in the corner is Ben. A cheeky grin on his face. I'm speechless for a second or two.

"How did you get in here?" Actually, who cares? I toss the ugly dress onto another chair and throw myself into his arms as he stands.

"Back lanes and bribery." He folds his arms around me and buries his face in my hair.

I'm torn between relief at seeing him and fear Marco could find out.

"Is it safe?"

Ben laughs quietly. "I don't think Marco's reach extends to expensive bridal shops. By the way, what is that hideous thing you brought in with you?" He lifts the dress off the chair and holds it up in front of me. "No. Just no."

I grab it and toss it back on the chair because the only thing I want his hands on is me. It seems Ben feels the same, because he sits back down and pulls me into his lap, resting my head against his shoulder, his fingers sifting through my hair. It's a long time before either of us speaks.

"How are you holding up? Can you bear it for another week or two?" Ben's lips move on my forehead as he speaks, as though he doesn't want to take his mouth off me.

"It's horrid. He's horrid. But I can bear it. As long as I know you're not in any danger." Which sounds absurd to say. It's like we've stepped into an alternate reality.

"I'm not in any danger. And Marco is so arrogant he's not even bothering to properly cover his tracks."

I can't wait any more. The feel of his strong thighs under my bum, his hard abs against my breasts. It's all too much. Lifting my head from his shoulder, I grab his cheeks and press my mouth to his.

Ben doesn't need any more encouragement. His tongue slides into my mouth, one hand buried in my hair and holding me close, the other sliding down my back, spreading across the top of my arse.

The heat and hardness of his cock is pressed against my leg, and all I want is to be back in his apartment. In his bed.

I know there are people—Ben is probably one of them—who wouldn't think twice about having sex in a brightly lit dressing room with sales staff right outside. But despite what happened at the burlesque club, I'm not one of them. Maybe one day I will be. But I'm not quite there yet.

I don't know whether Ben senses my hesitation or whether he feels constrained too, but he pulls back with a sigh. Bracketing my head with his hands, he searches my face, one thumb coming up to trace across the blue shadows I know are under my eyes.

"Can you arrange to have lunch with Lulu on the weekend? At Nick's apartment? Come up with some excuse to spend the afternoon there?" he murmurs, pressing his lips to my forehead, my cheeks, my eyelids.

"Yes. I think so."

"Good. Saturday. One o'clock." And with a last swift kiss, he stands, deposits me on the chair, and disappears through the heavy curtain. Moments later, Lulu's grinning face pops through the opening.

"I never would have thought it, but you know what? I'm really liking Ben for you, Rosanna."

My cheeks heat, and I can't quite meet her eyes.

"Me too."

"Now hurry up; we need to at least have a shortlist of ugly bridesmaid dresses so you can tell Marco and the Mother of Dragons mission accomplished."

CHAPTER THIRTY-TWO

BENEDICT

After I leave Rosanna at the bridal shop, I head home for a summit meeting. We have lots to discuss before Pete's appointment with Marco on Monday.

Seeing Rosie was bittersweet. It's been not much more than a week since I last saw her, but even in that short time, she appears to have lost weight. And Marco will pay extra for those purple shadows under her eyes.

The joy and relief that sprang to life on her face when she saw me in the dressing room was a balm to my soul. Not only because I saw for myself that she's okay, but I saw for myself that the sudden and unexpected feelings I have for Rosanna are reciprocated, at least on some level. I can work with that. She may not be ready for anything deep, and who could blame her after this experience. But when she is, I'll be there, offering my heart. And whatever else she wants besides. Because one thing I know. I knew it the moment I laid eyes on her. Rosanna is it for me.

By the time Pete arrives, Will, Nick, Josh, Tama and I are already deep in conversation. Will helps himself to my beer fridge and hands me one while I dial a video call into Sabrina, who is in London at the moment.

"Did we really have to do this at the arse crack of dawn, guys?" she moans, clearly having tumbled out of bed for the meeting. I can see by the window behind her that it's still dark outside. I feel a little mean, but not mean enough to postpone. This shit needs sorting. Now. And let's be honest. It's winter in the UK. It's always dark.

I lift my beer at her. "It's not the arse crack of anything here, Sabbie." I grin because she hates it when I call her that. Her current girlfriend, who I have yet to meet, appears behind her and hands her a cup of what I presume is the Turkish coffee Sabrina is addicted to. This is all very domestic for Sab, and I'll be happy for her if it works out. She's an awesome person who's endured a lot of adversity in her life. She deserves the best.

"Fuck off," she mutters, lifting her cup at me. Showing exactly how awesome she is. She might be cranky right now, but I know by the time she gets to the bottom of the first cup she'll be firing on all cylinders.

"Right. With the pleasantries out of the way, how about we get started?" Will suggests with a laugh at my expense.

"How about we start with you, Tama? What have you got for us?"

Tama leans his enormous bulk back in the chair, making it creak alarmingly, but it holds. "This guy is the dumbest fuck I've ever had the pleasure of tailing," he says, looking like he's stepped in something nasty. And I suppose he has, metaphorically. "Thanks to Sabrina hacking his credit card account, I have a log of his movements. I've reached out to a couple of club and pub managers I know and pulled footage from nights we know he's been in their establishments. So far, we have three dodgy-looking meetings with guys who may or may not be councillors. Sab's running the facial recognition. Problem is, there's no law against meeting in a pub." He takes a swig of his beer before carrying on. "But in one video, there's a pretty clear handover of an envelope. From Marco to the guy we think is a councillor."

"Great. Anything else?" I'm pretty sure there is, based on the brief chats we've had.

"Oh yeah. Take your pick. This is a bit trickier, from a legal standpoint, because these cameras are City of Sydney security. But I know a guy, so ... Anyway, multiple videos of blow jobs, one of some pretty rough sex, and one of him actually hitting a woman. The quality of these is really good, much better than the cheap cameras from inside the clubs."

"The problem is, whilst it's abhorrent behaviour, and likely to get him a fine for public indecency, none of this is going to get him locked up. Unless the woman he hit makes a complaint," Nick interrupts, swishing his beer in his mouth a little, as though to wash away the awful taste of discussing Marco.

"Well, let's keep at it. Something will turn up. We've set up additional high-res cameras on the table for when he meets with Pete on Monday. Hopefully, he'll be desperate enough to let something slip." I turn to the computer screen where Sabrina is finally looking like she's awake. "Sabbie, what have you got for us?"

"As T said, running facial recognition on the videos, but it's slow going. Meanwhile, it will shock you to know he has a whole second life set up. Apparently, Moretti's employs a tech expert by the name of Robert Pacino. So lame. Does this guy fancy himself as a cross between De Niro and Pacino? Anyway, Bob doesn't exist. But he draws a biiiig salary, and the company pays for a fancy car. Apparently, his role requires a lot of schmoozing because his company card is brimming over with restaurant and hotel charges."

"How can you even do that in this day and age?" Pete asks.

"Easy. He's ostensibly a contractor. Paid through his business. Which, wait for it, is owned by Marco's mother. Guess who the signatory is? Marco. He's so sure he'll never get caught that he hasn't even bothered to distance himself. Fuck-knuckle."

"I think you'll find the correct term is cockhead," Tama amends and we all laugh.

"Great. Sabrina, that's enough to get him investigated by the NACC," Will chips in.

"No. We can't tip his hand. Investigated won't be enough. He needs to be locked up tight. If he's out on the streets, there's no telling what he'll do." Panic stabs sharply at my chest.

"Okay, okay." Will puts his hand on my arm to calm me. "I'll start putting a submission together, so when we're ready, it's all there. Meanwhile, I've reached out to a guy I know in the fraud squad. Off the record for now, but he's primed. Send me what you have, Sabrina. Is there any evidence at all that Rosanna's father has any idea about this?"

"Hard to prove a negative. But no. None so far."

"Sadly, that won't necessarily absolve him. So, we have to tread carefully. Keep digging and watching. What we need is clear evidence he's doing this on his own. An email, voice message, anything," Nick pipes up. He's so pissed over what's happening. I wouldn't want to be Marco when Nick gets a hold of him. Because messing with Rosanna is messing with Lulu. And Nick's having none of that. Assuming I don't get there first.

"On it. I'll let you know if anything pops up. So far, most of his electronic communications have been pretty circumspect. But, Pete, if you could get him to admit something, either at your meetings or over the phone, that would be great. I've got his phone tapped, so we'll pick it up."

"Right." Pete rubs his hands together. I think he's getting a kick out of this.

I hand him a pen, a tiny black button, and a fine navy silk tie.

"Fuuuck." Will whistles at the high-tech gear I've procured.

"The pen has a video and audio camera that transmits straight back to my phone and laptop. So does the button." Maybe it's overkill, but I'm not leaving anything to chance. "Slide the button inside the knot of your tie so it's pointing right at him. The fabric of the tie is fine enough that we should be able to pick up a shadowy shot. Leave the pen on the table."

The gear gets handed round the table for everyone to have a look. Boys and toys, after all.

"It's unlikely he'll say anything to incriminate himself at your first meeting. What we're looking to do is build some trust. Don't push. We don't want to make him suspicious."

"No worries," Pete says. "I'll talk about a new development I've got going on the North Shore, which is all above board, and once he thinks he's got the inside track, I'll let slip how much additional money we could make by going above and beyond the development application. That should get him talking."

"I really appreciate your help, mate."

"It's all good. To be honest, I'm enjoying myself. It's like being part of the Scooby Gang."

"The what?" Tama asks.

"You know, *Scooby Doo*? Crime fighting cartoon? No?" Pete's a few years older than us but even I know who *Scooby Doo* is. Tama must have been living under a rock.

"More like *Ocean's Eleven*," Will suggests. "Bags being Brad. No, wait. I think I'd rather be George."

"Fuck off. I'm George. He's the mastermind." I shove Will, almost unseating him.

"As long as I'm not Matt Damon," Josh adds, setting off a torrent of bickering. Fuck I love these guys.

"Aaand now that the dicks have started swinging, I'm out," says Sabrina with an eye roll, telling us she's had enough and is going back to bed, despite having downed two Turkish coffees in quick succession. Pete and Nick head home. I'm left alone with Will and Josh, finishing our beers and shooting the shit.

This afternoon I told Rosanna it was all coming together. And it is. What I didn't share was my fear. My terror, really, that this could all go sideways.

Will must see the concern on my face.

"You know, Ben, we've got this. *You've* got this. If it wasn't for you, Rosanna would be looking at life with—what did Sabrina call him?—that fuck-knuckle. Or cockhead. Take your pick. I'm really proud of you."

I can't remember the last time someone said that to me. The lump in my throat stops me from answering, but I give Will a grateful smile and a nod. I'll be proud of myself too. If we pull it off. *When* we pull it off. Because I can't bear to think about the consequences of failure.

CHAPTER THIRTY-THREE

ROSANNA

By Saturday morning, I'm jumping out of my skin with a combination of excitement and nerves.

I told Marco that Lulu and I are going to clear the last of Nick's personal possessions out of his apartment before it's sold. Since he'd rather be playing golf, or whatever the hell he does on a Saturday, he was fine with it. As long as I'm at my parents' place this evening to meet his mother for 'wedding planning'. Again. He won't be there of course. No doubt he'll be out tying up some poor unsuspecting blonde.

Meanwhile, his mother will report back to him every word and look. I know she's not responsible for his actions, but her slavish devotion to her son grates on my already frayed nerves. As do the constant texts about what colours, flowers, fabrics, blah, blah blah.

If there weren't more important things to worry about—like the fact I might end up married to a psychopath—I'd take the time to be annoyed. Who does she think she is? I'm a goddamn costume designer. This shit is my jam.

Lulu is loving the cloak and dagger stuff and puts on a big display of carrying flattened boxes into the apartment building from her obvious parking spot on the street.

"I really don't think Marco is having me followed," I gasp, struggling under the weight of the boxes and a wickedly sharp packing tape dispenser.

"You never know," she whispers back, looking over her shoulder to make sure we're alone in the lobby. "Besides, we do need to pack the rest of Nick's stuff sometime. But not this day," she squeaks with an un-Lulu-like giggle. I remember a time many months ago when she said those same words when talking about her tumultuous relationship with Nick. God, I love this woman. If we weren't laden down with all these boxes, I would hug the life out of her.

"I'll sneak out the back, and be back at four to pick you up," she says, keying in the passcode for the door and dropping the boxes in the front hall of Nick's apartment. "Have fun." She darts back to the lift, sliding her hands between the doors seconds before they close.

"Ben?" I call, unsure if he's here yet. And then he's there. Right in front of me, smiling like I'm the best thing he's ever seen.

"Should I even ask what that's all about?" He points to the pile of boxes beside me.

"Lulu thought we needed a disguise. In case Marco was watching." I roll my eyes and walk into his open arms.

"As talented as she is, she's wasted as an artist. She could have a brilliant career with ASIO," he murmurs against my neck, causing a delighted shiver to run up my spine and tingle my scalp. "I should feed you. I have lunch ready. But all I want to do is ..." He pauses, running his hands down my back to my arse, pressing me against him. Against his rock-hard erection.

I can barely breathe. "All you want to do is ...?"

"You," he growls, lifts me up, wraps my legs around his waist and carries me through the apartment to a bedroom. I don't have time to take in anything more than the softness of the cool sheets because Ben is laying me down, stretching out over me, his hands and mouth everywhere at once.

He rises above me, and his gaze roams my face, blue eyes so alight with emotion it seems like they're shooting sparks.

"How do you want it? Hard and fast, or slow and gentle?"

I take a moment to gather my thoughts. To find my words. "I want it all."

And I think, I hope, he knows I'm not just talking about now. About sex. Because for the first time in my life, I understand what having it all could be. And I really do want it all.

"All it is," his voice is a low rumble. Like magic, my clothes disappear item by item until I'm naked. And he's covering every inch of my skin with wet, open-mouthed, sucking kisses. As though he wants to devour me. Inhale me.

My hands shove at his clothes. It's clumsy and desperate, but I can't wait and it seems he can't either.

Once his pants are gone, chucked carelessly across the room to who knows where, he grinds his cock against my mound. Short, sharp, hard movements that beg me to match them.

By the time he reaches for a condom from the box on the bedside table, moisture is trickling down my thighs.

With a quick flick, Ben turns me over and slides an arm under my hips. Hoisting my arse in the air, he groans as he slams into me. It's so fast and furious I can barely catch my breath. His thrusts are sharp and hard. One hand holds my hip, while the fingers of the other find my clit to press and rub in time with Ben's frantic thrusts.

It's over for both of us in minutes. No sooner do my muscles reach maximum tension and then release with a jolt, like a tightly coiled spring, than Ben is roaring, buried deep. I can feel the pulse of his orgasm filling the condom as my muscles twitch and spasm around him.

Gently, he slides me forward so I'm stretched out on top of the doona. Ben's draped over my back, our skin stuck together with sweat.

How I've gone all my life without experiencing this kind of release is beyond me. Because as useful as bedroom toys, and my own hand, have been, nothing compares to the hands and mouth and dick of Benedict Carter.

After taking care of the condom, Ben gathers me close and we snuggle. Catching our breath and enjoying the post-coital bliss.

Until Ben weaves his fingers through mine and finds Marco's engagement ring.

Lifting my hand, he tries to slip it off my finger. But as I've already discovered, it's stuck tight.

"I hate that you're wearing this when you're with me," he mutters.

"Me too. But it's stuck." I turn my hand, marvelling at how gaudy it is.

Without a word, he slides his fingers through my folds, still swollen and sensitive and very wet. And before I know what he's about, he's smearing my finger with the moisture he picked up. Along my finger and around the ring before twisting and working the white gold up over my knuckle and off. He drops the ring onto the bedside table, then pulls my now red and slightly swollen finger into his mouth, licking and sucking away the sting and my own moisture. It's not a lie to say I almost come all over again, because that was so damn hot.

"Much better," he mumbles around my finger.

Suddenly I want to be sucking him, and not his finger. Pushing him onto his back, I climb between his thighs. He's already at least half-mast when I lick from base to tip before taking the head in my mouth and sucking. It was only a couple of weeks ago I first did this, but I got plenty of practice that weekend, and judging from Ben's response, I picked it up quickly. I don't know if the key to giving a good blowjob is enjoying it, but I love the feel of him in my mouth. The control and the power it gives me.

I suck rhythmically, inching my way lower, working him towards the back of my mouth. His hips rise off the bed in time with my sucking, soft moans building, letting me know he's getting close.

And then Ben's pulling away, rolling on top of me and handing me a condom to put on him before he slides into me. Long, slow glides. Fingers working my nipples. Gaze glued to mine.

My orgasm builds. Layer by layer. Inch by inch, until it rolls over me like a warmed blanket, stealing my breath and bringing tears to my eyes.

Ben pulls out, tears off the condom and, searching for my left hand, strokes himself to completion, coming across my palm and ring finger in long, hot bursts.

"Better still," he gasps, closing my fist around his cum.

That was the sexiest, hottest, most romantic thing I've ever heard of, much less experienced.

Back-to-back orgasms take it out of you, and we drift into a lazy, spoony cuddle, barely awake. It's on the tip of my tongue to tell Ben how I'm feeling. But my gaze catches on the ring Marco gave me, sitting big and ugly on the bedside table. Symbolising the big ugly thing keeping Ben and me apart. Now is not the time. I don't want the first time to say I love you to be tainted by Marco and all that's going to happen over the next few weeks. You only get to say it the first time once. And I want it to be perfect. Because I might not have much experience with relationships, but I know enough to understand that for me, Ben is it.

The rumbling of a stomach rouses us from our doze. Ugh. Embarrassing. It's my stomach.

"Hungry are we? Lunch should still be warm."

We have a quick shower, and once we're dressed, Ben takes my hand and leads me through the apartment to an enormous dining table set for two. Complete with flowers, a bottle of champagne in an ice bucket, serving plates under domed cloches, and a baking dish on a warming tray.

I can't believe how much trouble he's gone to, although he claims it was nothing since it was ordered in.

Lunch is a luscious cherry and burrata salad, followed by chicken breasts in a light lemon butter and a green salad. It's delicious. For the first time in over a week, thanks to Ben and the orgasms and food he so beautifully delivered, I'm relaxed. Despite everything that's hanging over us, dark and unresolved.

We're finishing our coffee, curled together on the sofa, when we hear the door open.

"I'm baaack. Is it safe to come in?" Lulu calls

"Yes, it's safe," I respond. But as she appears in the lounge-room, she jumps and slaps her hand against her mouth, eyes round and brimming with mischief.

"What?" I look down at myself and Ben. We're both fully clothed. Nothing to see here.

"That sofa. That's, well ... *the* sofa."

I can barely breathe for laughing. Ben and I are sitting on the very same sofa where Lulu and Nick first consummated their relationship.

"What am I missing?" Ben is bemused.

"You know what happened on that sofa, don't you, Ro? You'd better get up. Quick smart." Lulu gurgles.

"What happened on this sofa?" Ben makes no move to unfold his long legs from mine.

"Isla the Wonderchild, that's what," Lulu answers, and now all three of us are laughing.

"I hope you've had it dry-cleaned since then," Ben bursts out.

"Never mind the dry-cleaning, just keep a track of your dates, people." Which cracks us up all over again.

CHAPTER THIRTY-FOUR

BENEDICT

My afternoon with Rosanna was pure bliss. Not much beats orgasms, good food and a good laugh. I'm pretty relaxed when I arrive home, despite the niggling worry. Rosanna is coping with this whole situation like a boss. And I'm confident that once Pete gains Marco's trust, things will move quickly.

It's good to know Lulu is on the inside with her. She agreed to go with Rosanna this evening to try and be the voice of reason and slow the train down as much as possible. She'll let me know if Rosanna is struggling. We agreed Rosie can't push back too hard and risk stirring Marco up. To some extent, she'll need to go along with it all, which means keeping up a brave front, regardless of how hard this is getting for her. It can't be easy worrying about her father's failing health while all this shitfuckery is going on.

I spend the rest of the weekend pacing and fretting and combing through the evidence we have so far. Whilst it's enough to get him into trouble, and possibly enough for the police to investigate, it's not enough to ensure Andrea doesn't get hit with the backwash. Protecting him is almost as important as protecting Rosanna.

On Sunday night, Pete comes over to talk through the plans for his conversation with Marco tomorrow in detail. I'm leaving nothing to chance. And there's something else I need to discuss with him.

Because if—no, when—Marco is taken out of the picture, Moretti's will be left with a big vacuum. Rosanna won't want to take it on. And Andrea isn't in a position to return to the level of work required to run a company.

I've invested in all kinds of things. Apps, clubs, restaurants, even a band that blew up on Spotify and now make huge bank. But I've never invested in property development. I don't know anything about it. Lucky for all of us, Pete does. He develops property all over Sydney. If Pete isn't the solution, he'll know where I can find one.

I don't want to take over Rosie's life. Or make her feel like I'm trying to control her or her family's business. But if I could give her some viable options on what to do with the business once Marco is gone, I'd be happy.

Monday morning dawns with ominous black clouds on the horizon. If I was the superstitious sort, I might be worried. But I choose to believe the clouds are a reflection of Marco's soul. Or lack thereof.

At five to eleven, Pete is in place at the café where they've agreed to meet. Sitting in the seat that will ensure Marco has to sit where we get the best camera angle for him. I'm in the upstairs office of a café a few doors down, watching the feed already up on my screen. It's a handy thing to be so well connected in the hospitality industry.

In the kind of powerplay only used by the desperately insecure or unbelievably arrogant, Marco arrives ten minutes late.

"Sorry I'm late," he mutters in a tone that indicates he's anything but.

"No problem, Marco. I was catching up on some emails," Pete says jovially, standing to shake the snake's hand.

"So, what can I do for you?" Marco settles in with a short black, leaning back in his chair and crossing his legs like he hasn't a care in the world. Which I guess he doesn't. Yet.

"I've got a deal in the works on the North Shore. Right between the train line and the highway." Pete opens up a map on his tablet, showing a prime site, outlined in red. "Problem is, I've got all my spare funds tied up in other projects at the moment. This needs to move fast. So, I'm looking for a partner." Pete runs him briefly through his ideas for the site.

Through the hidden pin and pen transmitters, I see Marco's eyes light up. I'm not a developer, but even I know a location like that is a licence to print money if you do it right.

"I was wondering if you might take it to Andrea and have a chat. See what he thinks." Oh, Pete is good. Give Marco the opportunity to talk himself up. Perfect.

"No need to take it to old man Moretti. I'm in charge. Have been for a while now. We're waiting on some final paperwork to be sorted out, but the business is mine. I make all the decisions." Marco's chest puffs up like a deluded pigeon.

"That's good news. Having a hungry young buck like you at the helm." It's lucky I'm a couple of doors away because I can't hold back the laugh. Wait till I show Rosie this footage. She'll wet herself.

"I'm glad you can appreciate the change, Pete. So, what were you thinking, deal-wise?"

"I was thinking seventy/thirty."

"Nah, I don't think so. A development of this size will tie up a lot of my funds and my trades. I'd need at least fifty/fifty," Marco counters.

They get down to haggling, and Pete puts up a good fight, but Marco is relentless. Finally, they reach a handshake agreement on fifty-five/forty-five. Pete was born to this caper. If I didn't know firsthand what a tough negotiator he really is, I'd be impressed by Marco's ability to grind him down. Based on Marco's smirk, he's plenty impressed with himself. If I'd written the script myself, it couldn't have gone any better.

Like a pro, as they're leaving the table, Pete throws out the bait.

"It's a shame we had to amend the original DA. Council wouldn't come to the party. For another couple of hundred thou, we could've banked another mil at least. Still, it's a good deal as is."

And then he's out of there. Leaving Marco with nothing more than a whisper of an idea. A seed that needs watering.

Tomorrow, or maybe the next day, we break out the watering can.

CHAPTER THIRTY-FIVE

ROSANNA

I t's torture to sit at the dining table with my mother and Fernanda on Saturday night, trying to show enthusiasm for a fake wedding I know won't be going ahead. Surrounded by bridal magazines, fabric swatches and bonbonniere samples. It almost ruins the high I'm on from spending the afternoon with Ben. Almost.

"*Cara mia*, you are glowing. It must be excitement about the wedding," Fernanda observes. If only they knew. I try to hold back a snort, and Lulu claps me on the back.

"Went down the wrong way, did it?" She takes the glass of wine I'm sipping from my hands.

Thank goodness for Lulu.

It's tempting to abdicate all responsibility and decisions to the mothers, but I can't do that without raising suspicions, so I use my 'wilfulness', as Fernanda has started to call it, to attempt to delay and postpone.

I spent a lot of time this week searching for things that were out of stock, difficult to produce or generally unavailable for delivery on such short notice. Much to the confusion of the suppliers, who are used to brides begging for delivery. As it turns out, the stationery I *have to have* can't be ready in time. Shame. The *only* florist who can do the flowers I want isn't available on the date Marco has picked. Damn. The fabric I *need* for the dress has to be ordered from overseas. No! But for every roadblock I put up, Fernanda offers a solution.

I pout and sulk and turn myself into a bridezilla, refusing every alternative, while Lulu pretends to mediate.

"The wedding is not the important thing, *cara mia*. The marriage is what is important," Fernanda says, squeezing my cheeks like some 1950s nonna. "And soon you will be married to my beautiful Marco. Making me pretty grandbabies. This is what you need to focus on."

I throw up a little in my mouth. Christ knows what horrible STI could be lurking on Marco's peen. Even if by some horrible stroke of fate the wedding did go ahead, there is no way I'd be letting that thing anywhere near me.

"This is my wedding. I'm the bride. I should get to choose." I stop short of stamping my foot. I'm really getting into this bridezilla thing. Maybe I missed my calling. If it weren't for the underlying fear that all our efforts might fail, I would almost say I'm enjoying myself.

"Of course, you're right, Fernanda. But what girl doesn't dream of the perfect wedding?" Lulu interrupts. "Surely an extra week or two for Rosanna to have the wedding she's always dreamed of isn't too much to ask?" She flashes her sparkly dimples at Fernanda.

Apparently, it is too much because Marco is immediately consulted, no doubt interrupting a blow job or spanking, and he holds firm. So, Ben now has three and a half weeks to get this wrapped up.

I feel guilty about my parents paying deposits for caterers and cars and flowers for no reason whatsoever, but it can't be helped. Marco wouldn't hesitate to carry out his threats. Assuming the news of his treachery didn't kill Dad first. I have to be patient and wait for Ben to get the evidence he needs to sort all this out.

I make sure everything I suggest is the complete opposite of what I would want at my actual wedding. I don't know when or if I'll ever get married, but I want there to be no reminders of this debacle when I do.

Sometimes I catch my mother looking at me oddly as though she knows something is amiss, but she never says anything. She's so worried about Dad, who spends a good part of the day in bed now; I don't think she wants to say or do anything to cause an argument.

Dad's breathing gets more laboured every day, and the only time he seems truly peaceful is when he talks about how soon I will be Marco's wife and he can rest easy knowing I'm taken care of. Which is the only thing that stops me from running to him for support in postponing the wedding. I need to tough this out myself.

It boggles my mind how such a clever man has been so thoroughly hoodwinked by a snake like Marco. Then again, I guess I was fooled for a while too. Never in my wildest dreams did I expect the depths of his hideousness.

I've done a lot of thinking as I lie awake at night, missing Ben. It's embarrassing to realise I've been going through life with my eyes closed for the past few years, and it's my own choices that have led me here. Initially, my insecurity, which Marco spotted and used to manipulate me, and then my need to keep my father happy. Ben's analogy of the frog being put into cold water is right. Looking back, I can't pinpoint the moment when the gaslighting and control started. It crept up on me. Which is a hallmark of narcissistic abuse. I thank the universe every day for that visit to the bathroom. And for Benedict.

One thing that strikes me as odd is that Mum never mentions Ben, not even to Lulu. She clearly took to him in the hospital, but she hasn't once asked after him since then. I wonder if my mother has a suspicion, but I have no idea how to bring it up. We're rarely left alone since Fernanda has made it her mission to control the entire wedding and, by extension, me. I'd never noticed until now what an interfering and domineering woman she is. I guess I know where Marco gets his sparkling personality.

On the way home, I think about the grief I gave Lulu when she and Nick were dancing around their feelings, and I want to curl up in a ball. Or call her and apologise. Which I do as soon as I get home.

Lulu laughs.

"It's much easier to see other people's shit for what it is than your own. Don't beat yourself up. Besides, I needed to hear everything you said. If it wasn't for you, I'd probably be a single mum, and Nick would be clueless about his baby girl." Who takes this moment to squeal down the phone at me.

"That is absolutely not true," I disagree. "*You* might not have pulled your head out of your arse, but Nick came after you, and he sure as shit wasn't going to take no for an answer." Which is absolutely true.

"Fair. But the fact remains, it's easier to see the situation when you're not living it yourself. The important thing is, you've seen it now. And all this will soon be ancient history we can laugh about."

"I hope so."

On Monday night when Marco picks me up from work, his smug grin would tell me everything I need to know about how Pete's meeting with him went if Ben hadn't already filled me in. It's hard to keep the smile off my face. If he had any idea what was about to happen, he wouldn't strut into my parents' house like a rooster with a new hen.

It's this puffed-up confidence that causes him to overplay his hand as Mum brings out the desserts.

"Andrea, since it's only a matter of weeks until your daughter and I are married, I think now is a good time to take care of the paperwork for the business."

I nearly choke on my panna cotta as Marco brings his brief-case to the table, pulls out a sheaf of papers and hands them to Dad with a flourish.

I stand and read over Dad's shoulder. Transfer of Business Ownership. Right there in big, bold letters. And my name? Nowhere to be seen. Just Dad transferring full ownership and operation to Marco. Holy crap, this guy has some balls.

"No, Marco. *Questo non è giusto*. We will do this on your *giorno del matrimonio.*" Dad hands the papers back, confident that will be the last word on the subject.

I can't believe nobody else can see the glittering malice in Marco's eyes.

"But Andrea, our wedding day will be so busy. We will be focused on our joy. Not business. It's best to get this done now." Of course it is. Before he signs a deal with Pete. Or so he thinks.

"No, there will be time on the day. And these papers, they are *sono sbagliati*. The business will go to you both."

Marco now looks in danger of having a stroke.

"That is ridiculous, Andrea. Rosanna has no head for business." Oops. Marco's emotions are getting the best of him.

"*È ridicolo lasciare i miei affari alla mia unica figlia?*" Dad is getting impatient. He might be old school, but of course he's questioning why Marco would expect the company to be left to him alone. He's also not used to being questioned. Mum is scowling. She doesn't like it when Dad's pronouncements are questioned.

Marco is now scrambling to recover the situation. "I only meant that Rosanna doesn't need to be worried about the business. She will be busy with the babies."

But Dad won't be moved. Despite his age and ailing health, my father is still a stubborn man.

"No. It will wait." Dad crosses his arms, and even Marco knows that means the discussion is over. I can see him weighing his next move. Whether to push or let it slide.

The decision is taken out of Marco's hands by my mother, who picks up the sheaf of papers and hands it back to him.

"We will do as Andrea says."

I'm torn between glee that Marco has been thwarted and fear it will cause him to lash out. Because it will probably be me in the firing line.

The rest of the evening passes in tense silence, with Fernanda trying in vain to interest us in wedding planning. I'm relieved when, as soon as the table has been cleared, Marco makes his excuses and we leave.

Marco doesn't say a word in the car on the way home until I'm climbing out of the car in front of my building.

"Your father is being ridiculous. I expect you to speak to him and convince him to sign those papers." The desperation in his voice almost makes me laugh.

"Hmm. Now, why would I do that?"

"Because it won't go well for you if you don't."

Now I do laugh.

"It's not going well for me already, you bastard. Force his hand and you might lose what leverage you have. I'd tread carefully if I were you."

I turn my back, walk up the steps and let myself into the building without a second glance. I can't wait to tell Ben about tonight's developments.

The rest of the week drags by. Ben keeps me posted about the progress they're making with their investigations.

Marco keeps me locked down tight, often picking me up from work and taking me to either my parents' or his mother's for dinner and to discuss the preparations. His mood is sullen, but there's no more mention of signing over the company. Maybe Marco isn't always as dumb as we think.

Ben tells me that, after Marco drops me home each night, he heads out to all sorts of nasty nightclubs and does things I don't even want to think about.

My appetite has completely fled. Lulu teases me about why her appetite disappeared, but I get my period mid-week, so I know it's not that.

"You've lost weight," Julie, the receptionist, observes as I arrive at work on Thursday morning. "Trying to squeeze yourself into a smaller size for the wedding?" I turn and run my gaze up and down her bony frame.

The vague impression I've had about her relationship with Marco coalesces into knowledge. I have no hard proof other than the flirty vibe I've only just twigged to. But now I know what I do, I can see she's exactly his type. Duh. How clueless I've been.

"Some men like a woman to look like a woman, not a twelve-year-old boy." My response is catty, but this woman has always rubbed me the wrong way, and now I know why. It's also not entirely accurate, because a twelve-year-old boy wouldn't typically have a double D cup. Even if they are artificial.

"Not Marco," she mutters as she turns away, confirming there was, and maybe still is, something going on between them. The thought Julie has probably slept with my then-boyfriend—and supposed fiancé—is humiliating, to say the least. But she's welcome to him. Maybe I should give her the number of the local sexual health clinic. She's probably going to need it.

When Marco comes to pick me up that evening, I make sure I'm waiting in reception and I don't miss the look they give one another. It's so obvious, now that I'm looking for it. This guy is the gift that keeps on giving. Hooking up with one of my colleagues? He's got to be kidding. But it's a good reminder to be careful what I say and where I say it. Because the walls could well have ears.

CHAPTER THIRTY-SIX

BENEDICT

Why does the shit always hit the fan on a Friday afternoon?

The week had been inching along with slow but steady progress. Tama was reporting Marco's continued odious behaviour. Pete was dropping subtle hints, which Marco was gobbling up, and it was business as usual from Sabrina.

Until it wasn't.

"We may have a problem, Ben." Sabrina's words are not at all welcome. My spine stiffens, and I reach for my laptop.

"Speak to me." I'm logging on to our encrypted share drive as I speak.

"Cockhead has just received an email from the tax office. They're opening an investigation into his tax returns and those of the consultancy he runs Bob Pacino through."

That gets me up out of my chair.

"Fuck," I shout.

"Yeah. Fuck," Sab agrees, somewhat less violently. "He hasn't seen it yet, but when he does, he'll go nuclear."

"Okay. I need to think. Let me know if and when he sees the email. In the meantime, I'll get everyone together. You free in half an hour or so?" I'm pacing and pulling my hair so hard it hurts.

"On standby." Sab hangs up, and I throw my coffee cup at the wall. At least it was empty.

Forty minutes later, Will and Nick are in my apartment, Pete is on speaker phone and Sabrina is on video call. I'm so grateful to these guys. They all drop everything whenever I need them.

My first action after throwing the coffee cup and calling a team meeting was to message Rosanna and ask her to call me when she can. I need to speak to her. Warn her Marco might be more volatile than usual. But she hasn't seen the message yet, which worries me. When she first got the phone, we agreed on no unannounced calls in case she was with Marco, or someone else who might get suspicious. She always calls back as soon as she can.

This whole thing is coming to a head faster than any of us expected, thanks to the Australian Tax Office.

"Once the ATO get their teeth into you, there's no letting go," Will pipes up from his seat at what we've been referring to as Command Central. Otherwise known as my dining table.

"No shit, Sherlock." My frame of mind hasn't been improved by my inability to get in touch with Rosanna.

"He opened the email about twenty minutes ago," Sabrina confirms.

Checking my phone, I realise that would be about the time he typically picks Rosie up from work. The confluence of those two events scares me.

I check with Tama, who confirms they left Ro's office a couple of minutes ago, and Marco appeared agitated.

"Stay close," I tell Tama unnecessarily, knowing he wouldn't dream of losing sight of them.

"I've given Jeff Williams at Fraud the heads-up that things have escalated. Just in case. He's standing by." Will drops into the tense silence. Thank Christ, he thought of that. I have a feeling we might need him.

Nick has been quiet. Listening to the tape of Pete's conversation with Marco earlier today, in which he reiterated he'd been running Moretti's solo for nearly two years and boasted Andrea Moretti had no input whatsoever. But the nugget of gold was his suggestion he has a good relationship with certain councillors, and if Pete could send him the original DA, he was sure he could get them to take a more 'favourable' view of it. Not quite a smoking gun, but with everything else we have, it's pretty close.

"I want to run through this again," Nick starts, handing the headphones to Will for his opinion. "But I think we might have enough in this conversation to keep Andrea's name clean. What do you think, Will?"

There's a tense silence as Will listens to the audio, exchanging a couple of loaded glances with Nick.

"Yeah. It's line ball."

"It is. But if we get the right prosecutor and judge ..." Nick pauses.

"Given today's developments, I think it's a risk we have to take," Will finishes for him.

It's late Friday afternoon. But we've already primed the Fraud Squad. Do we move or do we wait? For several long heartbeats, we look at each other, weighing the risks. I see the moment we come to the same conclusion, all at once. Will laughs. Actually laughs.

"The shit is going to hit the fan tonight, guys. Time to get our hazmat suits on."

CHAPTER THIRTY-SEVEN

ROSANNA

It's obvious something has happened when Marco picks me up on Friday afternoon. He's in an even fouler mood than usual and drives like a madman. He's an aggressive driver at the best of times, which combines beautifully with the overpowering smell of his cologne to make being in a car with him less than pleasant. But today he's tailgating, speeding, running very orange lights. To the point where I have to grab the handle above the door as he sails through a stop sign without stopping.

"Marco!" I can't hold in the gasp of fear.

Another coat of paint and we'd have collected a minivan full of school kids.

"Shut the fuck up," Marco snarls, shoving the car into fifth gear and swerving back and forth between lanes.

By the time we get to my parents' place, I'm shaken, both physically and emotionally. Something has set him off. I desperately want to talk to Ben, but I'm not game to sneak a peek at my burner with Marco in this explosive mood.

Normally, it's like a switch flicks. In the car with me he's rude, dismissive and arrogant. But as soon as we walk through the door of my parents', or his, the smooth, suave façade goes up. Not today. He's surly and uncommunicative.

Mum looks anxious and keeps darting worried glances at me. Trying to sweeten his mood, she fusses, offering his favourite snacks and drinks one after the other. Only to be met with a curt no. Dad looks confused. He's used to Marco being polite to the point of obsequious.

By the time Fernanda arrives, there's so much pressure in my head I feel like it might split like a dropped watermelon.

Oblivious to Marco's mood, Fernanda launches into wedding chatter. How many guests. The invitations must go out on Monday, Tuesday at the latest. The bonbonnieres I've chosen are not 'impressive' enough. We need something better. One band is insufficient. We should hire a second one. Or perhaps a DJ? On and on and on.

It only takes a few minutes for Marco to break.

"*Merda, basta!* We don't need all this ridiculous expense. I am cancelling the entire thing." My heart soars. He's had enough. I'll be free. Dad will be safe. "Rosanna and I will go to the registry office on Monday and get married without all this fuss."

There's a moment of silence, during which I'm sure I hear my heart, which had taken flight and was circling the ceiling, splat on the floor at my feet. Then chaos erupts.

Crying, pleading, shouting, demanding, wheedling, whining, cursing. English. Italian. I'm the only one who's silent. Until Marco bellows, "*Tranquillo!*" And again, there's silence, except for the wheezing breath of my father, whose face is a mottled red. He's trying to stand, grabbing at the worn old arms of his recliner.

"I don't wish to wait. I don't wish to spend so much money on stupid things like bands and sugared almonds. I have decided. There will be no more discussion," Marco continues to shout. I'm about to respond when time lurches into slow motion.

My father topples forward, clutching his chest.

Mum screams and falls to the floor beside him.

I drop to my knees.

Somehow, I find the presence of mind to check Dad's oxygen levels.

Check his mask.

Wrap my fingers around his wrist to feel for his pulse.

It's bouncing around erratically. His oxygen levels are way too low.

His eyes start to roll back in his head as though he's going to lose consciousness.

Mum is crying, stroking the thin strands of his silvery hair back from his sweaty forehead.

My heart is thundering in my ears as I stand and turn to Marco. Something explodes inside me. The last fragile piece of me that was scared to stand up to him. Scared to fight. For fear of the consequences. All the venom that's been simmering in my soul pours out with my next words.

"If your greed and selfishness has caused my father any harm, I will make you regret the day you were born," I spit with all the virulence I can muster. Without a single thought to the outcome. Because if something happens to Dad, Marco's threats will mean nothing. This charade has gone on long enough.

There's a gasp from everyone as Marco's hand flies high. It's clear his intention is to backhand me. Part of me wants it. Wants him to show us all what he's capable of. Wants to have something concrete for *me* to lay at his feet. For *me* to destroy him with.

"I dare you," I growl, moving towards him so we're nose to nose. His arm falls, but the fury on his face remains.

Mum is weeping, and Dad is still struggling for breath on the floor. I grab my phone and call 000, ignoring Fernanda, who clings to Marco's arm, pleading with him in rapid-fire Italian to see sense.

No sooner have I hung up from the operator than Marco is turning to me. Like the narcissist he is, he doesn't yet realise his reign is over.

"You will never speak to me in that tone again. We will marry on Monday at the registry office, and I will hear no more about it. From any of you." His words— which would have scared me mere hours ago—flow past me like nothing more than filthy water in an overflowing gutter.

"Go to hell, you lying, cheating bastard. You no longer call the shots around here." I hear Fernanda cry out, but I can't worry about her now. All I can think about is Dad, whose chest is heaving, fingers digging into the carpet beneath him. And Mum, who is sobbing as though her heart is breaking. Neither of them even register what I've said.

"Mum, go and get his hospital bag." I pick her up off the floor and give her a gentle push towards their bedroom. I need to keep us both calm, and she's better with something practical to do. It's a sad thing that he has a permanently packed hospital bag these days.

The whole episode can't have taken more than a minute, but in that single minute, my heart has beat enough for twenty. My system is so flooded with adrenaline that I can't stop the shaking. However things go from here, I know the course of our lives has changed. I have to trust Ben has enough to protect Dad. I have to believe the ambulance will get here in time.

I hear sirens in the distance. It's a strange tableau, all of us standing around my parents' living room, silent now except for Dad's desperate gasps, Mum's quiet praying in Italian and Fernanda's sobs.

Marco stands immobile. Like a true bully, he has no idea what to do now I've stood up to him. I wish I'd done it years ago, instead of letting my insecurities and need to please others stop me.

The ambos clatter up the drive. They're the same guys who have been here a couple of times before.

"Hey there, Andrea. I hear you're not doing so well tonight," the older one says cheerfully, opening his bag and loading up a syringe, oblivious to the cause of the tension. "Remember me? I'm Gavin. Don't worry, we'll have you out of here and off to the Ritz in time for jelly and lukewarm tea."

Todd rattles up the steps with a trolley. As they're loading Dad onto it, we hear more sirens.

We're navigating the front steps when suddenly, the quiet, boring little suburban street is filled with blue flashing lights;

three unmarked cars screech to a stop on either side of the ambulance.

A tall, middle-aged guy shaped like a bear, with thick grey hair, a close-cropped beard and an ill-fitting suit strides up the front path.

"Marco Silvestri?"

We all turn to Marco, who looks terrified.

"Jeff Williams, Central Sydney Fraud Squad. You are under arrest for fraud, bribery, and tax evasion ..."

I hear another car door slam. I know before I even turn around who I'll see.

CHAPTER THIRTY-EIGHT

BENEDICT

I've hardly even had time to take in the chaotic scene in front of me when Rosanna is hurling herself into my arms.

"Ben. Thank God you're here," she sobs.

"Where else would I be, Rosie?" I whisper into her hair.

One of the detectives is slapping cuffs on Marco and bundling him into the car, while another drops Marco's phone into an evidence bag, and a third starts a search through his flashy sports car. Not far away, I know there's a team searching his apartment. Bundling up his computers and no doubt finding stashes of cash, cocaine and a whole host of other nasties. I hope they've had their shots.

I give Marco a contemptuous once-over, and before the cops have had the chance to slam the door on him, I lean down.

"Who's telling who what to do now, you piece of shit?" I ask with a wide grin.

Will and Nick are already deep in conversation with Jeff, no doubt consulting on the long list of accusations we have lined up against Marco.

A middle-aged woman I assume is Marco's mother is huddled on the front steps, sobbing into her hands. Andrea is being loaded into the ambulance, with Flavia talking a mile a minute to the ambos. She takes a moment as they get her husband settled to scuttle over to me.

"Oh, *Benedetto*. It is good you are here. You will bring Rosanna to the hospital, yes?"

"Of course, Flavia. Don't worry. You go with Andrea. We'll see you there shortly."

She turns and makes a spitting motion towards Marco, who is cowering in the back seat of the police car.

"Marco is a bad man. A man who would hit a woman deserves to rot in hell." After dropping that little bomb, she climbs up the steps of the ambulance and disappears.

"He hit you?" I screech, searching Rosie's face for signs of damage.

"No. He raised his hand, but he didn't hit me. I'll tell you about it later."

"You bet your arse you will," I respond, following her up the path to the house as the ambulance pulls away. She doesn't even spare a glance at Marco's mother. Whatever has gone on here tonight has pushed her way past her limit. "Grab your bag; I'll drive you to the hospital."

By the time we lock up the house and come back out, Marco's mother is gone, as are Marco and all but one of the police cars. All that's left of the madness is Nick and Will, still chatting to Jeff.

"I'm going to take Rosanna to the hospital. I'm assuming I can leave Marco in your capable hands?"

"Absolutely. Do what you gotta do. We've got this. I'll let Pete know what's gone on. And don't worry, Rosanna, Marco won't be seeing the light of day for a while." Will's grinning like a loon as though this has been the most exciting night of his life.

"Oh, by the way, you can add attempted assault to the list," I tell them.

"Might need another page on the charge sheet," Jeff jokes. It would be funny if it wasn't so true. And if it hadn't been such a close call.

Andrea is still in Emergency when we arrive at the hospital—it's a Friday night, after all—and since they only allow one person with the patient, Rosanna and I sit in the crowded waiting room while she tells me all about the events of the evening. I have to fight down the urge to throw up or throw a punch.

"If that fucker ever even looks at you again, I'll make his life such a living hell he'll wish he was dead." I've never before felt the kind of visceral anger and hatred I feel towards Marco. And I've dealt with some shady characters over the years.

"You'll have to get in line behind me because we crossed the Rubicon tonight. There will be no more trying to keep the peace or keep others happy. I'm done." Rosanna arcs up and with good reason. It soothes my anxiety to know she's angry rather than scared. "By the way, what made you bring the plan forward to tonight? I thought you were going to tell me when you had enough on him to arrest."

"Yeah, that was the plan, but events kind of overtook us." I fill her in on the email we intercepted from the ATO and how we realised there was no time to waste. I figure she doesn't need to know the roasting we got from Jeff about 'interfering with a carriage service'. I have no doubt Will and Nick will smooth it over somehow. "I did message you, but I'm guessing you were already with Marco."

I find I can't take my hands off her. One arm is over her shoulder, holding her close, the other rests across her lap, fingers entwined with hers.

The idea that Marco nearly hit her has me vibrating with rage. But hearing how she stood up to him? This woman has become a force of nature.

And all I want is to spend the rest of my life standing beside her.

CHAPTER THIRTY-NINE

ROSANNA

I t's well after midnight before Dad is settled in a ward and we leave the hospital. In the end they had to sedate him because every time he asked about Marco, he lost control of his breathing. But he's right where he needs to be for now.

Mum is exhausted, and I'm so grateful Ben is here to drive us home. A large part of me wants to go home with him and curl up in his arms. But I can't leave Mum alone. After checking in with Nick and Will to make sure Marco will not be out on bail until Monday at the earliest, Ben reluctantly agrees to go home. As long as Tama is out the front.

As I'm putting Mum to bed, she clasps my hand against her cheek.

"*Tesoro*," she says. "In the morning, you and Benedetto will tell me everything."

"Ben has gone home, Mum."

"*Si, si*. But he will be back. I see the way he looks at you, *cara mia*. I see the way you look at him. He will always be back."

Suddenly the reason Mum never mentioned Ben hits me. She knew. All along. Yet she was just as trapped as me. I kiss her forehead softly in wordless thanks.

"I love you, Mum," I whisper.

Mum was right, as mothers often are. Ben's back again at eight am, with coffee and pastries and the news Marco has been formally charged with a long list of monumentally bad decisions.

We sit at the kitchen table, and Mum gets the G rated version of the events that have unfolded over the past few weeks. I don't hold back on dropping shit on Marco. He earned it fair and square.

Recounting everything reminds me of Marco's threats. Everything happened in such a rush yesterday that I forgot Dad could be in trouble. I have no idea if Ben and his friends had time to sort that out. A lead weight forms in my stomach.

"What about Dad, Ben? Will you be able to protect him? Will he be implicated?"

"When he's well enough, the police will want to interview him. But it's clear he had no idea what was going on. Given his ill health, we don't expect any consequences."

"Who will run the company now?" Mum starts to fret. "Andrea is too ill. Now Marco is gone, who will take care of things?"

"It's okay, Mum. We'll work it out," I say, although I have no earthly idea how.

"How will we work it out? I know nothing about business." Tears are leaking down her face, and she's wringing her hands. She's tired and emotional. It's no wonder she's working herself up into a state. I need to nip this in the bud.

"We'll hire someone." I realise how lame that sounds. This is so far outside my wheelhouse that I know I'll be lost, but I also know I will do what needs to be done. "Ben will help us. He's very clever with business. He'll give us the right advice." I say it without a second thought. It occurs to me I've assumed Ben will be able to help, will *want* to help, and I look across the table at him. I'm about to apologise for making an assumption when I notice the pride on his face, and I realise how much my faith in his ability means to him.

"You don't need to worry, Flavia. When Andrea is well enough, we'll talk to him, but I have a friend who might be interested in buying the business. If that's what you all want."

"*Molto bene*, this is good. You are a good man, Benedetto." Mum pats him on the cheek and hops up from the table, grabs her handbag and goes to the front door to wait for us to take her to the hospital.

"A friend?" I ask quietly. Maybe there's a friend. Maybe it's Ben. I'm not sure I like the idea it might be him bailing us out because Dad and I couldn't see Marco for the lying, cheating thief he is.

Ben grins. "We'll talk about it later, Rosie." I smile at the nickname only Ben has ever called me. It feels like safety.

At the hospital, Dad is agitated. We had planned to avoid talking about Marco, but he won't settle until we fill him in on all that's happened.

"*Mi dispiace tanto*," he weeps. "Flavia warned me. She said she had a bad feeling about Marco. But I wouldn't listen. And now look." Which is news to me. I shoot Mum a quick glance, and she shrugs. Dad has always been the boss. I wish she'd stood up to him more. I wish I'd questioned him more.

"No need to be sorry. He had everyone fooled," Ben tells him, before leaving Mum and me to spend the rest of the morning reassuring Dad.

Ben insists Mum and I visit the police station on Sunday morning and take out an AVO against Marco. This confuses poor Mum, who has had more excitement in the past two days than in her entire life. And not the good kind.

"But Marco is in prison," she says as we sign the paperwork. "This is just a piece of paper. What good can it do?"

"Yes, it is just a piece of paper. But he may get bail, Flavia. And if he does, this paper means he can't come near you, or he'll be sent right back to jail. Tama will be keeping a careful eye on you, but it's best to be safe, isn't it?" Ben is so patient with her.

I've heard too many horror stories of AVOs being ignored to have faith in the 'piece of paper'. What I do have faith in are Tama and his boys. And Ben.

She beams at Ben, pats his cheek and hands him the forms. "You know best, Benedetto."

It looks like she's gone from deferring to my father to deferring to Ben. Which she never did with Marco. She might be the obedient Italian wife, and she might be clueless about business and the law, but my mother is no dummy.

Bloody hell. She's fallen in love with Ben too. I can't blame her.

It's Monday morning before the doctors think Dad is stable enough for police questioning. Will and Nick insist on being present while Mum, Ben, Lulu, Isla, and I all wait in the noisy hospital cafeteria. We choose a table with a clear line of sight across the foyer to the bank of lifts and wait. We pick at friands nobody—other than Isla—wants, making tense small talk. All except for Ben, who appears as relaxed as ever. Very little seems to faze him. Except for coming face to face with Marco. And I'm with him there.

It's an anxious couple of hours before the lift doors open. Will emerges, grinning from ear to ear, followed by the police officers. Nick brings up the rear with his customary serious expression. I can tell the minute he spots Lulu and Isla. It's corny, but it's like the sun comes out, a rainbow appears and unicorns dance across his eyes all at once.

I never had that with Marco. Not once did he look at me like that. I guess now I know why. But I want it. In fact, I want it from Ben.

I know it's too soon. We've made no promises on either side. I know he spends his life jet setting around the world. I know women hit on him constantly. Hell, he could have anyone he wants, I'm sure. None of that means anything to me. Because I want Ben. I want to be the unicorn in *his* eyes. Once all this shit with Dad and Marco and the business is sorted out, I'm going to tell him so.

The officers join the line for coffee, no doubt exhausted by my father's rantings about Marco, and leave the rest of us standing in the cavernous, echoing foyer. Will and Nick assure us things went as well as could be expected with Dad. I see the exhale of relief from all of us before everyone starts asking questions at once. One minute it's all friendly chatter, and the next, Ben's face morphs into a mask of hatred as he stares over my shoulder.

"Well, well, well. What have we here?"

Sadly, I'll never forget that spiteful voice.

I turn and face Marco.

Before anyone can react, he charges at me, screaming. "You bitch. You'll pay for what you've done to me."

Pandemonium breaks out.

Nick pushes Lulu and Isla behind him.

Will darts off towards the coffee line, presumably to alert the officers.

Ben steps in front of me and my mother, arms wide in protection. But right now, I don't need his protection. I need closure.

I step out from behind Ben's arms.

"You will never speak to me in that tone again." Before he has time to react, my hand is flying through the air, connecting with his cheek with a satisfying crack that reverberates around the entire foyer.

I hear a 'whoop' from Lulu as one of the uniformed officers grabs Marco from behind before he can even raise his clenched fist, and Ben steps in front of me again, ready to take the blow. The plain-clothes officers who interviewed Dad finally converge on our dramatic little tableau.

"Looks to me like you've violated the terms of your parole, Mr Silvestri." It seems Jeff has a dry sense of humour. "Not to mention two AVOs. And in full view of multiple witnesses and security cameras. Not the sharpest, are you?"

"She hit me. That's assault," Marco screams.

"Yeah, it looked more like self-defence to me," Jeff says calmly. "But you're welcome to take it up with your lawyer," he finishes as a junior officer slaps the cuffs on Marco again.

· ♥ · ♥ · ♥ · ♥ ·

The police take our statements about what happened while we sit in the coffee shop. They get Mum's over with first so she can go back upstairs and sit with Dad.

Marco is in the corner, handcuffed and flanked by the junior officers while they wait for a paddy wagon. Most of the fight seems to have gone out of him. Jeff Williams has let him know in no uncertain terms he won't be walking free anytime soon, thanks to this morning's little stunt.

Lulu gets a cold compress for my hand from the café staff, who had front-row seats to the show, and bring me a complimentary cup of tea and a muffin. Surprisingly, the appetite that had been missing earlier is back in full force and I wolf it down.

I don't use the compress. I relish the sting of my palm. It's a reminder to never again allow anyone to treat me the way Marco did.

CHAPTER FORTY

BENEDICT

I've walked a fine line all weekend. Actually, it was more of a dotted line where stuff kept leaking through the gaps. I wanted to be there to support Rosanna and her parents, but I also wanted to give them the space they needed as a family.

The Marco bombshell won't be easy for them to navigate. The tangled web of business and personal. The breaking of trust. The worry about Andrea's health. The precarious situation this has left the business in. I came and went. I picked them up and dropped them off. I made sure they ate. I arranged for AVOs on Marco. And I held in all the rage I feel about him. About how Andrea didn't see what a liar he is, and how Flavia kept quiet about her fears and let her husband make decisions that ultimately put Rosanna in danger.

I know there is no way they could've predicted the lengths Marco would go to, but that doesn't mitigate my anger.

What does help is seeing Rosanna take control and slap him from here to Christmas in front of dozens of onlookers when he stupidly arrives at the hospital. I make a mental note to get a copy of the security footage because that will be worth watching over and over again. Between that and the footage of his meetings with Pete, I'm gathering quite the movie night collection.

Once the police have taken our statements and carted Marco off—again—Nick and Will finally have the time to fully debrief us on the outcome of the police interview with Andrea. I'm checking with Rosanna about what she wants to do now when Will takes me aside.

"Nick and Lulu are going to take point with the Moretti's this afternoon. You're coming with me."

"What? Where?"

"To the nearest bar. We're going to get shitfaced, and you're going to let it all out."

"All what out?" He can't possibly know how much I've been bottling up.

"All everything. The anger, the resentment, the fear. All of it. And then, if we're sober enough, we're going to work out how to tell Mum and Dad what you've been up to for the past ten years without Dad having a stroke and Mum having a nervous breakdown."

I want to argue. I want to stay with Rosanna. But Will is having none of it. At least I know I can trust Nick and Lulu to keep her safe.

We say our farewells. I kiss Rosanna on the forehead, and her chocolate gaze finds mine. She doesn't need to ask if I'm okay. And neither do I. Because we're not. Yet. But we will be.

The bar Will chooses could best be described as scungy. It's dark and quiet, and the barman gives us a bottle of top-shelf whisky and two glasses without batting an eye. Which might have something to do with Will's sharp suit. Or his ostentatious Tag Heuer Nanograph watch. Or maybe it's the black Amex he slaps on the bar without a second thought.

"So. Hit me," Will says, pouring until my glass is more than half full before doing the same with his own.

"Fuck. I have no idea where to start." I gulp down half the glass and shudder. Not a big fan of whisky. These days I don't drink much beyond the occasional beer or wine. But when I do, tequila is more my speed.

"How about I start then? I need to tell you again how badly I feel. An apology doesn't seem like enough. All those years you felt like you couldn't talk to me. Couldn't confide in me. I let you down. I'm your big brother, and I should've had your back. Should've been there for you. Should've known there was much more to you than you let on. I'm sorry."

I don't want Will to feel bad, but fuck if those words aren't a balm on a hurt I've been nursing for a long, long time. I don't know what to say. I'm not sure I could even get words past the lump in my throat. Lucky for me, Will seems to understand.

"I'm also sorry about the shit I gave you the first time you brought Rosanna around. I can see what she means to you. Sorry I implied you would use her as a fuck buddy. If I'd taken the time to look, or to listen, maybe I would have spotted it."

I find my voice. "Water under the bridge, bro. And I get why you were worried about Rosanna. But if there's one place I need to start, and I guess it's where I'll finish too, it's that I love her more than I can express. I have no idea what to do about it, but it's as much a fact as I have red hair and Marco is a cockhead."

"Seems to me you've been handing it pretty well so far. You know, riding in on your white horse and saving her from the evil duke, rescuing her father's estates and saving the family from ruin."

That gets a loud laugh out of me. "What the hell? You've been reading too many romance books, man."

Despite the low lighting, I can see Will's ears going pink. We have the same tell. There's a story there. One day I'll get it out of him.

"I can neither confirm nor deny. But the fact remains, you've been there for her when she needed you most."

And there's the rub. "Yeah, but what if that's it for her? Nothing more than gratitude that I've been around? What if, once everything's sorted out, she moves on?"

"Are you kidding me? Have you seen the way she looks at you?" Will leans back in his chair, rolling his eyes at my apparent stupidity.

"Emotions are running high. I couldn't blame her for imagining her feelings are more than they are."

"You mean like transference?" Will asks, topping up my glass.

"No idea what that is."

"Kind of like Stockholm Syndrome, but with rescuers instead of kidnappers."

"Right. Well, yes then. Like transference. Also, she's been with Marco all those years. Shouldn't she, you know, go out and stretch her wings a bit?" The thought of it makes me nauseous. But I also don't want to be the overbearing arsehole she rightly accused Marco of being.

"From what I've seen, she wants to stretch her wings right around you. Don't be a tool and let her go because you're afraid. And don't insult her intelligence by thinking she can't sort out her feelings. She's quite capable of working out what she wants all by herself. If she says that's you, take her word for it." I guess I've been told.

"The thing is, *I* need to know she's choosing me freely. With a clear head. I don't want to spend the rest of my life wondering if she would've chosen *me*, without all the other noise."

It strikes me how good Will is at this relationship advice, given he's never had a serious girlfriend in his life.

"You have nothing to worry about with Rosanna. What you should be worried about is Mum and Dad," Will says with deep foreboding.

By the time we're looking at the bottom of the bottle, I'm so loose I can barely stand up. Which is what I needed. A trip into complete oblivion.

My last thought as I fall face down on my bed is if I live through fessing up to my parents, Rosanna and I are going to have a serious talk.

CHAPTER FORTY-ONE

ROSANNA

Ben arrives on Tuesday morning much quieter than usual. Seems he has a hangover, thanks to Will. I'm glad he got a chance to relax and let his hair down. The past few days, weeks, I guess, have been stressful for all of us.

Fernanda has not shown her face since Friday night, which is a relief. I don't know whether or not she knew, or had a suspicion, about what Marco was up to, and I don't care. The last thing we need to hear right now is a defence of his behaviour. It's all still too raw. Honestly, maybe I'll never be ready to hear it. Which is fine by me.

"The police called this morning," I tell Ben as Mum pushes him into a chair at the kitchen table and deposits a heaped plate of food in front of him.

"Eat, Benedetto. You are too thin," she says. It doesn't take too much encouragement.

"And?" he manages between mouthfuls.

"Marco's bail has been revoked. He'll be held in custody until trial." The relief I felt hearing those words from Detective Williams cannot be overstated.

"Did Jeff talk to you at all about compensation?" Ben asks.

"He mentioned criminal compensation and something about civil compensation. I have no idea what the difference is." I still don't have a clear handle on all the ins and outs of what Marco did. Between my personal problems with him, managing my mother's anxiety and worrying about my father, I haven't had the time or the mindspace to fully comprehend what he's done.

"Marco defrauded Moretti and Co. of hundreds of thousands of dollars. This has been going on for a number of years, Ro." I don't miss the fact that Ben doesn't call me Rosie. I try not to read too much into it. We're all tired and overwrought.

"Essentially, you'll be entitled to both victims of crime compensation and civil compensation, if you choose to launch a case against him."

Mum looks from me to Ben, clearly not understanding the gravity of what Ben is saying. I don't care about the money. But that's my father's hard work. It's their retirement savings. It's his misplaced trust in Marco. I don't want Marco to see a cent of my father's money.

"What if we want to launch a civil case?"

"You'd need to engage a lawyer." Ben pats Mum on the hand as she starts to weep into her hanky, whispering her worries in Italian. "It's okay, Flavia. I know a couple of really good ones."

That brightens her up. "Oh. Yes. Nico. Nico is a very smart lawyer. He will know what to do."

She actually has no idea. In fact, Nick doesn't handle this sort of thing; he's more of a corporate lawyer. But if thinking Nick can help gives her comfort, I'm not going to correct her.

"Yes. He is. And so are my brother and father." Ben looks at me. "I've spoken to Will, and he's happy to come and chat through your options any time."

Mum's face takes on a mutinous expression. "Yes. Good. Marco should not get to keep the money he stole from us. We will fight him."

That gets a much-needed laugh out of all of us.

Ben insists on coming to the hospital with us, but only stays long enough to check on Dad and reassure him that Mum and I are fine and Marco is no longer a threat. Of course, I told him all this yesterday. Several times, but it seems it's more believable coming from Ben. Something to do with him having a penis, I expect.

Ben kisses my forehead as he's leaving, and I'm reminded of the way he called me Ro earlier. I don't think I'm imagining it. He's pulling back. Who could blame him? My life is a dumpster fire right now. Anyone would be crazy to get involved.

We never talked about our relationship being more than friends with one-time benefits. He did what I asked. He gave me the experience I wanted. It's entirely fine for him to move on. Even if my poor, battered heart is screaming for more.

As Ben leaves the room, I notice my mother passing him some folded papers.

"What was that?" I ask in a whisper, trying not to wake Dad, who has dozed off now that someone in authority—Ben—has reassured him.

"What was what?" Mum responds with faux innocence.

"Those papers you gave to Ben. What were they?"

"Nothing. They were nothing." Mum busies herself straightening Dad's blankets so she doesn't have to look me in the eye while telling me a bald-faced lie.

I sigh long and loud. "Mum, we're going through hell. All because of secrets and lies and nobody being honest about what they were feeling." She looks crestfallen. "That's on all of us—including me. So, no more keeping secrets. What did you just hand Ben?"

"Alright. It was the bills. For the wedding. Benedetto said to give them to him and he would take care of them." I'm horrified.

"What?" I whisper-shriek. Mum's cheeks flush, as they should. "I can't believe you did that. After everything Ben has done for us. Now you give him the *bills*?" My shrill tone alerts the nurse who comes over and asks us to take our argument elsewhere. I stride down the corridor to the stairwell, Mum trotting behind.

I'm so embarrassed.

"I'm going to call Ben and get those bills back. *I* will pay them. I don't care what he says or how much he wheedles, you will *not* allow him to give us one single cent. Am I clear?" Phew. This taking your power thing is a bit addictive.

"Si, si. Alright. But—"

"No buts, Mum."

I send her back to sit with Dad and call Ben.

"I'm not letting you pay those bills, Ben."

"Honestly, it's fine. Some of them I can get you out of, thanks to my contacts, and the rest don't add up to much, Rosanna." There's that word again. Not Rosie or honey. Rosanna. The edges of the tape holding my heart together are starting to peel off.

"It's not fine."

"It wouldn't have got that far if I hadn't asked you to play along with him," Ben suggests as though any of this is his responsibility.

"If it wasn't for you, my father would be looking at jail time, and those bills would be for an actual wedding. I need to take care of those bills myself, Ben."

He must hear the steel in my tone. There's a long pause.

"Okay. I'll bring them back with me tomorrow."

I make a snap decision. In the past few weeks, I haven't had a single moment to myself. The past three or four days have been complete chaos. I need some time. Some space to think. To just be. I need to go home to my own apartment.

I'm also not sure I want to see the version of Ben who is pulling back to nothing more than friends. I'm not ready for that.

"No. Please don't. You've done more than enough. I'll take care of things from here."

"What do you mean?"

"I think ... I think I need a bit of space, Ben. My head is spinning. I need some peace and quiet to think. Wrap my head around what's going to happen from here."

There's a long silence from Ben. "Okay. Well, call me any time if you need me."

I can't speak for the lump in my throat. Is this it? Have I given him the exit he needed?

"Take care, Rosie." He hangs up before I can take any of it back. Which I want to do. Because he called me Rosie.

My stress and lack of sleep, my shame over how I let this happen, and my fear that he's slipping away have led me to hurt the one person in the world who has never once given me cause to doubt him.

CHAPTER FORTY-TWO

BENEDICT

I hang up the phone from Rosie, feeling sick to my stomach.

I know I've pulled away from her a little over the past couple of days. All I wanted was to give her some space. To be with her parents. To come to terms with what Marco has done. To her father and his business. To her. There's no way anyone could be thinking clearly after what she's been through.

It also felt wrong to be too affectionate with her in front of her parents, given less than a week ago she was engaged to another man. Did she take my putting some distance between us as a rejection? Or was it the opportunity she needed to walk away gracefully? I've been walking a tightrope here, and I think maybe I've overbalanced.

I call Will. He gave me good advice the other day. Which it looks like I should've taken. The thing is, it's important for me to know Rosie is choosing me for me. Not because of some kind of transference, as he called it. That comment has stuck in my mind like a strawberry seed in my teeth. I can't get past it.

"You're an idiot," he says.

"Yes. Thanks. I'm aware." I'm in danger of wearing a hole in my carpet from all the pacing I've done over the past couple of weeks.

"What you need is a night out. Oh. I know. Let's get the band back together. I think we all deserve a celebration after what we pulled off. I'll call everyone. We'll start at your place. Eight o'clock."

Which is how we all end up in a nightclub at three am, singing Cold Chisel songs at the top of our lungs. Even Nick.

The next morning, I wake to find Will asleep in one of my guest bedrooms. He says he was too drunk to go home, but those pink ears tell another story. He's worried about me.

Neither of us are fit to be seen, so we order in a big hangover breakfast and sit at my dining table with our sunglasses on, blinded by the sun glinting off the harbour.

"Right. Now that the Rosanna thing has been sorted, you need to get onto telling Mum and Dad about your activities," he says as he polishes off a second large coffee and wipes the remaining egg yolk off his plate with the last piece of sourdough toast.

"What? I don't get a day or two to decompress?"

"Nope. No time like the present. Hop onto the family chat. Maybe organise it for tomorrow night. I've got a hunch I'll still be feeling a little ordinary tonight." He passes my phone from the counter behind him. "Are you going to invite them here?"

"Nah. That might be a bit too much all at once. I'll do it at their place. That way, I can get out quickly if Dad starts yelling and throwing things."

"Good point. Although, to be fair, he hasn't thrown anything since I hot-wired the headmaster's car in high school." We both laugh at the memory. Although it wasn't funny at the time.

"Hey. Shouldn't you be at work by now?" I check the time. It's nearly eleven o'clock.

"Perks of being a partner, bro." He smirks and watches as I send the text that will cause all kinds of chaos in the family.

I know it's ridiculous to be so tense about telling my parents what they don't know about my life. It's not as if it's bad news. They're not monsters. They're supportive, loving people.

I know they'll be hurt by the secrets I've been keeping. If I don't miss my guess, they—well, Mum, at least—will also feel guilty that I wasn't able to tell them. The last thing I want is for them to feel bad.

Actually, no. That's not true. The last thing I want is for my life to continue the way it's been for the past ten years. I want to be able to talk about my life with the people who are important to me. I want my father to be proud of me. My mother to not worry about me.

Despite where things stand right now, I want all that with Rosanna by my side.

So, after this shitshow is over, she and I are going to sit down and have a heart-on-your-sleeve chat. If she needs space, or time, or whatever, I'm okay with that. As long as I know at some point, hopefully in the not-too-distant future, there's a chance we can have a life together.

But first things first.

The entire family, including Nick, Lulu and baby Isla, are around the outdoor table. It hasn't escaped my notice that Will took the seat to my right. The pizzas I ordered have been delivered and we're about to tuck in when the doorbell goes. Lulu leaps from her seat and rushes to open it, which is weird. Until I see who follows her onto the back patio. Rosanna.

"You're here," I whisper. Duh. "How did you know?"

"Will called me. You didn't think I'd leave you to do this by yourself, did you?" she whispers, as a chair is shoved into the space to my left for her. I've never loved my brother more than I do at this moment.

"Thank you," is all I can think to say. I take her hand under the table and squeeze. I'm overjoyed when she squeezes back.

Everyone is speculating and asking what this is all about, but I wait until we've all got a drink and some pizza before I start.

Dad, being Dad, can't wait any longer.

"What's all this cloak and dagger routine, Ben? Are you in trouble? Is this about whatever Will and Nick have been working on in secret these last couple of weeks?"

It's typical of my father to assume the worst. I nearly back off, but Rosanna's hand holding mine under the table reminds me to take the leap.

"No, Dad. I'm not in trouble. But there is something you all need to know." I hesitate.

"You've got this, bro," Will mutters from the corner of his mouth.

"I haven't been entirely honest with you over the past few years," I start. Rosanna gives Will a sharp look when he snorts. "I let you all think I've been living off Granny's money, and that's not true."

Dad rolls his eyes, clearly expecting the worst, and I nearly falter, but Rosanna squeezes my hand again, and I carry on.

"I've been investing in startups. It turns out I have a knack for it." You could hear a pin drop. All eyes are on me as it all comes pouring out.

By the time I'm finished my story, minus Operation Marco, as I've come to think of it, the table has gone from gasps of 'What the hell?', 'Are you serious?' and an 'Oh my goodness' from Mum to stunned silence, mouths agape.

"As for what's been going on the last couple of weeks, that's all my fault," Rosanna lays out the Marco debacle to more gasps. More exclamations. More stunned silence and gaping mouths.

Finally, Greer gets her thoughts in order.

"You knew about this?" she screeches at Josh, backhanding him on the arm.

"Only for the last couple of weeks. And it wasn't my story to tell. What kind of brother-in-law would I be if I blabbed?" They take no shit from each other, those two.

"Sure. But ... I'm your wife. Well, I will be."

Josh grins and kisses her square on the lips. "And I can't wait."

I make a mental note to thank Josh and Nick again for keeping my secret.

Then all hell breaks loose. Dad is bellowing about the idiocy of keeping secrets in a family; Ethan is demanding specifics; Will is embroidering details into Rosanna's brief telling of the events of the last few weeks. I'm fielding questions left and right until I notice Mum's absence. I find her in the kitchen, face dropped into her hands, shoulders shaking.

"Mum, Mum. Please don't cry." I want to cry myself, seeing what I've done to her.

She looks up at me. Face awash with tears. "Oh, my darling boy. I'm so sorry. We let you down. You should've been able to tell us. We should've known."

I wrap her up in my arms, and the flow of comfort that runs from mother to child is reversed.

"You're right. I should've been able to tell you, but that's on me as much as you." There's plenty of blame to go around if we want to be honest.

"This is all so terrible."

"Is finding out I've got more money than I know what to do with that bad, really?" I ask, trying to lighten the mood.

It works to a point. "No. Not that part. I'm happy I don't have to worry about you. I mean the secrets. Then there's the Rosanna thing. I'm so proud of you for what you did for her."

I don't get the chance to answer because there's a bellow from the kitchen door.

"What the hell were you thinking, Benedict James?" Oops. Dad's broken out the full name. I'm an adult and it still scares the tripe out of me. "You've lied to us, you've made your mother cry, and then you toss off an explanation like it's nothing important."

"Don't speak to Ben that way," comes a firm voice behind him. Rosanna strides into view, steps around my father and lines up next to me. "He's a grown man, and it's past time you started treating him like one." Wow! Rosie really has stepped into her power since confronting Marco.

Dad's eyes nearly pop out of his skull. Nobody speaks to him like that.

"Obviously, it's not ideal he's kept these secrets, but he had his reasons. It's not like he's done anything illegal or immoral. He deserves your understanding and forgiveness in the same way he's forgiven you for your mistakes. Maybe even an apology for not seeing who he is. For underestimating him. And for not giving him the safe space he needed to be honest."

Whoa.

My tiny little mother straightens her shoulders, tears drying on her cheeks.

"She's right, Harry. I think you should take some time to think about how you've contributed to this situation," she says.

With a harrumph, Dad turns on his heel, stomps down the hall and slams his study door behind him.

"Don't worry, dear. He's just feeling guilty and embarrassed. He'll get over it." Mum pats Rosanna—who's looking like she swallowed a slug—on the arm and darts back out onto the back patio.

"Oh my God. I can't believe I spoke to your father like that." Rosie covers her face with trembling hands.

"Me either. But it was awesome. I'm just sorry Will, Josh and Ethan missed it." I can't keep the grin off my face. Partly because someone stood up to my larger-than-life father, and partly because it was Rosanna ... standing up for me.

CHAPTER FORTY-THREE

Rosanna

By the time we leave the Carters', it's late and we're all talked out. Now that Marco has been dealt with and Ben's secret is out, the emotional roller coaster of the past month is slowing down, ready for us to disembark.

We climb into the Uber, and Ben looks at me with a raised eyebrow.

"Where to?" Despite my appearance at dinner, he's not making any assumptions, and I love that about him.

"Your place, I guess. You still have a whole lot of my stuff there. I have to get it back sometime." Ben had brought a bag with a couple of changes of clothes to Mum's, but it hadn't escaped my notice not everything was there.

"Oh." His face morphs from hopeful to sad in a millisecond.

"I'm kidding." It's comical how fast his face breaks into a mile-wide smile.

Ben laughs. "Haha. I suppose you think you're funny. We'll see who's laughing when I get you upstairs, woman."

As soon as we hit the pavement outside his apartment, Ben grabs me and, with a whoop, swings me over his shoulder before darting into the foyer.

"Put me down. I'm too heavy," I manage to squeeze out through my compressed diaphragm as the lift doors open and Ben carries me inside.

"And give up the opportunity to fondle this fine arse? Not a chance." His hands roam across said arse and down my thighs till they reach the hem of my skirt and delve under to slide back up my bare legs and tease at the elastic of my knickers.

"You know, if they didn't have cameras in these lifts ..." he teases.

"I'm surprised you'd let a little thing like a camera stop you."

"Once upon a time, you'd have been right. But I don't want anyone else seeing what's under this flirty little skirt but me." There's a growl in his voice that goes straight to my lady parts, and I thank the universe when the lift doors open and he shoves through the door into his apartment and presses me up against the wall.

Wrapping my legs around his waist, he pushes my knickers aside and slides his fingers up and into me.

"Looks like someone's ready to take her punishment," he whispers.

I can't answer because my breath is stalled, but my hands push between us, and I somehow manage to unbutton his jeans and slide the zipper down enough to get his erection out and into my hand.

"Condom. Back pocket," he rumbles, continuing to work his fingers in and out while sucking and biting my neck. It takes a moment, but as soon as the condom is in my hand he's leaning back, watching me roll it over his length. And then he's driving up and in. My head falls back against the wall with a thunk, but neither of us care.

The pace is brutal. Short, sharp, fast jabs. It's the lack of finesse, the lack of control, from this man who has always taken such gentle care with me, that excites me almost as much as the sensation of him filling me. He roars his release seconds before I find my own, gasping for breath as spots dance before my eyes.

"Will that discourage you from giving me sass?" Ben asks once he has his breathing under control.

"Hell no." And I use what little breath I've managed to catch to kiss him senseless.

Sliding me down the wall, Ben carries me to the bedroom and falls to the bed with me in his arms. We cuddle in silence for a long time before I say what I need to say.

"I'm sorry, Ben. I'm sorry I pushed you away. I'm sorry I told you I needed space. I was just overwhelmed. And so ... so ashamed of what I put up with from Marco. What I hadn't been able to see."

"Hush," he whispers against my hair. "You have nothing to be sorry for. We'll work it all out. Tomorrow. Right now, I need to sleep."

"Sleep? Are you sure? Because ..." I reach down and grasp his cock. It only takes a second or two to show me sleep is not on the agenda any time soon.

CHAPTER FORTY-FOUR

BENEDICT

I t's almost noon before we surface.

Rosie checks in quickly with Flavia and Andrea, who is coming home tomorrow, while I brew some much-needed coffee.

I sit on the side of the bed and hand her a cup as she hangs up. She's so beautiful. Soft and dishevelled and looking well used. Nobody looking at her now could mistake what we spent most of the night doing.

"It's a beautiful day out. I thought maybe we could take a walk in the park. See if the gelato van is there?"

We order the same flavours we had last time we were here, sit on the same secluded bench and sample from each other's cones.

"Last time we were here, you had just propositioned me to take your virginity." I gaze out at the sparkling water, spotted with white sails, even on a weekday.

"You didn't take much convincing." She leans over and licks the side of my cone which is about to drip onto my bare thigh, exposed by my shorts. Come to think of it, maybe she should have waited.

"I might have dyslexia, Rosie, but I'm not stupid. Only an idiot would have to think twice about that offer."

A glorious pink creeps up her cheeks.

"So, no regrets then?"

"Yes, actually. I do have one regret."

She raises her eyebrows, waiting for me to continue.

"I regret I didn't warn you that once I'd had you, I'd never want to let you go. Because I knew it even then." I turn to face her on the bench, my eyes searching hers. "I knew if you let me have even a tiny piece, it wouldn't be enough. Now I find myself in a quandary."

"You do?" she asks, more a sigh than a sentence.

"I do. You've been through so much with Marco. Been controlled and neglected and let down. Abused. Spent so long doing what you thought was right by others. You deserve some time to heal. To spread your wings. Work out who you are. Maybe play the field. Do what it is you want." She nods for me to continue. "I want you to have exactly what you need, with a clear conscience and an open mind. But my dilemma is, I want me to be what you need."

Tears are starting to leak down her face.

"I mean it when I say I want you to have the life you want. But I can't let you walk away without telling you the truth. In case maybe it's what you want too."

"And what is the truth?"

"The truth is, I love you. I've loved you since the moment I laid eyes on you. I never thought it would happen to me. Had never felt even a stirring. I always assumed I didn't have the capacity for that kind of love. And then, there you were. And I realised why I'd never felt it before. Because I was waiting for you."

Emotions are flying across her expressive face too fast for me to recognise them. Finally, after what seems like hours, she speaks.

"I've never met anyone with more capacity for love than you, Benedict Carter. And maybe, after everything I've been through, I should be wanting to go my own way. Live life on my own terms. But you know what? Turns out life on my terms is spending it with you."

I'm secure enough in my masculinity to admit tears are trickling over my cheeks now too, and the gelato has dripped all over my leg.

"Are you sure? Because I'll wait if you need me to. It might kill me, but I'll wait. As long as you need."

She shakes her head, and her beautiful hair catches the sunlight.

"No waiting. I love you. I don't want to waste another minute of my life. I lost eight years thinking I was doing the right thing. Now it's my turn to choose. And I choose you."

EPILOGUE

BENEDICT

The bridal party at Ethan and Jessie's wedding ends up being enormous. He does have two brothers, an almost-brother-in-law and a pseudo-brother, after all. There was no way Jessie could leave Lulu or Rosanna out. The four of them, not forgetting my sister Greer, have become super tight. They had a bit of a scramble to find a partner for Will, but luckily Jessie has a cousin.

Rosanna struts down the aisle, hips swaying, in the beautiful dress she designed and made for herself and the other bridesmaids. It looks gold to me, but apparently, it's bronze. I don't know, but if Rosanna says so, it must be true. Whatever the colour is, she looks stunning. As always.

Rosie worked her fingers to the bone to get four bridesmaids' dresses and a wedding dress ready in time, with the help of Flavia, who was the one who originally taught her to sew. In the end, Greer, Lulu and Jessie were conscripted on 'beading duty' whatever the hell that means, and they finished the last of the dresses late last night. My apartment looks like a haberdashery store. But it was better than nice, after so many solitary years, to have people I love coming and going at all hours. And it was worth it to watch four of the most beautiful women I've ever seen walking down the aisle.

It's three months since Rosanna and I ate our second gelato together. It's become a regular thing since she migrated to my apartment. I say migrated because we never even talked about her moving in, it just happened. One day we were confessing our love, the next neither of us could remember what it was like *not* to live together. Nor do we want to.

Andrea was a bit unhappy about it at first, but Flavia reminded him how it could be worse, and Rosanna could be married to Marco. Which shut him up pretty quick.

Marco. The hole he has dug himself keeps getting deeper. Jeff Williams keeps me updated on the progress of their investigation. He's of the opinion that by the time they've finished, Marco will have a list of charges as long as his arm. Good riddance. The trial is set for some time next year, and I can't wait for Rosanna to get her day in court.

Pete White bought Moretti's as promised, with a little silent-partner help from me. Which gave Flavia and Andrea a nice retirement nest egg. Without the worry of the business, his health has improved slightly.

Rosanna sold the ugly ring Marco gave her, and donated the money to a local women's shelter. Then sent a copy of the receipt to Marco. I was happy to see the back of it, and even happier it helped a worthwhile cause.

Having made Lulu's wedding dress and now Jessie's, Rosanna has discovered a love for wedding design and is in the process of leaving her job at the ballet and setting up her own business designing wedding dresses, drag outfits and surprise, surprise, burlesque costumes. It's been great fun helping her find the ideal location, set up her website and come up with a business plan. She even has her first client. Sabrina and her girlfriend are getting married and have asked Rosie to design both dresses, so she's off to a great start.

It took Dad a couple of weeks, but eventually he calmed down enough to take me out for lunch one day and apologise for his reaction and his part in our relationship breakdown. I won't say we're as close as he and Will or Josh, but we're working towards it. Even though she tore him a new one, Rosanna has become one of his favourite people. No surprise to me. She's adorable. Only last week he declared her a keeper and warned me not to screw it up. Old habits.

Finally, the ceremony is over, and Rosanna and I meet at the top of the aisle, waiting to file out behind the happy couple.

"How about I meet you here again in one year?" I whisper. Rosie turns to face me, horror on her face.

"*That's* your proposal?" she hisses.

As if.

"Nah, that's just a place-holder. Believe me, honey, when I propose, you and the whole world will know it."

"I don't need a big proposal, Bee. I just need you."

Right back atcha.

THE END

AUSTRALIANISMS & TRANSLATIONS

A ustralian-isms

NACC- National Anti-Corruption Commission
ATO- Australian Tax Office
AVO- Apprehended Violence Order
ASIO- Australian Secret Intelligence Organisation (not unlike the CIA)
DA- Development Application for building
Seccie – Security Guard
Jelly – in America this would be called Jello

Italian Translations

un matrimonio – a marriage
una bambina – a baby girl
è bellissima /molto bellissima – she is extremely/very beautiful
Benvenuto alla casa nostra – Welcome to our home
non è un problema – it's no problem
Questa è la figlia di Lulu, Isla. Non è bellissima? – This is Lulu and her daughter, Isla. Isn't she beautiful?
Si, si. Che belli capelli rossi – Yes, what beautiful red hair
Cosa c'è? stai bene? – What's wrong? Are you okay?
Si. Si. Vengo subito – Yes, yes. I'm on my way
Comè sta? – How is he?

È molto bello, ma dov'è Marco? –It's very nice. But where is Marco?

Si. Si. Un bravo ragazzo – Yes. A good boy.

Bella mia.– Beautiful

Basta, Flavia, per favore – Stop, Flavia, please

sfogliatelle – Italian puff pastries

Due coni per favore, uno di ciocalato fondente e fior di latte e uno di biscotti e zabaglione. Grazie – Two cones please, one dark chocolate and sweetened cream and one almond cookie and cream and sweet wine.

Un momento, Tesoro – One moment, darling

Grazie mille – Thank you very much

Baciala – Kiss her

Alla fine, alla fine. Posso morire in pace sapendo che mia figlia ha un brav'uomo che si prende cura di lei. Sono così felice – This is good. I can die in peace knowing my daughter has a good man to take care of her. I am very happy.

Si, si. È molto saggio, Marco – Yes, Marco knows what's best

Non possiamo organizzarlo – We can't arrange it.

Si, Tesoro, Marco hanno ragione. Aspetteremo -Yes, my darling. Marco, they are right. We will wait.

Tre mesi sono sufficienti? – Is three months enough?

Questo non è giusto – This is not right

giorno del matrimonio – wedding day

sono sbagliati – wrong

È ridicolo lasciare i miei affari alla mia unica figlia? – Ridiculous to leave my business to my only daughter?

Cara mia – My darling/dear

Merda, Basta – Shit. Enough

Tranquillo - Be quiet

Tesoro - My treasure

si - yes

molto bene - very good

stupido - stupid

Mi dispiace tanto - I am so sorry

ACKNOWLEDGEMENTS

'I can't write without a reader. It's precisely like a kiss –
you can't do it alone.'
John Cheever

Is there a more appropriate quote for a romance writer to use in thanking her readers?

Writing a book is one thing, but the life it is given by readers is where the magic happens. So thank you, from the bottom of my heart, for reading my words. I hope they brought you joy.

Before a book ever gets to a reader, there are a whole raft of people who have a hand in its creation, and I'm lucky enough to have found a team who challenge me, encourage me and support me in equal measure.

Once again, big love and thanks to Kelly Rigby, for helping me take this from a skeleton to a fully-fleshed, living, breathing story. Thanks to Jo Speirs. Your patience with my disdain for commas is much appreciated! And to Ryan Gilchrist – thank you for bringing the personality of my characters to life on the cover.

Thanks to my critique partners and beta readers Karen, Emma, Frances, and especially Antonella, who checked my less-than-perfect Italian. Any errors are entirely my own.

Michele, Deb, Lisa, Mary, Angela, Kay, Linda, Sue and Michelle – my personal cheer squad – love you all.

Finally, thanks to RWAus and all the wonderful writers I've met through this fantastic organisation. Finding your tribe is so important in helping you grow as a writer, supporting you through the inevitable insecurities, and in celebrating your successes, big and small.

If you enjoyed this book, I'd love it if you could leave a review on Amazon or Goodreads.

Thanks for reading,

Carrie x

ABOUT THE AUTHOR

Carrie Clarke is native of Sydney, Australia and has been writing stories, in her head and otherwise, since she first picked up a Georgette Heyer as a tween.

Five Fun Facts about Carrie:

1. After writing (and reading), Carrie's favourite thing to do is travel
2. Carrie loves history, bonus points if it's Egyptian
3. In Carrie's world the most important meal of the day is dessert
4. She would love to speak French, but has no talent for languages
5. Carrie firmly believes sleeping in is the only acceptable use for the mornings

Join Carrie's mailing list via her website to receive advance news about upcoming books, exclusive extras and special content: www.carrieclarkeauthor.com.au.

KEEP IN TOUCH

If you would like to keep you up to date on when the next book in the Falling in Love Series is coming out, receive exclusive bonus content for each of my books, plus a subscriber-only short story 'What Happens in Singapore', I'd love you to join my mailing list at: **carrieclarkeauthor.com.au**.

Follow me on:
Facebook.com/CarrieClarkeAuthor
Instagram.com/carrieclarkeauthor
X: @CarrieCAuthor

ALSO BY CARRIE CLARKE

The Falling in Love Series:

The Art of Falling in Love – Book 1

It's irritation at first sight when Lulu destroys Nick's shoe, and his peace of mind, with a wicked stiletto. And that's just for starters.

Lulu – He's so annoying. Okay, so maybe he is the sexiest man I've ever met in real life. I mean, those lips ... And maybe he did give me the best O of my life. But it absolutely won't happen again. Until it does.

Nick – She's infuriating. And not my type. Definitely not my type. But the smell of her wildflower hair goes straight to my boxers. I barely recognise the man I become when I'm with her. In the best of ways. It can't last, of course.

Battling to overcome their lifetime of baggage is one thing, but will taking on a meddling mother, an ex-girlfriend who won't take no for an answer, and a wicked set of bovine horns prove too much?

This story features a buttoned-up, buttoned-down lawyer with a hidden talent for dirty talk, a sunshiny artist with a morbid fear of commitment, and more highland cattle than you might expect.

Blueprint for Falling in Love – Book 2

Sparks fly and the air sizzles when Josh meets Greer disembarking a flight from London. Sparks, and a strange sense of familiarity...

Josh – I can't believe I hit on my best friend's little sister. In my defence, she's changed since I last saw her ten years ago. A lot. I wish things were different, but there's no way I'm going there.

Greer – Josh may think denying our connection is the right thing to do, but I've got news for him. And working together on renovating his new house gives me the opportunity I need to prove it to him.

Giving in to temptation puts everything Josh holds dear at risk, but not giving in might just break both their hearts.

This story features a reluctant hero with abandonment issues, a determined heroine with an unshakeable belief in love, a family who knows much more than they're letting on and a grand gesture the whole of Sydney gets behind.

Coming Soon:

The Nature of Falling in Love – Early 2024

Short Story – only available to Subscribers:

What Happens in Singapore